Runaway Bus . . .

In the rearview mirror, I saw the top half of the driver's face as he glanced back to the carriage. The driver's hat was pulled down low over his forehead, nearly obscuring his eyes, but the reflected image struck me cold.

I'd seen those eyes before—on a face that wore a feathery red mustache.

"Monty!" I called out, trying to warn him, but the sound of the bus's roaring engine drowned out my voice.

Thirty seconds later, midway down the next block, the bus lurched to a sudden stop, throwing me chin-first against the back of the bench in front of me.

Rubbing my jaw, I looked out toward the windshield on the front of the bus. The road in front of us suddenly dropped off, rolling down toward the flatlands of the Mission. We were at the top of 22nd Street, at the crest of one of the steepest hills in the city.

I watched in horror as Monty staggered forward and reached out to tap the driver on his shoulder. Just as Monty's arm swung out, the driver cut the engine, yanked out the key and leapt up from his seat. Monty stood, stunned, as the driver hurled himself down the steps and out the front door.

Frank Napis glanced back at the bus, a smirking sneer on his flat face, before he scuttled away down a side street. As Monty and I stared at his fleeing figure, the bus began to roll, driverless, down the hill . . .

Titles by Rebecca M. Hale

HOW TO WASH A CAT
NINE LIVES LAST FOREVER

NINE LIVES
LAST FOREVER

REBECCA M. HALE

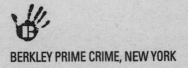

BERKLEY PRIME CRIME, NEW YORK

THE BERKLEY PUBLISHING GROUP
Published by the Penguin Group
Penguin Group (USA) Inc.
375 Hudson Street, New York, New York 10014, USA
Penguin Group (Canada), 90 Eglinton Avenue East, Suite 700, Toronto, Ontario M4P 2Y3, Canada
(a division of Pearson Penguin Canada Inc.)
Penguin Books Ltd., 80 Strand, London WC2R 0RL, England
Penguin Group Ireland, 25 St. Stephen's Green, Dublin 2, Ireland (a division of Penguin Books Ltd.)
Penguin Group (Australia), 250 Camberwell Road, Camberwell, Victoria 3124, Australia
(a division of Pearson Australia Group Pty. Ltd.)
Penguin Books India Pvt. Ltd., 11 Community Centre, Panchsheel Park, New Delhi—110 017, India
Penguin Group (NZ), 67 Apollo Drive, Rosedale, North Shore 0632, New Zealand
(a division of Pearson New Zealand Ltd.)
Penguin Books (South Africa) (Pty.) Ltd., 24 Sturdee Avenue, Rosebank, Johannesburg 2196,
South Africa

Penguin Books Ltd., Registered Offices: 80 Strand, London WC2R 0RL, England

NINE LIVES LAST FOREVER

A Berkley Prime Crime Book / published by arrangement with the author

PRINTING HISTORY
Berkley Prime Crime mass-market edition / July 2010

Copyright © 2010 by Rebecca M. Hale.
Cover illustration by Mary Ann Lasher.
Cover design by Diana Kolsky.
Interior text design by Kristin del Rosario.

ISBN: 978-0-425-23432-7

BERKLEY® PRIME CRIME
Berkley Prime Crime Books are published by The Berkley Publishing Group,
a division of Penguin Group (USA) Inc.,
375 Hudson Street, New York, New York 10014.
BERKLEY® PRIME CRIME and the PRIME CRIME logo are trademarks of Penguin Group (USA) Inc.

PRINTED IN THE UNITED STATES OF AMERICA

10   9   8   7   6   5   4   3   2   1

For my mother, Carol

One of the striking differences between a cat and a lie is that a cat has only nine lives.

—MARK TWAIN, 1894

PART I

Wednesday Morning
The First Occurrence

A SLIPPERY INTRUDER

RUPERT'S FUZZY WHITE body meandered sleepily across the Green Vase showroom. With each step, the soft padding on the soles of his feet squished against the creaky wood flooring.

Wreek. Wroight. Wreek. Wroight.

He squeaked across to the far side of the room, taking care to rub his neck and shoulder against the corner of a bookcase he passed along the way.

The first rays of early morning light were beginning to pierce the predawn fog and shine through the wall of windows that lined the storefront, causing the green vase icon inlaid into each square pane of glass to gleam brightly.

Rupert stepped gingerly through the shadows, carefully avoiding the beams of light that stretched across the floor until he stopped in front of a particularly wide swath of sunlight. His chunky white feet kneaded a loose floorboard as he considered his selection.

Wreek. Wroight. Wreek. Wroight.

This was it—the perfect spot. Rupert prepared himself to take the plunge.

He shook his head, setting off a violent vibration that spread throughout his entire body. A snowstorm of loose hair floated up into the air before drifting down onto the surrounding surfaces. Now suitably fluffed, Rupert smacked his lips together and stretched his mouth open to its widest yawn.

Still standing on the shadow's edge, he pulled all four feet in under his pillowy stomach and prepared to launch. His long fluffy tail waved back and forth as he focused on the selected beam of light.

At long last, Rupert lunged forward onto the sunlit floorboard. In a single smooth motion, he rolled over onto his left shoulder and flipped a right paw up and over his head—perfectly beaching his pudgy form so that the brightest section of sunlight baked the paunch of his upturned stomach.

Rupert heaved out a deep, satisfied sigh, the pouches of skin above his mouth whiffling gently as he expelled the air. A look of intense satisfaction spread across his furry face as his eyelids narrowed into slits.

It takes a great deal of skill and training to achieve such an immediate state of complete relaxation.

Rupert's soft, whistling snores mingled with the comforting rush of piped water flowing from a shower in the upstairs apartment. The seconds ticked slowly by as Rupert slipped deeper and deeper into his early morning slumber, rotating slightly to maintain optimal solar absorption. His thoughts drifted peacefully in and out of his favorite images: a freshly poured litter box, a set of warm bedsheets pulled out of a hot dryer, an unattended plate of leftover fried chicken . . .

But just then, the sonar of his sleeping senses picked up on a disturbance—an unexplained movement on the opposite side of the room. The orange triangle of Rupert's right ear rotated in the direction of the sound.

A slight, splatting *plunk* thudded against the floorboards near the bottom of the stairs.

With a disgruntled half snort, Rupert's head jerked up. His eyes glazed with sleep, he rolled up onto his stomach and glanced around the room.

Plunk.

Rupert's claws dug instinctively into the soft wood surface of the floor. His shoulders stiffened as his body tensed into a stalking lion stance. His eyes and ears widened, searching for the creature who had made such a curious noise.

Plunk.

This time, he matched a movement with the sound. There was something small and springy in the shadows at the back of the room—something staring back at him with googly, round alien-eyes.

Rupert eased forward, the white fur of his stomach sweeping the floor as he snaked between a pair of bookcases and around a worn leather dentist recliner, cautiously approaching the intruder.

Even in the dim light at the back of the room, the moist sheen of the creature's skin shimmered. A dank mustiness oozed out of its pores.

The flat bottom of Rupert's chin hovered barely an inch over his front feet as his round back end rose upward, the plume of his feathery orange tail curving skyward into an intrigued S shape.

The creature inched toward Rupert, eyeing him warily. Its webbed feet suctioned against the floorboards as its bulging eyes squeezed shut and then reopened.

Rupert and the creature were now nearly nose to nose. They stared at each other for a long moment, the slight twitching of Rupert's delicate white whiskers the only movement in the room.

Holding his breath, Rupert slid one paw forward, cupping it sideways. The long feathery hairs that stuck out between his toes neared the creature's pulsing, elastic sides.

"Ribbit."

Rupert jumped back, setting loose another explosion of

hair. The frog closed its wide, lipless mouth and blinked once more.

Rupert hunched down again, his ample stomach carpeting the floor as he scooched back toward the frog. The frog stared anxiously at the advancing cat, its flat green face pinched with concern.

Plunk.

Rupert whirled around, his blue eyes chasing the springy form as it sailed up into the air, easily leaping over him.

Plunk.

The frog was wasting no time now. It hopped toward the front of the store, looking for an exit.

Plunk.

The frog eyed the iron-framed door leading to the street, searching for an opening in its glass panels. It could sense the crisp outside air on the opposite side of the glass; it could smell its freedom—but it saw no way to reach it. Looking up, the frog changed course and sprang up toward the top of the cashier counter.

Now in an uninhibited hot pursuit, Rupert scrambled wildly across the slick wood floor, his claws scraping into the surface as he accelerated. He fixed all of his concentration on the frog's soaring figure, closely following its path through the air. With reckless abandon, Rupert hurled himself up after the frog, his front feet butterflying out as he tried to swat at the slippery little beast.

Another *plunk* sounded against the top of the cashier counter as Rupert caught its carved edge with his flailing front feet. The rest of Rupert's heavy, round body slammed into the counter's vertical front paneling. Undeterred, Rupert scrambled to pull himself up, the claws of his back feet digging tracks across the paneling's decorative scrollwork.

Plunk. The frog jumped halfway across the counter, heading toward the nearest bookcase.

Rupert dashed after it, his wide middle brushing against a slender green vase sitting on the edge of the counter. A bouquet of fresh violet-colored tulips poking out of the top of the vase swayed back and forth, rustling nervously. The rim of the vase's round base began to roll precariously.

Rupert paid no attention to the wobbling vase. He perched himself on the edge of the counter, trying to size up the distance to where the frog now crouched on the upper shelf of the adjacent bookcase.

Secure in its position of vertical advantage, the frog peered down at Rupert and blinked mockingly.

"Ribbit."

Rupert's feathery tail swished against the teetering vase as he launched himself into the air.

The crashing sound of tumbling books and breaking glass echoed through the showroom to the apartment above.

A woman's muffled holler issued from the bathroom as ancient water pipes screeched, and the shower's faucet was wrenched off.

"Rupert!"

PART II

Sunday Morning
Four Days and Several Frogs Later

AN UNEXPECTED GUEST

IT WAS AN early Sunday morning in the middle of June, pseudo-summer on the tip of San Francisco's peninsula. The arrival of the summer months signified more the end of the winter's soggy, rainy spell than the beginning of a season's warmth. Each afternoon, a crisp, cool, tourist-chilling wind buffeted off the Pacific, stealing the heat from the sun's bright rays.

The mornings, however, were governed by a different beast entirely. In the wee hours of half darkness, the air stood still as a damp ghost of fog slid its oozing fingers through the streets, gripping the ready-made handles of the city's steep hills. You could almost taste the dense, salty moisture that seeped in through San Francisco's countless open windows—including the one on the third floor bedroom of the apartment above the Green Vase.

The rest of Jackson Square still snoozed in languid silence as I crawled out of bed, stumbled into the bathroom, and turned on the shower. The first trickle of water spat violently from the faucet, gradually increasing into a steady stream as air pockets hiccupped out of the pipes.

I stood sleepily outside the shower stall, waiting for the water to heat up, while Rupert trotted into a shiny red igloo-shaped litter box to begin his early morning ritual. Within seconds, the box began to rock spastically back and forth, propelled by the efforts of the energetic digger inside. In a triumph to his well-honed technique, an occasional clump of litter gained sufficient height and spin to breach the interior rim and spray out the front of the box onto the bathroom floor.

Isabella hopped up onto the counter by the sink, yawning as she kept watch over the bathroom. With sharp blue eyes, a shiny white coat, and an orange-tipped pipelike tail, she was a sleek, slender mirror of her plump brother. She glanced down at the litter box as his fluffy white blur burst out of its opening and galloped down the stairs toward the kitchen.

With a sigh, I climbed into the shower and let the warming water soak my head and shoulders. Still half asleep, my thoughts drifted down to the Green Vase showroom, two floors below. I had inherited the shop, along with the living quarters above it, from my Uncle Oscar a few months earlier.

Oscar had run the Green Vase as an antique shop, or at least that's how it had appeared to everyone on the outside—including me. Few customers had visited the Green Vase during Oscar's tenure; those who had dared to enter were quickly shooed away. As one of my Jackson Square neighbors put it, Oscar "wasn't much into customers."

In the weeks following Oscar's death, I had learned that his fascination with the historical figures from San Francisco's past had been more than just an extracurricular pastime. He'd been searching for the hidden treasures those figures might have left behind.

The traditional antique storefront of the Green Vase had provided an easy cover for Oscar's treasure hunting activities. The relics and artifacts that filled the showroom were all clues he'd collected to the location of much more

valuable items, many of which were still hidden throughout the city. Unfortunately, Oscar had kept most of the
details regarding his historical research in his head, so the
underlying significance of the seemingly random articles
within Oscar's vast collection had died with him.

After Oscar's death, my two cats and I moved into
his old apartment above the antique store. At that time,
the showroom was crammed with dusty, decaying boxes,
cracked display cases, and piles of what could only be
described as junk. Two months into the arduous task of
sorting through the scattered remnants of Oscar's investi-
gative efforts, I had only processed a fraction of the heap.

Most of the items related in some way to the Gold
Rush, Oscar's favorite period of San Francisco history. It
was no coincidence that Oscar's treasure hunting headquarters was located in the heart of Jackson Square, a
neighborhood known during the Gold Rush years as the
Barbary Coast.

The brick buildings that line these streets are some of
the few in San Francisco to have survived the massive
1906 earthquake and subsequent city-sweeping fire. The
area's historical significance is further enhanced by the central role it played during the Gold Rush's massive population influx.

From 1849 onward, millions of desperate would-be
miners rushed past the building that now houses the Green
Vase on their way to the Sierra gold fields. Little of the
precious mountain dust the gold-seekers collected stayed
in their pockets. Most of it ended up back here in Jackson
Square, in the hands of saloonkeepers, thrift shop owners,
and a cunning swarm of freewheeling swindlers, pick-
pockets, and thieves.

The Green Vase had seen a lot of history over the
years, but Jackson Square's rough and rowdy Gold Rush
days ended long ago. The historic brick structures up and
down the street are now occupied by high-end antique
stores with highly polished merchandise displayed behind
expansive glass windows. The line of fancy cars parallel-

parked along the street gives notice of the sophisticated clientele who shop here.

Uncle Oscar had been the lone holdout to this high-brow trend. With the help of his vampy but effective lawyer, Miranda Richards, he'd managed to fend off the neighborhood's attempts to force him to clean up or sell the Green Vase—its cracked, glass windows and crumbling, brick exterior had matched the dusty piles within. By the time I took over the place, the residents of Jackson Square were so relieved at my willingness to renovate that I met little resistance obtaining permits for the necessary construction work.

The majority of Oscar's Gold Rush antiques were now packed up, or at least haphazardly stacked, down in the basement. I had selected what I hoped were the most marketable items from the collection and cleaned them up for a more flattering display.

To be honest, I had no idea what I was doing, trying to run an antique shop. Prior to Oscar's death, I had worked as an accountant in San Francisco's nearby financial district. I'd spent my days hunched down in an office cubicle, drearily crunching numbers and plotting them out onto spreadsheets. It was a dull but comfortably predictable existence, one that I had wholeheartedly immersed myself in. Few vestiges of that previous life survived the aftermath of Oscar's death.

Oscar had been buried less than a week when I was dismissed from my job at the accounting firm—thanks to the misguided interventions of my new neighbor, Montgomery Carmichael. To be frank, I was fired. Finding myself suddenly unemployed, I consolidated my meager savings with the proceeds from Oscar's estate and moved into the apartment above the Green Vase.

Despite pressure from Oscar's attorney to sell the antique store, I decided to hold on to it. A part of me, I think, couldn't bear to let it go. Oscar had been a gruff, grumpy old man, but he'd been my last remaining family tie, the only relative with whom I still had any relationship.

Almost every Saturday night in the years before his death, Oscar would fix dinner for the cats and me in the apartment above the Green Vase. His signature dish was a skillet full of crispy, pan-fried chicken paired with a heaping bowl of creamy mashed potatoes. The succulent smell still oozed out of the cracks and corners of the upstairs kitchen. If I stood in just the right spot in front of the stove, I could soak in enough of the scent to trick my taste buds into thinking that a hunk of that delicious chicken was passing through my lips. Those Saturday night meals at Oscar's had been the highlight of every week.

So, for reasons more sentimental than practical, I'd decided to try my hand as a Jackson Square antique dealer. The store had reopened a couple of weeks ago, but I'd had little luck, thus far, reversing the negative flow of traffic into the showroom. Even with its new red brick exterior flanked by bright green, freshly painted iron columns, the Green Vase just didn't have the reputation, the cachet, of its competitors up and down the street. I was going to have to come up with another source of income—and soon.

There was one potential recourse to save me from bankruptcy: a substantial, if illiquid, asset that Oscar had tucked away for me in one of the building's many hiding places. Two months after its discovery, I still hadn't come up with a way to leverage the item's value. Nevertheless, it was comforting to know that I had something, however tenuous, to fall back on should my efforts to run the antique store result in a complete failure.

But as the hot shower pulsed down on me that morning, my thoughts wandered away from the gloomy financial prospects of the Green Vase. I began to puzzle, instead, on the strange events of the previous couple of days.

Whispered rumors and speculations of the potential gold mines mapped out in Oscar's legendary collection of antiques had begun to circulate through Jackson Square.

Oscar had not been the only one in this neighborhood, it seemed, with an interest in hidden fortunes, and I had been unwittingly drawn into the hunt. So far, the search had unearthed nothing but questions about my mysterious uncle and his life prior to becoming the caretaker of the Green Vase.

It was as the last suds of shampoo were slipping down the drain that this second train of thought was interrupted by a series of sharp, thudding bangs that echoed up from the first floor. Concerned, I wrenched off the faucet and reached for a bath towel. I peeked nervously out through the shower curtain and looked around for Isabella. She was nowhere to be seen.

"Oh, good grief," I muttered, anticipating the source of the sound. My cats had been up to some strange behavior lately.

Another loud bump echoed up from the ground floor as I struggled into a sweatshirt and jeans—a troupe of elephants appeared to be rampaging through the Green Vase showroom. I made my way across the bathroom, gingerly stepping around the red igloo and its surrounding sprinkling of litter.

"You two better not have broken anything else," I called out as I descended to the second floor, crossed the kitchen, and headed down the wooden staircase leading to the back of the showroom. In the past couple of days, I'd lost several pieces of pottery, including a green vase, to the recent outbreak of feline mayhem.

Drops of water slid off of my sopping hair, leaving a polka-dotted trail on the steps behind me. Midway down the flight of stairs, I heard the telltale scraping sound of claws scrambling on wood flooring, followed by a swishing whomp of unidentifiable origins.

I pushed off the bottom step and stood for a moment at the back of the showroom, listening for the location of the feline mischief-makers. There was a scuttling sound near the front of the store, but my view was blocked by the rows of tall oak bookcases that forested the room's long rectangular cube. I reached up to push the wet bangs off of my forehead and marched resolutely into the store.

Isabella's head poked out from behind the bookcase closest to the cashier counter. She flashed me a quizzical, "Guess what I found" look before ducking back out of view.

"Isabella," I called out sternly. Then, reflecting on the more likely culprit, I broadened my accusation. "Rupert! What have you two gotten into now?"

A furry presence appeared at my feet, his long, fluffy tail curling around the back of my leg. Rupert looked innocently up at me, his blue eyes, as always, guilt free.

"Hmnh," I harrumphed down at him.

I took another step toward the cashier counter, causing the worn wooden floorboards to creak beneath my bare feet.

The last remnants of the morning's fog still draped the shreds of its thick, gauzy veil over the sun. Isolated rays of sunshine stretched across the floor intermixed with hazy arcs of shadow, creating an eerie half-light that didn't fully illuminate the room. Next to the counter, I noticed with a start, the front door stood slightly ajar, its curling wrought iron frame rotating slowly on the morning's thin breeze.

The blood drained from my face as I realized that the noise that had summoned me from my shower might have been caused by something other than my cats.

I crossed my arms over my chest and tried to will my feet forward, but they refused to part with the floorboards. Cautiously, I inched toward the counter.

Wreeeeek. Wroooooight. I couldn't hear anything but the increasing pounding of my heart and the annoyingly loud squeak of the floorboards.

Isabella's white head poked out again. She chirped at me, clicking her vocal cords instructively. "Come on," she seemed to be saying. "Come see."

I relaxed, suddenly feeling silly for my moment of panic, and released the volume of air I'd involuntarily sucked up into my lungs. Trying to think of alternative reasons for the front door being open, I stepped briskly up to the counter, rounded the bookcase—and stopped short.

I couldn't believe it. It wasn't possible.

A man sat on a stool behind the counter. Isabella paced back and forth on the floor in front of the stool, purring up at him adoringly. Rupert sped past me to join her, his tail fluffed up in greeting.

I could do nothing but stare at the man on the stool, my legs immobile, my head unable to process any thoughts or emotions.

He smiled—in a way that only unsettled me more.

"You seem surprised to see me."

It was all I could do to gasp out my response.

"I . . . I thought you were dead."

PART III

The Days—and Frogs— in Between . . .

Chapter 1

A MILITANT MUSTACHE

LATE WEDNESDAY MORNING, a grungy, off-smelling man hobbled down Jackson Street toward the Green Vase. His pace appeared slow and painfully labored. He paused every ten or fifteen feet, as if to rest a sore hip, and scanned the nearly deserted street.

A pair of recently purchased overalls hung loosely over the man's bony frame, but the crispness of the fabric had already begun to wilt from several days of repeated sweaty wear. The few pedestrians he passed turned their heads to avoid making eye contact. That was fine with Harold Wombler; that was the whole purpose of the outfit.

Harold raised a rough, wrinkled hand to his face and wiped the dribbling underside of his nose with the back side of it as he paused outside of an empty storefront. Sheets of brown kraft paper covered the floor-to-ceiling windows, sealing off the inside showroom from view. Harold stared into the sheeted plates of glass, looking for any indication of recent activity, but there was no sign of the previous occupant.

No one had seen Frank Napis—or his elaborate

mustache—since mid-April, when he had poisoned, and nearly killed, the niece of one of the Jackson Square shopkeepers. Local gossip speculated that Napis had escaped police capture by hiding out in the network of sewage tunnels running underneath the streets of San Francisco. He'd skipped town, many assumed, and fled the country for a sparsely populated outpost in South America.

One of the neighbors even insisted that Napis had accessed the sewage tunnels through a secret entrance in the basement beneath the Green Vase antique shop. Napis, this gossipy person was convinced, had made off with an enormous diamond previously owned in the late 1800s by San Francisco finance magnate William Ralston. But since this individual was prone to exaggeration and any number of tall tales, most dismissed his story.

Harold Wombler had turned a deaf ear to all of it. Senseless drivel from a bunch of ninnies, as far as he was concerned. He'd been there, at the scene of the crime, and he had seen Frank Napis run *up* out of the basement, and not *into* the tunnel entrance. Moreover, Harold was quite certain that Napis had not managed to get his hands on the diamond. No, the rumors circulating Jackson Square—on this particular issue at least—were wrong.

Harold had a different theory regarding the whereabouts of Frank Napis, but he kept it to himself.

Napis's store of Far Eastern antiquities had been surreptitiously cleaned out the day after his disappearance, the locks changed, and the windows papered over. The place had appeared vacant ever since. Harold Wombler knew better.

"I'm onto you," he grumbled under his breath before limping on to the next store. "You haven't fooled me."

Harold stopped next in front of a red brick edifice that was flanked on either end by iron crenellated columns covered in bright green paint. The top half of the brick wall featured several rows of square windows, every other one of which contained the inlay of a green vase icon.

Harold fingered one of his many riveted pockets as he looked in through the windowpanes at a woman seated on a stool behind the cashier counter. Scattered papers filled with doodles and an uneven pile of books cluttered the counter in front of her. The closest book lay on top of the pile, open-faced but ignored, as the woman stared upward, unseeing, into the rafters, her bifocal glasses tilted slightly off kilter.

"This is going to be easier than I thought," Harold muttered with satisfaction, patting a rectangular shape bulging inside one of his larger pockets.

IT WAS ANOTHER still, quiet day inside the newly reopened Green Vase. Oscar's antique cash register sulked on the counter in front of me, glowering in reproachful silence. Every now and then, a wary pedestrian would stop on the sidewalk and peer in through the windows, but so far I had been unable to lure anyone inside. My new business venture was off to a decidedly inauspicious start.

Isabella sat, sphinxlike, on top of the nearest bookcase, staring intently at the front door. Rupert occupied the bottom shelf, curled up in the dark space behind the row of books. One white foot poked out between the spines, offering the only evidence of his location.

To pass the time—and to distract myself from the realization of my obvious shortcomings as an antique dealer—I had begun reading through a selection of books I'd culled from Oscar's collections: numerous tattered texts on the city's history, political, and social movements, along with several anthologies of famous San Francisco writers.

On that day, however, concentration was fighting a losing battle with distraction. Several discarded books littered the counter in front of me. My mind kept drifting off, floating up toward the wooden rafters in the ceiling. Shielded from the wind billowing down the street outside, the warmth of the sun soaked into the room, coaxing me into the hazy film of a daydream.

Though my thoughts started out on their own random course, each one eventually fell into the same well-trodden path—a course my dreams had worn bare through the thicket of my imagination. For the last two months, my subconscious had been fixated on a single disturbing image.

A feathery orange mustache flitted through the rafters of the showroom—unattached to its human face, each half of the hairpiece fluttering like the wing of a small bird. The strange, runty beast seemed almost cuddly at first, pausing for a moment on one of the ceiling beams, as if to preen its feathers.

Seconds later, however, the mustache took on a more militant persona. Its body hardened into a sharp, arrowlike shape as it dove down from the rafters, aiming for my head. My arms flailed about as a hidden beak snipped at my hair. I picked up the nearest book and swung it around at the vicious orange blur, catching enough of its body to send it spinning across the room. The nasty little critter circled back to the rafters to regroup, all the while chattering angrily at me.

I was preparing to fend off another assault from the warring mustache when a glass-cracking knock jolted me loose from the dream. Someone was banging on one of the windows that ran along the street.

Startled, my weight shifted, and the stool I'd been sitting on tipped backward and slipped beneath me. I grabbed onto the edge of the cashier counter, but it was too late. I landed with a loud thump, rump first, on the floor. Somewhere, in the far corner of the room, I could have sworn I heard that wicked mustache laughing at me.

Isabella looked down, concerned, as I righted the stool and pulled myself up. I coughed and straightened my glasses, allowing my eyes to focus in on the crumpled face pressed up against the nearest pane of glass. The end of the man's perpetually runny nose smushed into a puddinglike circle as he peered in at me.

Blushing with embarrassment, I slid around the counter

and reached for the knobbed, tulip-embossed handle of the front door. I twisted it open in time to be greeted by a loud snort as Harold Wombler pulled back from the glass and readjusted his nose.

"Uh, hi, Harold," I said, grimacing as he wiped a gnarled hand across the lower half of his face.

Harold grunted a response and pushed past me, shuffling his way through the front door with a stilted, lurching gait resembling that of an arthritic crab. A foul, decaying odor seeped into the air as Harold tipped his dingy baseball cap up to scratch the scalp of his greasy black head of hair. I carefully edged around him to return to the stool on the opposite side of the cashier counter.

"What's going on in here?" he asked, mockingly flapping his hands above his head, mimicking my daydreamed efforts to stave off the dive-bombing mustache.

I mumbled something about a pesky fly as my eyes averted his dubious glare.

Harold gummed his teeth, pushing forward the bottom frame of his ill-fitting dentures. His sunken, bloodshot eyes bored into me suspiciously.

Steeling myself for his inevitably caustic reply, I mustered a smile and asked, "How can I help you, Harold?"

Harold glanced up at Isabella and then down to the bottom shelf of the bookcase. The still sleeping Rupert had rolled over, creating a cat-sized wave in the line of books.

Harold's thin upper lip rumpled into a flat, squiggling line as he returned his gaze to the counter. "Place smells like old books," he said, scowling at the pile in front of me.

My smile weakened to a cringe.

Harold jabbed the bottom shelf of the bookcase with the ragged toe of his boot, smacking his lips together derisively as the white bullet that was Rupert leapt out from behind the row of books.

"Old books and *cat*," he cried out with a sudden impish delight.

I bit back a retort on the scent Harold was contributing

to the room. I was, unfortunately, familiar with his surly nature and even more objectionable smell.

For reasons that still escaped me, Oscar's attorney had recommended Harold for the remodel work on the Green Vase. The renovations were now complete, but he still stopped by every now and then to grumpily deliver his negative assessment of my progress with the store.

"What brings you by today, Harold?" I asked, forcing the pleasantry out through tightly clenched teeth.

Harold leaned across the cashier counter, whisking more of his rank body odor in my direction.

"Seen your next-door neighbor around lately?" he asked, his voice rasping creepily as he tipped his knobby head toward the far wall.

"No," I replied briskly, the two-letter word taking the brunt of my discomfort. "No, of course not."

I got up off of the stool and slipped around the counter, pacing quickly into the showroom to put as much distance as possible between us. Harold sure knew how to give me the heebie-jeebies.

Frank Napis had run an Asian-themed antique shop in the building next door, but no one had seen him since the night, almost two months ago, when he had nearly killed me with a spider venom poison. The police had arrested his accomplice, but the man known as Frank Napis—among many other aliases—was still on the run.

Frank's face was a flat, featureless landscape that he frequently altered with the skilled use of facial putty. He could thicken his nose into a bulking beak or plump out a heavier brow to darken his eyes. Overlaying the makeup, he often applied a distracting layer of facial hair—most memorably, a feathery orange mustache.

Shuddering, I turned back toward Harold. He was still leaning against the cashier counter, drumming his stubby, knotted fingers across the stack of books. The edges of his mouth curved upward, lifting the loose, pouchy skin of his cheeks.

"I wouldn't worry about it if I were you," he said, the

coarse grinding of his voice incongruous with his curious, grinchlike smile.

The statement did little to ease my anxiety.

Harold waved a dismissive hand in my direction and turned toward the exit. Numbly, I watched him gimp out the door to the street.

I stumbled back to the cashier counter, trying to ignore the odor that now hung in the room like the pungent aftermath of a startled skunk. I scrunched up my nose, trying not to breathe it in.

As I sank back onto the stool, my watering eyes lit on the scattered pile of books. On the top of the pile, the worn cloth of an emerald green cover glimmered in the afternoon sunlight. Despite the wear evidenced by its frayed corners, the surface of the book was almost the same shade of green as the vase that had, until just that morning, stood on the edge of the cashier counter.

This book had not been there before.

"Harold must have left this here," I said out loud, trying to make sense of it.

"Mrao," Isabella confirmed from the top of her bookcase.

I rounded the counter and stepped out the front door, craning my neck to look up and down the street, but Harold Wombler had already disappeared.

Chapter 2

A FAVOR FOR DILLA

I WALKED BACK inside the Green Vase and picked up Harold's conspicuously discarded book from the counter, examining it more closely as I turned it over in my hands.

It was small, rectangular-shaped, and tightly covered in a bright green cloth that, despite the dulling effects of age, still shone when a direct ray of light hit its surface. Gold-colored script embossed into the cover identified the contents as a collection of Mark Twain essays from his early years in San Francisco.

I cupped the spine in my right hand and thumbed open the cover with my left. The adhesive binding creaked as I turned the yellowed sheets of brittle paper. It had been a long time, it appeared, since this book had been read.

I scanned the pages, trying to recall the tidbits I knew about Mark Twain's adventures in San Francisco.

Twain headed west in the early 1860s, besotted by the get-rich Gold Rush tales that had inundated his hometown of Hannibal, Missouri. One of his first stops was Virginia City, Nevada, a silver mine boomtown near present-day Reno. Twain worked in the mining trenches for less than a year before he gave up on the mirage of easy riches and returned to his true talent, writing.

The months spent suffering in the mines were not wasted, however. Twain's experiences in the Sierra mountain communities provided ample fodder for many of his early publications. These essays found a receptive audience in San Francisco, the unofficial capital of the mineral-crazed West, a town that came to love Twain's caustic wit and sarcasm. Even in its youth, San Francisco was a city confident and secure enough in its identity to enjoy a laugh at its own expense.

A muffled ringing from beneath the stack of books and papers interrupted my Mark Twain musings. Isabella hopped down from the bookcase as I dug through the pile on the counter to find the phone buried underneath. She nosed roughly through the heap, trying to beat me to the jingling creature hiding within.

On the fourth ring, I managed to swipe the receiver out from under a pouncing Isabella.

"Hello, this is the Green Vase," I greeted the caller while keeping a close eye on my cat. Undeterred, she hunched near the phone's base unit. The whip of her tail swung back and forth, taunting the machine to ring again.

"Oh, hello dear," a woman sang back in a cheerful, warbling tone. "It's Dilla."

Not a customer, I thought ruefully.

The voice on the other end of the line belonged to Dilla Eckles—a friend, I believed, of my late Uncle Oscar. The details of their relationship were still a bit murky to me, but then I hadn't known much about any of Oscar's acquaintances.

I had assumed, incorrectly, that Oscar had always lived the hermit lifestyle I'd observed in the last years of his life. Even now, months after his death, I continued to stumble across unexpected insights into my uncle's previously undetected social activities. The essence of Oscar was inextricably enmeshed within the bricks and mortar of the Green Vase, but the once sharp edges of his memory had begun to blur as facets emerged of a much more complicated life.

I'd first met Dilla in the days immediately following Oscar's death. She had stopped by the Green Vase to convince me to let my cats model some rather unique jewelry for a benefit auction at the showcase Palace Hotel. A grand matron in the most elite circles of San Francisco society, Dilla loved to put on high-profile charity events, particularly if they gave her a chance to try to lure the city's handsome, young Mayor to attend.

Unfortunately, the evening had not gone according to plan—it had ended with my admittance to the hospital for treatment to clear Frank Napis's poison from my system.

Nevertheless, I'd found a close confidant in Dilla. Despite her eccentricities, she had an indulgent, grandmotherly way about her that was comforting and refreshing. More importantly, I had the feeling that she knew a lot more about my Uncle Oscar than I did.

The thing to watch with Dilla, however, was her tendency toward wild, elaborate schemes, which almost always fronted as a ruse for her to flirt with the Mayor. You never knew what kind of crazy circus she might have in mind. I had learned my lesson from the Palace Hotel cat auction.

"How've you been, Dilla?" I asked cautiously. "I haven't seen you since right after . . ."

I let the silence fill in the blank. I hadn't seen Dilla since I checked out of the hospital. She'd brought my cats back to the Green Vase from their temporary living quarters at the flower shop down the street.

She'd been wearing a memorable outfit—a strange but convincing costume disguising herself as an elderly Asian woman. A thick rubber mask had covered her face, concealing all but her distinctively Dilla voice. The drab, frayed clothing she'd worn on her body had been a shock compared to her typically bright, colorful garb. I hadn't quite known what to make of it.

"Yes, well, I had some things to take care of," Dilla replied evasively. "I did some traveling, visited some old friends."

Her bubbling voice deflated to a hushed whisper. "I thought it best to lay low for a while, so I took myself out of circulation for a couple of weeks. There hasn't been any sign of . . . ?" She paused, letting the question hang in the air, unfinished.

"Nope," I popped in the answer. There was no reason for her to complete the sentence. I could empathize with the strain in her voice; we both knew her reference was to Frank Napis. The poisoning event had really shaken up Dilla; for some reason, she'd been certain that he would be coming after her next.

"It's been nothing but quiet here." I sighed, glancing at the stolidly silent cash register.

Those last words were still zooming through the telephone line when a thudding plunk sounded at the back of the showroom.

Isabella leapt off of the counter, her ears alertly perked. The hair along her backbone spiked up as her tail stretched out behind her, both indications of the seriousness of her inquiry. I leaned over the counter to watch her stalk across the floor toward the stairs at the back of the room.

On the other end of the phone line, Dilla relaxed back into a perky chatter. "Did you hear about Monty's new position?" she asked conversationally, sounding more like her buoyant self. "I ran into him the other day. He told me all about it."

Montgomery Carmichael—Monty to everyone in Jackson Square—ran an art studio across the street from the Green Vase, but he spent little time manning its sales counter. He was far too busy nosing around in other people's business. His well-intentioned but often ill-fated efforts of assistance were a constant nuisance to his neighbors, me in particular. Monty's ubiquitous presence was a fact of life in Jackson Square, a daily vitamin with a strange aftertaste whose dosing it was pointless to protest.

It had been a couple of days since Monty's tall, stringy figure had stopped by to poke around the Green Vase showroom. Counting my blessings, I hadn't gone looking for him.

"He's so excited," Dilla reported cheerily. "The Mayor has appointed him as City Commissioner for the Historical Preservation of Jackson Square."

She spun the title out slowly, as if trying to make sure she remembered it correctly. "It's a new position. The Mayor's just created it—to replace the old neighborhood Board."

The Jackson Square Board had been responsible for managing the historical preservation of the buildings in our neighborhood. Uncle Oscar and his attorney, Miranda Richards, had tussled with it numerous times over the last couple of years, the result of the many complaints raised about the decrepit condition of the Green Vase.

The Board had disbanded a couple of months ago, following the mysterious disappearance of its disgraced chairman, Gordon Bosco. I was one of only a handful of people who knew that Gordon Bosco had actually been an alter ego of Frank Napis. It was information I would just as soon not have acquired.

There had been months of speculation in Jackson Square about how the Mayor would handle the Board's replacement, and I couldn't imagine how Monty had landed this position, but, at that particular moment in the conversation, I was far more interested in what creature my cats were chasing at the back of the store—Rupert had bounced down the stairs from the kitchen to join Isabella in the hunt.

I stretched the cord of the receiver to its furthest uncoiled length, trying to get a better view. I could just make out the orange tips of two furry tails swishing in the air as Dilla continued to rave about Monty's new appointment.

"They've given him an office in City Hall—that's why you haven't seen him around Jackson Square the last couple of days. He's been settling in, learning the ropes. I understand it's a really important position."

I hardly heard her. My eyes were fixed on the two white streaks of fur thundering laps across the back of the showroom. A moment later, both cats landed with a loud thump on the trapdoor to the basement.

Dilla regained my attention as her tone suddenly took a more serious turn. "I need you to go visit him, dear," she coaxed. "To pick up a package for me."

I felt my eyelids retract in rebuke to the suggestion; Dilla correctly interpreted the reluctance in my silence. Her voice trembled slightly.

"It'll be nice for you to get out of the showroom for an hour or two, won't it? You can see Monty's new office. I'm sure he'd love to show it to you."

"I can only imagine," I muttered under my breath before quickly clearing my throat to mask the comment.

"What's in the package, Dilla?" I asked with a faint hue of suspicion. Of all people, Dilla was the least likely to pass up an opportunity to visit City Hall, given the off chance that she might run into the Mayor.

"Oh, it's not very big at all," she replied, overtly dodging my question. "It'll fit right into your pocket."

A static of wind or water, it was impossible to tell which, crackled through the phone line.

"I'm sorry, dear, the line is breaking up. It must be the connection." Dilla's voice was barely audible over the roar of what sounded more and more like a waterfall. "Please, as a favor to me. Won't you?"

"All right—" I sighed, starting to concede.

"There's just one more thing," Dilla cut in, her words suddenly crystal clear. "Monty's been acting a bit . . . *odd* lately. I don't want you to be surprised when you see him. I'm sure it's just a phase he's going through."

"Odd?" I asked with growing alarm, sensing, too late, that the fix was in. "Odd in what way?"

With thick, curlicue locks that bounced like springs off

the top of his head and a curious collection of vanity cufflinks, Montgomery Carmichael had been "odd" since the day I met him. You could call him quirky, I guess, if you wanted to be charitable, but he had always been odd.

Each time Monty wandered into the Green Vase, he greeted me with the same question. "How's your uncle?" he would ask, a smug, impertinent look on his face. Monty had developed a bizarre and, I believed, irrational theory that Oscar had faked his death and was hiding out somewhere in San Francisco.

"Still dead," was my standard reply, usually accompanied by the strong impulse to throw something at him.

The static returned to the phone line as Dilla signed off. "That's wonderful, dear. You'll need to go over there this afternoon. If you can leave in the next couple of minutes, that would be fine. I'll be in touch soon."

And with that, the line went dead, leaving nothing but a droning dial tone in my ear.

"Great," I said resignedly to the empty showroom, already dreading this assignment.

I hung up the receiver and ambled to the back of the store in search of the cats. Whatever they'd been chasing was now long gone. Rupert was flopped sideways on the floor, his legs flung out into a tummy-stretching sprawl. Isabella sat on the floor next to him, carefully licking one of his ears.

I searched the entire area, peeking behind the nearest bookcase, searching for any crevice where a trapped creature might be hiding. I couldn't identify anything out of the ordinary.

"What was going on back here?" I asked, wondering if I should set a couple of mousetraps. "What were you two trying to catch?"

Isabella glanced up from her grooming project. "Wrao," she replied noncommittally.

I shrugged and shook my head. "I have no idea what that means."

Isabella gave me an appeasing look, as if to placate a

clearly less intelligent creature, and then returned her attentions to the hair in Rupert's ear.

TWENTY MINUTES LATER, I headed out the door for City Hall.

Let's get this over with, I thought, pausing for a moment at the cashier counter. Harold's green-covered text still lay on top of the pile of books. I picked it up and scanned through the index.

The featured essay in the volume was one of Mark Twain's more famous California pieces, *The Celebrated Jumping Frog of Calaveras County*.

Chapter 3

REDWOOD PARK

DILLA ECKLES HUNG up the pay phone and nervously scanned the area surrounding the booth. She stood at the edge of a small park tucked in behind the TransAmerica Pyramid building, a few blocks away from Jackson Square.

The outer struts of the Pyramid's massive concrete base flanked one side of the half-acre park, almost all of which shivered in the perpetual shadow of the building's cold, lumbering mass. A formation of redwoods ringed the park, their long, straight trunks rocketing skyward, racing against the Pyramid's pointed skyscraper to reach the warmth of the sun.

The vertical plumes of a fountain caught the few splashes of sunlight that filtered down to the ground level of the park. The statues of a half dozen gangly legged frogs hopped amongst the fountain's stone lily pads, their bronze, green-tinged legs outstretched, the wide span of their webbed flippers flying through the air.

The fountain's frogs were San Francisco's tribute to Mark Twain, who manned a newspaper desk in the downtown Montgomery Block building during the latter half of the nineteenth century. In addition to providing office space, the Monkey Block, as it was affectionately called, also featured bars, restaurants, and, in the basement, a series of steam baths where Twain allegedly met a San Francisco firefighter named Tom Sawyer.

The historic building was torn down in the 1950s; it was replaced first by a parking lot and later by the towering Pyramid structure.

Redwood Park was all that remained of San Francisco's former downtown artist haven. In modern times, the park was frequented primarily by early morning tai chi practitioners and lunching office workers. The two groups used the space in peaceful, noncommunicative coexistence. Consequently, no one in that day's crowd of lunchers took notice of the elderly Asian woman using the pay phone near the fountain.

Dilla Eckles shuddered in her oversized ratty wool sweater. The loose-fitting legs of her putty brown pants flapped against her ankles as she shifted her weight back and forth.

It was like splitting glue, Dilla thought, trying to get that woman out of the Green Vase showroom. Oscar had tracked down a sizeable bounty prior to his death. Much of that treasure, Dilla knew, still lay hidden throughout the city. If his niece were to pick up where Oscar left off, she was going to need a little push.

Dilla clapped her gloved hands together to ward off the chill, her mouth firming with resolve. She had assured Oscar that she would look after his niece, and she was determined to make good on that promise—no matter how difficult that vow was becoming to keep.

Dilla stretched her neck to glance down at her watch. She had difficulty reading the time; her eyes were impeded by the thick rubber mask plastered over her face. The slanted oval slits around her eyes cupped as she tried to look downward. She brought her hand up to her face and tugged on the ragged charcoal-colored scarf tied around her neck, using the motion to get a more direct viewing of the watch face. Satisfied that she had waited a sufficient amount of time, Dilla exited the back side of the park, hustled down Sansome Street, and headed toward Jackson Square.

If not inspected too closely, her outer shell emulated that of an elderly Asian woman. The only Dilla-distinguishing feature she wore on her feet: square-toed, ankle-high, neon green go-go boots.

THE AFTERNOON BREEZE whipped up my hair as I stepped out the front door of the Green Vase. I hopped off of the semicircular stone threshold and skipped down the two steps to the street. My efforts to tuck the loose strands of hair behind my ear blinded me to the elderly Asian woman in bright green shoes peeking around the corner from the alley behind Frank Napis's papered-up storefront.

A few minutes later, I rounded the corner of Columbus and began walking down Montgomery Street. The wind barreled through the canyons of the financial district's tall office buildings, whipping up loose pieces of trash into tiny tornadoes that slapped against the bumpers of passing cars.

I used the wait at the next stoplight to button up my jacket, smiling ruefully at the iced-down pair of optimistically dressed tourists standing next to me on the curb.

A block ahead on the right, a colorful display of flowers could be seen through a clear plastic sheeting, brightening Montgomery's otherwise cold, gloomy corridor. Wang's flower stall was tarped up against the day's wind, but it was still in business.

Mr. Wang had been as obsessed as my Uncle Oscar with San Francisco's history and folklore. It was an interest the two of them had apparently shared. In the days following Oscar's death, Mr. Wang seemed to have known more than anyone else about Oscar's clandestine treasure-hunting activities.

With his pallid skin, constant cough, and unchecked cigarette habit, it shouldn't have been a surprise when Mr. Wang himself passed away a few weeks after Oscar. But somehow, I still expected to see his frail, skeletal hand waving at me from the rows of flowers.

Instead, the jarring sight of an impatient female figure in a trim yellow pantsuit dominated the flower stall. The front lines of her slacks were ironed into perfect pleats; the silhouetting outline of a tight black knit sweater was visible beneath her fitted jacket. The woman's thick auburn hair curled neatly under a black headband and bounced smoothly out the back into a perfect bob. Heavy black liner etched the boundary of her eyes; a thick coating of bloodred lipstick glazed her lips.

I watched as Miranda Richards glowered threateningly at Mr. Wang's demure but defiant daughter, Lily.

"I won't be put off any longer," the voice of Oscar's attorney sliced through the crisp, chilly air. "You must know where she is."

My legs instinctively curled beneath me as I slipped behind a conveniently located blue metal mailbox. I had no desire to draw Miranda's attention, particularly if she were already fired up into her barracuda lawyer mode.

I nosed over the humped lid of the mailbox as an unfortunate shopper approached the dueling pair with a bouquet of fluffy daffodils. From his defensive hand gestures, it appeared that the man was trying to make a purchase. Sulking testily, Miranda stepped aside while Lily rang up the sale.

The long, curved claws of Miranda's expertly manicured nails clicked against the counter while she waited for the flustered man to count out the total from his wallet. Her pouty red lips spouted out a slew of inaudible curses as I grimaced behind the mailbox.

One of the most powerful attorneys in San Francisco, Miranda Richards worked in a prestigious glass-walled office on the top floor of one of the taller buildings in the financial district. I had never figured out why she had agreed to represent my Uncle Oscar—or, for that matter, how he had managed to pay her exorbitant fees.

Despite the verbal bruising and diminished self-esteem I suffered each time we interacted, Miranda had turned out to be an ally, of sorts. She had tried to warn me about Frank Napis and his collaborator, and, in the end, it was Miranda who had saved my life by providing the tulip extract antidote to the hallucinogenic poison.

That history notwithstanding, I didn't intend to interrupt Miranda and Lily's heated discussion, which had resumed upon completion of the daffodil transaction.

The nearest traffic light turned, releasing a small herd of pedestrians. This seemed like the best moment to relinquish my mailbox screen and slip past the flower stall unnoticed. I fell in amongst the crowd, carefully avoiding Miranda's direct line of sight. As I passed the main entrance to the flower stall, Miranda's venomous voice seared the sidewalk.

"Tell me where my mother is."

Gulping in panic, I increased my pace, almost running over an amorous couple strolling hand in hand in front of me.

Although other limbs of their family tree were still a mystery to me, the strained relationship between Miranda Richards and her mother was well-known in Jackson Square.

Miranda's harsh, driven, frequently barbed personality marked a sharp contrast to her mother's fluttery, eccentric one. Dilla Eckles seemed to enjoy tormenting—and embarrassing—her daughter at every turn.

I hadn't thought to ask Dilla if she was still wearing her elderly Asian woman disguise. Surely that precaution was no longer necessary, I mused. I was trying hard to convince myself that Frank Napis must have moved on to another city and a new alias by now.

Since meeting Mr. Wang, I'd only caught a couple of glimpses of the woman I presumed to be his wife, but

Dilla's mask, I thought as I scurried down the street away from the flower stall, had made her a dead ringer for Mr. Wang's widow.

After I'd cleared a safe distance, I glanced back toward the flower shop, searching the rest of the inside for the elderly Asian woman who sometimes helped Lily out with the flower stall—the woman I'd always assumed to be Mrs. Wang—but I didn't see any sign of her there that day. I dismissed the thought and hurried the remaining blocks to the BART station.

IT NEVER OCCURRED to me that Dilla had been the *real* Mrs. Wang all along.

Chapter 4

EN ROUTE TO CITY HALL

THE DOORS OF the BART train slid open, releasing a stream of passengers into a mammoth concrete cavern that formed the lowest level of the Civic Center Station. I fell in line behind the crowd, hopping over the short gap between the frame of the train and the lip of the platform. Echoes of voices and footfalls followed me up a maze of escalators to the street.

The subway probably wasn't the most direct means of public transportation from the Green Vase to City Hall, but I had yet to master the bus routes that passed through Jackson Square.

On my last ill-fated attempt, I had inadvertently boarded a bus headed straight into the middle of Chinatown—which, on that particular day, happened to be celebrating one of its larger festivals. Each stop had brought an endless line of would-be riders patiently pushing their way inside the bus until the driver managed to staunch the flow and clamp the door shut.

The bus had quickly packed beyond capacity. I'd found

myself squashed onto a bench seat next to an elderly gentleman with a battered cane and a wide, toothless smile. A
worn, wild-haired woman of indeterminable age crammed
in behind me. Without apology, she shoved a cloth-covered
cage into the nonexistent space between us. Every so often
the animal inside emitted a loud, protesting squawk, causing the toothless man to burst into giggles at my disconcerted expression.

It took several blocks and two more stops before I
could maneuver close enough to the door to burst free
from the melee. I had been walking through the financial
district to the Market Street BART stations ever since.

The last limb in the Civic Center Station's tree of escalators rose out of a slanted, concrete-walled pit and deposited me onto the United Nations Plaza, a couple of blocks
away from City Hall. The day's breeze had only strength-
ened while I'd been underground. The wind blasted my
head as soon as it rose above street level.

I proceeded down a red brick walkway, littered with
the scattered, leafy remnants of broccoli, cabbage, and
bok choy. It was just after midday on Wednesday, and
the Civic Center's weekly farmers' market was about to
wrap up.

At a nearby table, a few stragglers haggled over the last
remaining hunks of daikon root. Across the way, a worker
packed up a small pile of green onions, neatly tying their
slender green stems into two-inch round bunches. At this
point in the day's trading, the tented makeshift stalls were
nearly depleted of the fresh-picked produce that had been
unloaded on the plaza earlier that morning—a verdant
array of fruits and vegetables tailored to the recipes of the
market's predominantly Asian shoppers.

As I passed the last food stall, the red brick pavement
merged into a wide asphalt corridor populated by an
army of hungry pigeons. The birds swarmed in around
me, strutting fearlessly toward my feet, their beady black
eyes eagerly assessing my snack-dropping potential. One

of the leaders cocked his head and swiveled it sideways, giving me the leering, one-eyed ogle of a bird confident in his own machismo.

Stepping timidly through the pack of aggressively cooing birds, I approached the backside of a monument to the Latin American icon Simon Bolivar. His bronze figure was depicted seated astride a rearing horse. One of Bolivar's arms stretched out in a grand gesture, as if to beckon me on toward my destination, Civic Center Plaza.

The long width of City Hall fenced in the far side of the sweeping plaza. The main branch of the city's library, the Civic Auditorium, and several state and federal buildings flanked the other edges of the square. I crossed the windswept common, passing more statued monuments as my feet pointed toward City Hall's gilded dome.

The building had sustained extensive damage during the 1989 Loma Prieta earthquake, but top to bottom renovations had recently been completed, outfitting the building with state-of-the-art seismic fortifications.

The project was one of the most lauded accomplishments of our previous Mayor. He had meticulously ensured the restoration of the original building's grand structure, down to the last flourishing detail—with one bright and gleaming exception.

The building's original dome had been plated with copper. Over time, the copper had corroded, tingeing to a greenish hue. To provide a more permanently glamorous exterior, the newly renovated dome was covered in a special 23.4-carat gold-infused paint. The proud pigeons of City Hall now roosted on a gold roof worth nearly half a million dollars. Perhaps that explained the bravado of the pigeons I'd encountered.

As I approached the front entrance to City Hall, my eyes were drawn to its center second floor balcony, which fronted the curtained glass doors of the Mayor's office suite. From the far end of the square, the balcony was dwarfed by the mammoth Corinthian columns rising up from its terrace. As I grew nearer, my attention focused in on the abundance of leafy gold scrolling that wound in and around the balcony's front railing. From my spectator's distance on the pavement below, it appeared as if a multitude of gilded octopus arms were swarming into the Mayor's office.

I climbed up the front steps of City Hall, fending off the amorous advances of a last few pigeons. At the top of the stairs, menacing stone faces scowled down at me from the keystone of three arched entrances. I chose the ghoul on the far left and pulled open its thick glass door.

A serpentine of modern security equipment greeted me inside. The assembly of square metal boxes, scanners, and bulky computers looked decidedly out of place in the lobby's polished marble surroundings.

I surrendered my shoulder bag to a pair of security guards who absentmindedly poked inside it before waving me into the open doorframe of a walk-through scanner. As I retrieved my bag on the opposite side, I tried to catch the attention of the nearest guard, who seemed far more interested in the sandwich he had just picked up from behind the scanner's counter. Floppy blond hair dusted down over his eyes as he stretched his mouth around a large corner of the bread and chomped down on it.

"I'm looking for Montgomery Carmichael," I said hopefully. "Can you point me toward his office?"

The guard squinted a left eye at the ceiling and pumped his jaw up and down as he chewed on the massive hunk of sandwich.

"Don't think I've heard of that one before," he replied after a long moment of masticular consideration.

The guard looked as if he might still be considering my request, but I decided not to wait through the duration of his next bite. "I'm sure I'll be able to find him," I replied and proceeded through the lobby to the rotunda.

I'd driven past City Hall's mammoth block-long building several times, but this was my first actual experience inside. I'd heard people gush about the famous structure, but I was unprepared for its breathtaking panorama. Despite all of its gleaming gold grandeur, the outer shell of the building couldn't match the magnificent beauty of the cathedral-like interior.

My height seemed to shrink as I stood beneath the soaring dome. Enormous arches ringed the rotunda's upper walls, letting in such a flood of light that it was as if a part of the sky had been captured within. At its apex, the crown of the dome glowed a bubbling shade of pink, hovering over the rotunda like the underside of a gigantic jellyfish.

I tilted my neck upward, marveling at the myriad of carvings worked into every inch of ceramic, stone, and plaster. The skyward slant, however, quickly diminished my balance, and I almost lost my footing on the slick pink marble that decorated the floor directly beneath the dome.

As I was struggling to regain my balance, a pair of dark-suited men brushed past me. They crossed the floor of the rotunda with their heads bent close together in conversation; then they began to climb a sweeping marble staircase on the opposite side.

One of the men looked vaguely familiar to me. He had a smooth, fleshy, childlike face that was framed by limp mousy brown hair. A member of the city's Board of Supervisors, I thought as I squinted at his profile.

I followed the two men up the stairs, my own ascension much slower. I had to stop every couple of steps to let my eyes swallow another gulp of the elaborately decorated rotunda. Each step in elevation revealed more details of the figures carved into the surrounding walls.

A countless number of mythic deities howled into the chamber with spouting, circular-shaped mouths. Creamy stone lions with flowing manes and sharp, narrow eyes keenly assessed each passerby. Thick, curling ribbons of plaster fringed richly festooned frescoes mounted onto seemingly every surface.

Above it all, a flood of light flowed in through the stained glass windows that framed the arches of the rotunda's upper walls. Each wall of windows depicted the outlines of a ship, its sails rippling in the wind as it headed through the mouth of the Golden Gate and into San Francisco's treacherous bay.

Ten minutes later, I finally made it to the top of the stairs. I began wandering down the second floor hallway, which carved a circular path around the periphery of the rotunda. The search for Monty's office, I decided, could wait until I'd done a little sightseeing.

DILLA'S NEON GREEN go-go boots crept across the granite on the darkened corners on the main level of the rotunda. She stood next to a gilded lamppost, closely watching as a brown-haired woman in glasses climbed the central staircase and turned down the second floor hallway.

Once Dilla had ensured that the coast was clear, she scurried down a foyered hallway near the backside of the staircase and slid into a long coat closet that had been modified to accommodate several public telephones.

Dilla waited a moment for her eyes to adjust to the dimmer light in the windowless room; then she picked up the nearest receiver and began to dial.

The line on the other end rang only twice before a voice answered.

"She's here," Dilla whispered breathlessly through the thick lips of the mask.

Chapter 5

A NEW ACQUAINTANCE

I STROLLED THE length of the second floor hallway, following its route around the circumference of the rotunda. As I neared the central marble staircase, I paused for one more look up at the ceiling before I began my reluctant hunt for Monty's office.

"Wonder what the view is like up there," I murmured to myself as I leaned over a gilded iron railing and gazed toward the top echelons of the rotunda. A dazzling display of light flitted across the delicate crinkles and curls of the masonry, just beneath the opulent crest of the dome. My eyes scanned the highest tiered balcony several hundred feet above, checking for signs of tourists, but public access to that level appeared to be closed.

It was as I stood there, craning up at the dome with my back to the hallway, that I suddenly became aware of a presence moving in behind me—a putrid, smelly one that reeked of decaying fish and rotting garbage.

I spun around to ward off the source of the intruding odor and found myself face-to-grimy-smiling-face with a jumpsuit-clad man wielding a mop. A janitor, I presumed.

A wild mane of frizzy red hair covered the man's head like an overgrown weed. The same seed had sprouted thickly from his eyebrows and spread across the lower half of his face. It had been at least a week since his last shave, and, I suspected, shower. The stench was overwhelming—he was standing *way* too close to me.

"Can I help you, Miss?" the janitor asked genially, his stubbled chin inches from my nose.

He reached behind his back and pulled a beaten-up cart stuffed full of refuse into the space beside us. "Are you looking for something?"

I felt my toes curl inward as the edge of my spine pressed up against the iron frame of the balcony's railing. The persistent tickle of a sneeze began its curling ascent through my nasal passages.

"I-I was just looking around," I stuttered, pointing limply out at the rotunda.

"Ah, you're a visitor then?" He leaned back and looked me up and down. "A local though, I think. Not a tourist."

The janitor winked a rusty red eyebrow at me as I confirmed his assumption with a nod. A dingy layer of grit and grime covered the man's body, settling into every crack, crevice, and wrinkle.

"We try to take good care of our guests here at City Hall," he said pleasantly. He swung the business end of his mop through the air like a javelin and angled it into the cart. Then, he shoved his grungy hand toward me, offering it for a shake. "Nice to meet you. I'm Sam."

I shook his hand as gingerly as possible. My eyes scanned the faded nametag sewn onto the right chest pocket of the janitor's rumpled gray jumpsuit, confirming his identification.

"Nice to meet you, too . . . uh, Sam," I replied as his hand crunched down on mine, firmly stamping it with his soiled imprint.

Sam flipped a lever on his cart to brake its wheels. An air freshener cut in the circular outline of a piece of orange fruit swung, ineffectively, from the handle of the cart.

"Nice view, isn't it?" he asked, shaking his head in admiration as he leaned over the railing next to me. "I never get tired of looking at it."

The smell swilling in the air around him was almost unbearable. I managed a weak grimace in response as he continued.

"I've been here almost fifteen years now—took the spot over from my dad. He was in the job well over thirty years. He worked for *a lot* of Mayors, my dad did."

"Mmm," I hummed in response, anxiously becoming aware that I was pinned between Sam's smelly cart, the balcony, and the curving bulge of the nearest wall.

"I only go back two Mayors," Sam announced enthusiastically. He chuckled and bent his head toward me. "I've got to tell you, I liked the first one better." He grinned wryly at me, as if we were sharing a private joke. "I call him the First Mayor—on account of he was *my* first Mayor."

The corners of my mouth tightened with apprehension. I had the disturbing impression that Sam was settling in for a long chat.

"The First Mayor, he knew the name of everyone who worked here." Sam nodded his head up and down and pointed at his chest. "Even me. He always made a point to stop and talk with me. You know, it doesn't take much effort to make a person feel acknowledged. A little appreciation goes a long way."

Sam shifted his stance to gain a more comfortable and, I feared, permanent position against the railing.

"The First Mayor, when he'd see you coming, he'd touch the brim of his hat and tip it in your direction. Just like this."

Sam's right hand swung up to his own dingy, frayed cap and tapped the rim of its bill.

"Of course, he always wore a fancy hat, that First Mayor. Bowlers mostly. They gave him a dapper, smart look—not that he needed any help with that. That man was *born* with the smarts."

Sam returned his hand to the balcony, sliding it ever closer to the small of my back. "The First Mayor, he knew all about the janitorial business. That's how he started off when he came to San Francisco as a teenager. He got a part-time job cleaning the pews at one of the local churches. That was all the foothold he needed—he worked his way up from there. He went to law school; then he got himself into politics. He was the Speaker of the State Legislature before he became Mayor."

The combined rank odor of Sam and his cart had completely surrounded me. My eyes began to water as the sneeze forced its way closer to the surface.

"'Hey there, Sam. What's the news?' That's how the First Mayor would greet me. I made sure I always had a little tidbit of gossip for him." Sam's chest puffed out with pride. "I keep a close eye on everything that goes on here. Same as my father did. That's one of the things he taught me, before he passed the job on."

I stood there, crammed up against the balcony, struggling to remember what I had done to set loose this deluge of information. Sam continued on with the conversation as if we were both actively participating. He bobbed his head up and down, reinforcing his assertion.

"That's right. Everything that goes on here. Who's scheming with whom, which ones are in a tiff, and which ones are conspira-tating together. The First Mayor, he was *always* interested in that sort of thing. And not only about the Supervisors, but their staff, too."

Sam crossed his arms over his chest as he reflected.

"That's why the First Mayor was so good at his job. We'd have our little talk—you know, all secret-like—then, he'd pat me on the back and tell me how much he appreciated my assistance, my loyalty. Yes ma'am, he was a fine Mayor. He sure was."

"Aaah-chooo!" My nose made a valiant effort to expel the rancidly offensive odor tormenting it. The high-pitched sneeze echoed in the stone-walled chamber. Tourists on the far side of the rotunda looked up, startled.

"Bless you," Sam said reflexively, barely pausing his dialogue. "You know, the First Mayor would have been reelected, over and over again, no doubt about it, if it weren't for those term limits. He served out his eight years and couldn't run again. He's still around though. Still has his finger in the pie, so to speak. He knows everything that goes on in this city, *and* in City Hall, that's for sure."

Sam paused and stuck his thumbs through a pair of straps sewn onto the waist of his jumpsuit. "Now, the Current Mayor, I can't say much about him."

Thank goodness, I thought, momentarily relieved. Sam unhitched one of his thumbs and reached out for the handle of his cart. For a brief moment, I actually believed that he was preparing to depart.

I was sorely mistaken. Sam had been untruthful. He had plenty to say about the Current Mayor.

"Now, the Current Mayor, he keeps to himself—always walks through here with his head down, all closed off." Sam mimed an exaggerated head tuck. "He rushes right past people, as if he's afraid to talk to them. If you ask me, that's why he's had so much trouble with the Supervisors."

Sam pumped his eyebrows, as if daring me to challenge this proposition, but my face was blank. My feet were growing numb from standing so long without movement, and my nose was starting to pulse with the threat of another sneeze.

"You might think, well, the Mayor—he's the king of the city. Right? He doesn't have to worry about a bunch of silly Supervisors."

Sam tilted his head to emphasize his point. "But then you'd be wrong. You see, we've got a convoluted form of government here in San Francisco. Different parts have different powers; some of them overlap. It's all muddled together. Very complicated."

Sam shook his hands in the air, wiggling his grimy fingers at me.

"The Mayor has to work *with* the Board of Supervisors. He needs them to approve his budget and to enact legislation to support his programs and policies. They can be a right thorn in his side if they've got a mind to be."

"Ah-choo! Ah-choo! Ah-choo!" The sneezes were coming fast and furious now, each one in a high-pitched staccato. On the floor of the rotunda, another pair of tourists put their hands over their ears as they looked nervously up at the ceiling.

"Gesundheit!" Sam laughed and thumped me on the back. The force of the blow nearly threw me into the open mouth of his refuse cart.

"Where was I . . . ah yes. The Current Mayor. He used to be a Supervisor himself, so he should know better. But there's all of this anti-civility built up between him and them."

Sam tapped a grimy finger against his chin. "The thing is, not many of our Supervisors supported the Current Mayor when he ran for office the last time around. They plumped for this other fellow. Well, after he lost the Mayor's race, this guy ended up being the President of the Board of Supervisors."

Sam puckered his lips together and shot out a low whistle before shaking his head sadly. "The two of them—the Current Mayor and the Supervisor He Ran Against—they haven't been able to smooth things over since the last election. It's a shame. There's a lot of toxic air in the building these days." Sam wiped his brow. "You know, you just can't take political things personally. That's what the First Mayor used to say."

Sam paused to bemoan this unpleasant lesson in politics, and I decided it was time to make my escape. I'd had enough. I couldn't take any more.

"I've got to find a friend of mine." My words burst into the brief break in Sam's speech. "He's expecting me at his office." With effort, I pushed the braked garbage cart away from the balcony and leapt around it.

"Oh, who're you looking for?" Sam replied helpfully.

"I'd be happy to take you to him." He winked reassuringly. "I know every corner of City Hall."

I looked down the hallway, contemplating a sprint to the main staircase. There was no way Sam could keep up with me while pushing that heavy cart.

Sam smiled warmly. "It's easy for a newcomer to get lost wandering around this building."

I was trapped by a personality far stronger than my own. With a last, desperate glance at my escape route, I said weakly, my voice nearly a whisper, "I'm looking for Montgomery Carmichael's office."

"Ah yes, I know the place exactly." Sam grasped the handle of the cart and shoved it forward enthusiastically. "It's off the beaten path a ways—a little hard to find. Come on, I'll take you down there."

"Oh, I wouldn't want you to go out of your way," I stuttered as the cart zoomed toward me, its orange-shaped air freshener swinging wildly from the handle.

"No, no, it's no problem at all," Sam insisted. "I'm heading that direction anyway."

The cart sped past me, moving, I noted, at a clip that would have easily kept up with my contemplated escape sprint.

"Come on then," he called out over his shoulder, beckoning with a grimy hand.

Ruefully, I started off down the hallway, trotting to keep up with Sam and his smelly, speeding cart.

Chapter 6

COMMISSIONER CARMICHAEL

I WAS PANTING heavily when I caught up to Sam at the far end of the hallway. He stood next to his cart, patiently waiting for me in front of a bank of elevators.

"Ready?" he asked, carefully pressing the call button with one of his grime-blackened fingers when I nodded.

"All aboard, then," he called out cheerfully as one set of metal doors slid open.

I stepped into the elevator's cramped closet and flattened myself against the wall while Sam wheeled inside with his cart. The doors banged shut, and I held my breath as we began a bumpy descent.

The turbulence of the ride caused the air freshener tied to the cart's handle to sway back and forth. The previously ineffective orange scent began to concentrate in the elevator's ever shrinking compartment, the sweet, artificial smell overpowering even the stench of the cart's rotting rubbish.

"The paneling and flooring have all been restored to look just like the original," Sam explained as the elevator made a hiccupping lurch. He pointed to the floor beneath his cart. "The city symbol is inlaid in brass."

Each short, sudden drop of the elevator was accompanied by a loud grinding of gears, causing me to wonder if the elevator's mechanical components had received the same restorative attention.

I gripped onto the side railing as the elevator paused at the first floor. The metal doors slid open to reveal an elderly man in an expensive-looking suit and highly polished shoes.

Sam smiled broadly at the man, inviting him inside. "Plenty of room," he said encouragingly.

The man glanced at Sam's cart, took one whiff of the strange citrus-infused odor wafting out of the elevator, and waved us on.

"That's all right," he said, taking a wide step back from the opening. "I think I'll take the stairs." He swung his arms energetically back and forth. "Good for my health."

Another long minute later, we bumped to a stop on City Hall's basement level. The elevator doors opened to reveal a bland, windowless corridor with walls painted in a flat off-white paint. Dim artificial lighting hung from a prefab office-tile ceiling. The hallway's blank walls stretched out the length of the building, unadorned by even the smallest picture or painting.

Sam's effusive mood was undiminished by the drab change in decor. He pushed his cart toward the left leg of the corridor. "It's down this hall and around the corner," he assured me cheerfully.

I hesitated to follow him. The floor above us had been humming with activity, but here in the building's lowest level, not another soul seemed to be stirring. I was beginning to fear that the awful smell emanating from Sam's cart was due not to the refuse he had collected but from the decomposing body of the last hapless tourist he had lured down to the basement.

After several silent minutes anxiously passing door after tightly shut door, we approached one up ahead on the right that was slightly ajar. Light from inside the room stretched into the dim hallway.

The door was unlabeled, I noted when we reached it. Monty's appointment was so recent, his nameplate had yet to be affixed.

"This is it," Sam whispered into my ear, his hushed voice echoing in the vacant emptiness of the hallway.

I pushed the door open a bit further and poked my head into the office.

The room was sparsely furnished with a worn wooden desk fronted by a single guest chair that looked as if its legs might collapse if anyone were foolish enough to trust it with his weight.

Behind the desk, a man slumped back in a second, slightly more stable-looking seat. His closed eyelids fluttered with a deep, restful snore. I'd found my neighbor, Montgomery Carmichael, and I immediately saw the reason for Dilla's cautionary remarks.

Monty's long, pointed feet were propped up on the splintered edge of the desk, his toes rocking back and forth in time with his slumbered breathing. He wore a double-breasted black wool suit and a narrow pale blue tie. But it wasn't Monty's wardrobe that had caught my attention—it was his hair.

Monty's tightly curled locks had been combed out and straightened into the elevated wave of a pompadour that rose several inches up from his forehead. Every uncoiled strand was securely cinched into position with a shellacking tortoiseshell coat of hair gel; it was layered on so thick the surface appeared almost wet. The hairstyle's constrained formation was an amazing tribute to the molding capacity of modern styling products.

I started to speak to wake him, but Sam raised a hand to stop me. He put a finger to his lips and made a shushing sound as he clambered noisily around to the backside of Monty's desk.

Monty's eyelashes made a brief, off-snore flutter as Sam leaned over him, but his lids did not open. Slowly, gingerly, Sam brought his dingy left forefinger near the slick surface of Monty's eye-catching coif of hair.

Sam glanced conspiratorially back at me, grinned sheepishly, and then poked his finger into the cresting wave of Monty's shiny pompadour.

The entire mass of hair moved as if it were one being, a single slimy creature that had taken up residence on Monty's cranium. Sam licked his upper lip, concentrated on the target, and poked again, this time a little more vigorously. The second poke set off a Jell-O-like vibration that shook throughout the gelatinous mound of hair.

Monty's nose twitched, but otherwise, he did not stir. His snoring continued unabated.

Sam struggled to contain the giggles gurgling up inside him. He motioned for me to give his game a try, gesturing insistently at Monty's still slumbering head.

With a repulsed cringe, I crept around to the back of the desk and eased my right hand toward the coated surface of Monty's hair.

Sam bobbed his head up and down, enthusiastically urging me on.

I kept the rest of my body as far away as possible from the sacrificial hand as it hovered over Monty's head. Gritting my teeth, I let one fingertip drop into a half-hearted poke—quickly jerking it back as the off-putting texture snailed beneath my fingers.

Sam exchanged places with me and moved in for a second demonstration. But this time, just as his grimy hand neared the towering stack of hair, Monty's eyes flew open.

"Wha-haa . . . ha . . . ha!" Monty's tenor-pitched voice squealed as he awoke to the sight of Sam's looming fingers.

"Sam! Sam, Sam!" Monty wagged an admonishing finger as his long legs clattered off the edge of the desk. "What have I told you about the hair?"

Monty's chiding expression immediately changed when he saw me standing on the opposite side of the room where I'd retreated during Sam's second poking session.

"Well, hello," Monty said, his voice affecting a slick politician's unctuousness. "I was wondering when you would stop by to see me."

He winked as if I were an admiring fan and ran his hand over the top of his head, unnecessarily smoothing his immovable hair. "What do you think of my new office here in City Hall?"

I smiled, biting my lip. "Um, yes, it's quite impressive," I said placatingly. "Look, I'm here because of Dilla actually—"

Before I could ask about the package, Monty leapt up off of his chair and cut in. "How's your uncle?" he asked cheekily.

I sighed and rolled my eyes. "Still dea—"

"Let me give you the grand tour," Monty offered, not waiting for my response. He sidled past Sam and leapt around the desk. "This," he announced grandly, encircling my shoulders with his left arm, spreading his right one wide, "is my office."

"Mm-hmm," I acknowledged, as Monty swung me around to get a full 360-degree viewing of the room.

"This," Monty proclaimed with a sweep of his right hand, "is my desk."

"I see," I said blandly, still braced in position by Monty's left arm.

Monty was clearly not the first user of this piece of furniture. The finish on the surface had long since worn off. Something purple, possibly ink, had spilled across the top, creating a stain in the shape of a sprawling, many-legged blob.

Monty tapped a cracked plastic tray on the corner of the desk. "My in-box," he said importantly.

I attempted an appreciative stare at Monty's desk and empty in-box. After Monty determined that we had paid sufficient homage to his office furniture, he swung me toward the wall nearest the desk. A single picture hung from the short stretch of dingy, scuffed plaster.

It was an 8"x12" color photo of the Current Mayor, signed with a thick black marker in the bottom right-hand corner. The Mayor smiled handsomely in the frame as he posed leaning up against his own highly polished mahogany bureau. Several flags filled in the background behind him.

"And *this*," Monty said with majestic pride as he released my shoulders so that he could flourish both hands around the corners of the picture's frame, "is my boss. The man who made it all possible." He drumrolled his hands against the wall. "The Mayor."

Monty struck a pose beside the picture, leaning up against the edge of his desk to assume the same stance as the man frozen inside the frame. I clasped my hands to my cheeks, unsure of how to respond.

Monty had emulated the Mayor's style in every possible aspect. He wore the same cut of double-breasted suit and the same slim blue tie around his neck. Even his black, narrow, pointed-toe dress shoes were the same brand as the man's in the picture. He had captured every last detail—right down to the Mayor's swept-back hairstyle—although, I thought, perhaps he had gone a bit overboard on the hair gel.

This, I gathered, is what Dilla had meant by Monty's recent "odd" behavior.

"The window," Sam said insistently, breaking the spell on Monty's picture posing. "Tell her about the window."

Monty waved his hand dismissively. "Oh, there's nothing special to say about the window," he replied briskly, stepping in front of Sam to block him from my view. "It's just an ordinary window. We've got them all over City Hall."

"But, it's—" Sam protested over Monty's shoulder.

"Why don't I give you a quick tour upstairs," Monty said to me, his voice drowning out the rest of Sam's sentence.

"Thanks, but I've got to get back to the Green Vase," I tried to demur. "I'm just here to pick up Dilla's package."

"Got it right here," Monty replied, patting the breast pocket of his suit as he strode quickly toward the door of the office. "I'll give it to you upstairs."

I sighed resignedly and turned to follow Monty, taking one last glance back at Sam before I left.

Sam stood next to the desk, his face muddled with confusion. What, I wondered, had he been trying to say about the window? He registered the questioning look on my face and pointed up at the rectangular pane of glass that ran along the top of the back wall of the office.

The structure was reinforced with iron rebars that were welded to the outside of the frame; the pane of glass had been cracked open to let in some fresh air. Since we were standing in the building's basement, the window opened just over the surface of the grass outside. The feet of people walking by on the nearby sidewalk were barely visible from our vantage point inside the office.

I had to agree with Monty. It seemed like an ordinary window to me.

I shrugged and stepped toward the door, but Sam grabbed my arm and whispered urgently into my ear.

"That's the window," he said, his voice tinged with a solemn awe. "That's *the* window . . ."

One of Monty's long, stringy arms reached back and grabbed my wrist. With a sharp tug, he pulled me into the hallway. As he dragged me down the corridor, he whispered shortly, "I'll tell you about that *later*."

Chapter 7

THE GRAND TOUR ...
CONTINUED

"SAN FRANCISCO'S CITY Hall," Monty said proudly as the two of us walked up a flight of stairs from the basement to the first floor of the rotunda, "is now one of the most seismically sophisticated buildings in the state of California, if not the world."

We reached the first floor, emerging on the backside of the rotunda's central marble staircase. Monty waved his black-suited arms about like a tour guide, directing me around the base of the stairs into the rotunda as he continued.

"Of course, that wasn't always the case. San Francisco's first City Hall was destroyed by the 1906 earthquake." Monty shrugged, dismissing the loss. "To be honest, that building wasn't much to look at. Nothing like this," he said, dramatically sweeping his hands across the vast open space beneath the dome.

"They went all out when they drew up the plans for the replacement. San Francisco had something to prove. Not only would the city rise from the ashes of the earthquake's near total annihilation—it would do so with grace and style."

Monty stepped back on his left foot and angled his tall, slim body skyward. "The peak of this dome is one of the highest in the world—several inches taller than the one at the U.S. Capitol in Washington, D.C."

He turned his head back down toward me for an aside. "That's a huge claim to fame for us. We always make sure to mention it to the tourists, especially the ones from the East Coast."

I shook my head, amused, but not the least bit surprised, at how quickly Monty had assimilated himself into the City Hall "we."

Monty released his hold on the ceiling and motioned me toward one of the expansive, pavilionlike rooms that stretched out on the north and south sides of the rotunda.

"The 1989 Loma Prieta earthquake inflicted a fair amount of damage to City Hall. Extensive renovations were needed to repair the building and to bring it up to seismic code. On top of that, many of the structure's unique design elements had been neglected over the years and required refurbishment. Our previous Mayor led the fundraising efforts for the project. He ensured that the renovations were complete before he left office at the end of his second term."

We entered the side pavilion, which was identified by a small rectangular sign as the "South Light Court." Several displays dedicated to the renovation work had been set up on the far end of the large, open room.

Monty pointed me toward an exhibit in the corner, which showcased a massive round piece of rubber. A portion of the rubber device had been cut out to show the layers of its interior core.

Monty rested his right elbow on the edge of the display mount. "It was quite a challenge to retrofit a building of this size and age," he said, reveling in the authority of his newly acquired earthquake-retrofitting expertise. I cocked my right eyebrow at him skeptically as he continued.

"After extensive study and analysis, they settled on a form of technology called Base Isolation." Monty fondly patted the exhibit's lump of black rubber. "*This* is a base isolator unit."

I squinted at the hulking round mass. Despite the fancy terminology, it looked like nothing more than a solid chunk of rubber to me.

"The engineers went through the entire foundation and inserted these rubber base isolators into the middle of each supporting column, separating the top half of the column from the bottom of the foundation. The entire building is actually *detached* from the earth below us. Now, in the event of an earthquake—"

Monty stood back from the display and placed his feet parallel to one another, about two feet apart.

"In the event of an earthquake," he repeated, "the ground begins to move back and forth . . ."

Monty's hips began to gyrate as if they'd been activated by an internal jackhammer.

". . . some parts of it going one way . . . some parts of it going another . . ."

Monty's legs spasmed out in strange directions. His arms kept pace, causing his suit coat to flap about like an oversized bat trying to take flight. His hair, of course, held steady.

". . . but the building does not. It just kind of rolls along on top of the base isolators."

Monty's hips continued to move as he steadied his upper body. Slowly his shoulders slid sideways. He looked as if he were performing a strange new dance step. People in other parts of the room had started whispering and pointing at us.

"These isolators," Monty explained, his lower body still jerking wildly back and forth, "will allow the entire building to slide as one entity, up to . . ."

He leaned over to check a plaque mounted on the display.

". . . twenty-six inches. But, here in the rotunda, you wouldn't feel a thing. You wouldn't even know that an earthquake had hit."

Monty pointed to the floor beneath his dancing feet. "They built a four-foot moat around the base of the building to give the foundation plenty of room to move—it should be able to handle the biggest quake the earth can throw up at us."

One of the whisperers from across the room began walking toward us. The young man had squeaky white tennis shoes on his feet and a backpack squarely secured across his shoulders; a large camera hung around his neck.

Smiling shyly, the man approached Monty holding out a pen and a piece of paper. It suddenly occurred to me that he was about to ask Monty for his autograph. He actually thought Monty *was* the Mayor.

"Oh good grief," I muttered under my breath as Monty took the paper, pulled out his own artist-grade calligraphy pen, and signed it. From what I could see, the signature was practically illegible.

The excited man turned to me and began pointing and gesturing at his camera. Apparently, the misguided tourist didn't speak English; there was no way for me to explain that he'd been duped.

Begrudgingly, I accommodated his request. Monty and the man posed in front of the base isolator display as I focused the camera and clicked the button. Monty shook the man's hand and waved warmly at the happily tittering crowd of fellow tourists who had gathered around to watch.

"I bet you didn't know I was so famous," Monty jested at me. He arched his eyebrows in an elitist fashion. "Just one of the perks of the job."

I rolled my eyes with disgust. "That was pathetic."

"Here, let me show you something else," Monty said, predictably ignoring my comment as he pulled me over to another exhibit.

This display presented a wooden model of the upper half of City Hall's rotunda, cut out to show the interior structure of the dome. I was surprised to realize that the

pink-hued ceiling I had marveled at during my earlier
wanderings was merely a cap that sealed over the rotunda's central orifice, midway up the height of the dome.
The tiny balcony that I had spied from my earlier view-
point on the second floor hallway, I now realized, represented less than half of the dome's true height.

Hidden from the pedestrian view at the bottom of the
rotunda, a delicate spiral staircase stretched above the
faux ceiling, circling its way up into a steeple mounted on
the top of the dome. The winding staircase terminated
within the steeple at a small attic. I stared at the model,
trying to imagine the view from the magical little room
perched at the top of the dome.

"Have you been up there yet?" I asked, pointing to the
model.

"No," Monty sighed ruefully. "They're awfully restric-
tive about that area—afraid someone might fall out, I
guess." He winked at me. "I've been bugging Sam to get
me in. He's one of the few people with a key."

We left the South Light Court and walked back out into
the rotunda. I was hoping to extract Dilla's package from
Monty's suit pocket and start my trip back to the Green
Vase, but Monty wasn't yet finished with his tour. He began ticking off facts on his long, skinny fingers.

"Let's see, the floor design spreading out from the
staircase—that's done in pink Tennessee marble. And
those big gray walls surrounding us, they're all Colorado
limestone."

Monty pointed at a Hispanic couple walking across the
main floor of the rotunda. The woman was dressed in an
elaborate white wedding gown, decorated with yards and
yards of pearl-shaped beads. The man wore a black tuxedo, accented with a cummerbund brightly striped in reds,
greens, and yellows. A couple of attendants followed, each
of them dressed in formal attire, one of them carrying a
fiddle.

"That'll be a marriage queuing up," Monty said, glancing at his watch. "Come on, we should have enough time to check out the Ceremonial Rotunda before they get started. It's right at the top of the marble stairs." Monty grabbed my hand and pulled me toward the steps.

"All right," I replied wearily. "But then, I really need to get back to the shop."

Monty continued to pepper me with trivia while we climbed up the steps to the second floor. "Did you know?" he asked as we stepped into a smaller, more intimate cove formed in between the second and third floors. "This is where Joe DiMaggio and Marilyn Monroe got hitched. They call this the Ceremonial Rotunda."

A bronze bust had been placed at the edge of the cove. The head and shoulders of a man with a prominent nose, wide elephant ears, and a broad humorous smile had been positioned so that he overlooked the designated location for City Hall's marriage ceremonies.

I had noticed several similar monuments on my earlier walk around City Hall, but I had been so taken with the decorations on the walls and ceiling, I hadn't stopped to familiarize myself with any of the memorialized figures.

Monty sidled up to the bust and wrapped his right arm around its bronze shoulders. "This guy," Monty said, his voice dropping reverently, "is a legend in San Francisco politics. Most of these busts are monuments dedicated to former Mayors. But this one is for a former Supervisor, Harvey Milk."

Monty stepped back from the bust to let me examine it more closely. Thirty years after his death, Harvey Milk was still famous throughout San Francisco, not only for his politics—he was the city's first openly gay elected official—but for the tragic way in which he died. Harvey Milk and the Mayor of his time, George Moscone, were assassinated in City Hall by one of the other Supervisors. The horrifying event had shaken the city to its core.

A relief had been carved into the marble monument beneath the bust. The scene depicted a line of citizens marching through the streets of San Francisco holding candles in the air, commemorating the outpouring of grief that swept the city streets following the shootings.

Monty paced into the center of the rotunda while I bent down to study the base of the Milk monument. He was preparing to launch into the next topic of his lecture as I straightened and turned to face him.

But right at that moment, a strange feeling swept over me—an unsettled sensation, as if something were amiss.

I glanced around at the surrounding stone and then swept my eyes upward. A circular balcony, about ten feet or so in diameter, looked down from the third floor to the space where we were standing.

A movement on the edge of the stone balcony caught my eye as a tiny green figure shuffled to the edge of the railing. The slight echo of a meager croak floated down into the cove, barely audible over the drone of Monty's voice.

I felt my mouth fall open as the frog leapt into the air, his strong back legs propelling him into the center airspace of the Ceremonial Rotunda.

Monty noticed my gaping stare and turned his long, narrow face in the same upward direction I was looking— just in time to receive the splat of the frog's slimy body across his forehead.

Chapter 8

AFTER THE FROG ATTACK

THE FROG DUCKED into the slick helmet of Monty's hair, briefly dodging a flailing net of fingers as Monty's arms swung instinctively up over his head. A muffled *ribbit* issued from somewhere within the heaving heap of fingers, frog, and overstyled hair.

"Ah ha!" Monty exclaimed as he finally wrapped his hand around the frog's spongy middle.

But the extra lubrication of Monty's hair gel made the already slippery frog impossible to hold. The struggling frog popped out of Monty's grasp and shot up into the air, its hind legs stretching out behind it for full aerodynamic effect.

I stepped sideways to avoid both the fleeing frog and Monty's lunging effort to recapture it. The frog landed with a squishing plunk on the marble floor and quickly turned around to size up the oncoming pursuit of Monty's skinny, scrambling figure.

Monty stumbled forward, his long arms swooping down at the floor. The frog took off on a series of short, vigorous hops that took it straight between Monty's pointed feet. Monty swiveled the toes of his dress shoes on the marble, trying to reverse direction to continue the chase.

A small amount of hair gel had apparently transferred from the bottom of the frog's webbed feet to the center of the Ceremonial Rotunda when it first landed. As the sole of Monty's left shoe hit the slick spot on the marble, his legs flew out from under him, and he crashed painfully onto the floor. With a last triumphant *ribbit*, the frog disappeared around the corner leading to the second floor hallway.

The wedding party reached the top of the stairs, murmuring with concern at the sight laid out in front of them. The fiddle player peeked over my shoulder as I bent down toward Monty's lanky body, which was sprawled out in the middle of the Ceremonial Rotunda. His gel-coated hair had been hopelessly disarranged; it was now strangely spiked and ruffled as if he had just climbed out of bed after a restless night's sleep.

"Monty?" I asked tentatively as more members from the wedding party circled his prostrate body. "Are you okay?"

He didn't speak for a long moment. Slowly, he lifted his torso up into a seated position. His thin lips stretched out toward both corners of his narrow face as he turned his head to look at me. His expression was flat, unreadable.

"Was that . . . a . . . frog?"

A PAIR OF bright green go-go boots stood on the third floor balcony above the Ceremonial Rotunda, anchoring an elderly Asian woman who had leaned over the banister to watch the melee unfold below. Dilla giggled to herself, enjoying the scene. Then, she trotted off down the third floor hallway, heading toward the opposite end of the rotunda and the side stairs that would take her down to the Mayor's office suite.

Dilla was right on time for her afternoon appointment.

She could hardly wait to see the Mayor's response to her latest proposal—she just wasn't quite sure what he would think about her outfit.

IT WAS EARLY evening by the time I made it back to a now dark and chilly Jackson Square. Two hungry cats greeted me at the front door of the Green Vase, purring loudly as a reminder that it was time for their supper.

I crossed the showroom, stepping carefully around the furry bodies that eagerly herded me toward the stairs.

Dilla's package rested in my coat pocket. Wrapped up in brown kraft paper, it was a familiar book-sized rectangular shape. I patted the outside of the pocket, silently pondering as I started up the steps to the kitchen.

"Wrao," Isabella chirped impatiently, swatting insistently at my tired legs. She raced up a few steps and turned to glower down at me as I lumbered slowly up the ascent. Rupert brought up the rear, urging me along from the steps below, occasionally shoving his head against the back of my knee.

To the consternation of my starving feline companions, I stopped halfway up the stairs and pulled Dilla's package out of my pocket. Turning it over in my hands, I couldn't help thinking how similar the shape was to Harold's green Mark Twain book. I tested the pieces of tape that secured the folded flaps of the wrapping, but they were firmly attached to the kraft paper.

"Hmm," I sighed, wondering if I should open it.

"Wa-oourrrr!" Isabella demanded fiercely.

"Yes, of course," I replied. "Right away."

I skipped up the remaining steps to the kitchen. Isabella paced back and forth in front of the cupboard that held the cat food, making sure I knew where I was supposed to go next.

Four eager eyes fixed on me while I pried open the plastic lid of a container and poured out a meal's worth of dry food into each cat's bowl. Satisfied munching sounds filled the kitchen as I sat down at the table and dropped Dilla's package on its surface.

I leaned back in my chair, glancing at the room around me. While I'd done a lot of work on the Green Vase showroom since Oscar's departure, the two floors of the upstairs apartment remained much the way he'd left it.

The living quarters were vintage Uncle Oscar—which is to say the only maintenance that had been done over the course of the last fifty or so years involved the application of the cheapest available materials unrestricted in any way by building codes or construction guidelines. The kitchen was probably the best example of Oscar's creative handiwork.

From my seat at the table, I could count at least a half a dozen different patterns of wallpaper. Despite the liberal use of staples and tape to tamp the patterned sheets down, each one curled outward along its exposed edges.

There wasn't a square corner in the entire kitchen. The leaning walls somehow managed to meet up with the room's low ceiling, which sagged in places as if something large and bulging were sitting on it from above. On the upper half of one of the walls, a warped wooden board provided a shaky shelf for my uncle's large collection of cookbooks.

An ancient dishwasher commanded the space next to the sink. I had long since given up trying to use it. Every attempt had resulted in a nearly unstoppable eruption of foamy soapy water that spilled down its front and out across the uneven tiles of the kitchen floor.

My uncle's well-used wooden table dominated the center of the room. The grains in the table's wood planking had swelled and softened over its many years of service, providing a smooth, if not altogether flat, surface.

It was here where Dilla's brown paper package lay, tempting me to open it.

Smacking her lips to catch a crumb from her whiskers, Isabella sat back from her food bowl and gazed up at the table. Her immediate hunger satiated, she was now ready to investigate the package. Her sleek orange-tipped tail pointed into the air as she sauntered over to me, expressing her interest in the item that had so frustratingly delayed her supper.

She reached the table and hopped up onto the chair beside me. Her sharp blue eyes studied the package intently as she sniffed it with the pulsing pink cushion of her nose.

"I think, maybe, I should open it," I suggested. My arms crossed over my chest as I stared down at the package.

The white whiskers on Isabella's pixielike face twitched while she pondered my proposal. She raised a slender white paw and delicately poked at the package, jumping back when the paper crinkled beneath her touch.

Isabella hunched down into her chair so that her eyes were flush with the surface of the table. Her tail swung back and forth assessingly.

"Mrao," she opined after careful consideration.

I decided to interpret that as an assent. Sucking in my breath, I reached out for the package. Isabella watched as I slid my fingers underneath one of the folded flaps and pulled it up. Then, I spun the package around and freed the opposite side.

Isabella popped her head and shoulders up over the table as I lifted the edges of the packing paper and exposed the item wrapped inside.

It was a second green book of Mark Twain essays, nearly an exact replica of the one Harold had left on the cashier counter downstairs, albeit in a newer, more pristine condition.

Rupert issued a polite belch from the cat food station as I flipped through the pages of Dilla's book to the first selection. Isabella rested her head in my lap while I began to read her Mark Twain's tale about an excessively talkative miner and his Calaveras County frog.

Chapter 9

BENEATH THE DOME

LATER THAT NIGHT, deep within the substructure of City Hall's recently refurbished foundation, two pairs of round, protuberant eyes popped up from the surface of a stream of water that had begun to fill the moat circling the building's underground perimeter.

Unnoticed by almost all of City Hall's human occupants, a green garden hose had been poked down through an opening in the floor of a basement mop closet, threaded around several of the foundation's rubberized columns, stretched to the edge of the building's substructure, and fed into the surrounding moat. A steady trickle had been percolating out of the mouth of the hose for over a week, resulting in the accumulation of several feet of water in the moat's concrete base.

First one and then the other of two slippery, wet creatures emerged from the moat, splashing slightly as they hopped out onto the embankment. They crept slowly into the substructure, following the snaking path of the hose, their small mounded shapes mingling imperceptibly with the silky darkness that closed in around them.

A thick canopy of beams and joists sank down from the ceiling, providing an inverted topo-map of the building above. The two frogs crawled deeper and deeper into the substructure, passing a countless number of concrete columns, each one middled with an enormous black rubber isolator.

At long last, the hose led the traveling pair up a steep incline to an opening in the ceiling—a square hatch denoted by a weak, muffled light, emanating from a source somewhere in the basement level above.

The larger frog squatted beneath the center of the hole, sizing up the distance to the edge of its rim. The powerful muscles of his back legs pulsed, tightening the stretchy, elastic skin on the top of his knobby knees. With one explosive movement, the frog's back legs activated, and his body soared up through the opening, landing with a heavy, skidding plunk on the floor in the room above. The second, smaller, frog quickly followed, his tiny body springing lightly through the hole.

The pair sat silently for a moment, studying their new surroundings. The room held a mop bucket, a broom, and a strange-smelling cart with an orange-shaped air freshener tied to its handle. A long rectangular window ran along the top of the back wall. Scattered rays of light angled in from a streetlamp to provide a faint etching of illumination.

The larger frog led off on a hop across the tiled floor, and the second frog fell diligently into formation behind him. The frogs' feet suctioned against the flat tile surface as they progressed toward a door on the far side of the room. It was slightly ajar, its three-inch opening allowing more than enough space for the two frogs to pass through.

On the other side of the door, a long hallway stretched out to the left, dwarfing the two glistening figures with its emptiness. Without hesitation, the frogs set off, proceeding with long horizontal leaps. At the end of the hallway, the pair made a right turn into a wider corridor. Midway down this second hallway, they stopped in front of a short flight of stone steps and paused to catch their breath.

The larger frog waddled up to the perpendicular edge of the first step of the staircase, his ample girth jiggling as he moved. He gave a wise look to his smaller companion, blinked, and croaked hoarsely.

"Ribbit."

With that, the larger frog leapt up into the air. His hefty bulk barely cleared the top of the second step. Huffing slightly, he turned and looked down to encourage his sidekick.

The smaller frog shifted his weight back and forth, anxiously leaning from left to right. A long, stringy tongue zipped out of his mouth and smacked up against his right cheek. He squiggled his back legs eagerly; then his small form rocketed into the air—easily landing with one leap onto the top of the third step.

The larger frog considered this development, the wide rim of his lipless mouth curling inward as the smaller frog peeked down over the edge of the higher step.

The smaller frog pumped out his own, slightly higher pitched, croak.

"Ribbit."

The challenge issued, the duo vaulted up the stairs from the basement, their springing bodies slapping against the stone steps until they both landed, nostrils flaring for oxygen, on the building's first floor.

The frogs ambled amiably around a corner and continued on through the arched tunnel of a foyer, finally emerging at the edge of City Hall's cavernous rotunda. Their webbed feet slid across the pink marble floor as they crossed into the open center area under the dome.

The larger frog turned to offer a congratulatory croak to his froggy friend, but, before he could issue it, the sound withered in his throat—as he looked up at the towering marble staircase leading to the second floor.

AN HOUR LATER, two exhausted frogs panted together in the Ceremonial Rotunda at the top of the central marble staircase. The muscles in their legs pulsed wearily as they rested.

The smaller frog hobbled over to a bronze bust mounted on a marble block base. A jovial man with a protuberant nose and flapping ears looked warmly down at him.

The larger frog joined the smaller one and together they stared up at the quote inscribed on the block. It was a well-known catchphrase of the man commemorated in the bust.

You've got to give them hope.

As if inspired by the inscription, the frogs turned to look out over the rotunda. Moonlight soaked the soaring spaces of the room, playing eerily off of the carved stone faces, casting a myriad of shadows in the finely shaped plaster.

The larger frog lifted his head and nodded up toward the top of the dome, still hundreds of feet above them. The smaller frog gulped, and then turned, determinedly, down the hallway toward the next flight of stairs.

THE SOFT, GENTLE rays of dawn were beginning to glide through the arched windows of the rotunda when the two exhausted frogs hopped wearily up the last step. They had reached City Hall's highest interior room, a tiny attic space in the steeple that rose above the crest of the dome.

Human footsteps crossed the room to greet them.

They waited, patiently, as a grimy, freckled hand gently reached down and picked them up.

Chapter 10

AN EARLY MORNING RIDE TO THE CLIFF HOUSE

THE WEE HOURS of Thursday morning had yet to take hold when Harold Wombler's rusty pickup truck sputtered clunkily onto Jackson Street. Harold killed the motor halfway down the block, pushed in a knob to dim the headlights, and slowly coasted to a stop in the middle of the pavement outside of the Green Vase.

Harold turned his hunched torso to look across the cab through the passenger side window. Tilting up the rim of his faded baseball cap, Harold studied the darkened window of the apartment above the showroom across the street. There was a rippling in the blinds as a cat's tiny white face poked out from beneath the bottom slats. Otherwise, no one seemed to be stirring.

A shadow moved in across Harold's view. The passenger side door of the truck opened, creaking loudly with the protesting squeal of unoiled metal springs.

"Morning, Harold," a man's sleep-slurred voice mumbled as the shadow climbed into the cab and collapsed onto the passenger side of the truck's bench seat.

Harold tugged his cap back down over his head and glanced warily at the entrant.

The man's lanky form was cramped even in the truck's spacious cab. His freshly shaven face shone from the recent application of a citrus aftershave; damp brown curls bounced off the top of the man's head. He wore a pair of gray wool slacks matched with a long-sleeve sweater and a neatly pressed collared shirt. Metal cufflinks formed in the shape of merrily hopping frogs hung at both wrists.

"You got the message then," Harold grumped as his passenger struggled to fasten the uncooperative metal buckle of the seat belt.

"Yup," Monty replied, his sleepy voice waking with sarcasm. "Subtle, Wombler. Really subtle."

Harold allowed himself the pleasure of a smug grin; then he cranked the engine and rolled off down the street.

From the few bits of paint remaining on the truck's chipped and dented shell, it was difficult to guess the original color of its exterior. A jagged crack branched its way across most of the windshield. The plastic molding of the dashboard was blistered and hardened from years of unprotected exposure to the sun; the remains of the glove compartment rested at Monty's feet on the passenger side floorboard.

Monty carefully shifted his legs around the glove compartment and directed his half-lidded eyes toward the driver.

Harold wore a heavily stained T-shirt beneath a pair of quickly disintegrating overalls. A shredded flannel shirt that was missing the majority of its buttons draped over the bent curve of his shoulders.

Most of Harold's greasy, black, dandruffy hair was covered by a dingy baseball cap. The yellowed whites of his eyes sunk into dry, blotchy skin that sagged loosely below his jawline. Slumped forward in the driver's seat, gripping the steering wheel with his wrinkled, gnarled hands, it looked as if the truck were being piloted by a withered worm.

The streets of Jackson Square were dark and deserted as Harold swung the truck left at Sansome. Few cars moved along the city streets. Most of the residents of San Francisco were still tightly tucked in their beds.

A few blocks later, the truck slowed at an empty light for a left-hand turn onto Broadway. All the while, the truck's engine cycled roughly in a coughing, stuttering manner.

Monty shivered and wrapped his arms across his chest, trying to warm himself against the damp chill rushing in through the gaping passenger side window. He had given up wrestling with the immovable handle that would have been used to roll up the glass partition.

Monty stared out the open window at the silent street as the truck chugged up Broadway, passing through the poorly delineated convergence of Chinatown and North Beach. A gaudy collection of strip clubs, their neon signs flashing flesh-promising adverts, pressed up against a handful of sooty dim sum joints and specialty grocery stores whose banners were marked more prominently by their Chinese characters than the faint English subtitles printed underneath. The price of every inch of space in downtown San Francisco was at such a premium, there was no room for gradual transitions.

The truck rumbled with the roar of an escalating avalanche as it worked to pick up speed. The increased vibration threatened to dislodge the more loosely attached of its parts.

"Where are we going?" Monty tried to yell over the racket.

"Cliff House," Harold replied bluntly. The truck hit a deep pothole that caused the front bumper to scrape against the pavement before the cab jolted up wildly on the recoil.

"Why?" Monty hollered, straining his voice to be heard over the engine as he reached between his knees to steady the bouncing glove compartment.

"For the view," Harold spit out through pursed lips.

A taxi screeched by in the open left-hand lane as both

vehicles entered the Broadway tunnel. The brick and concrete walls swallowed the truck, amplifying the already
deafening squall of the motor.

The taxi quickly disappeared into the distance, leaving
the truck to trundle alone through the cave of the empty
tunnel. The round opening on the opposite end appeared
first as a blinding halo of artificial light before slowly soft-
ening into the contours of a streetlamp-lit street. Monty
tried to tuck his cold-numbed hands into the bottom hem
of his sweater as the truck emerged from the tunnel's exit
and a fresh blast of chilly air shot through his open window.

Once free of the tunnel, the road sloped upward toward
the wide boulevard of Van Ness. Harold scaled back the
engine to an uneven idle as they waited at the light. He
turned his stiff neck to look at the passenger seat.

Monty had wrapped every available limb over and around
one another in his attempt to fight off the chill. He looked
like a pale, sweater-clad pretzel.

Harold gummed his dentures; then he reached his right
arm behind the back of the truck's bench seat, grabbed a
dingy brown blanket, and tossed it into Monty's lap.

Monty sniffed at the blanket disdainfully. "Smells funny,"
he complained as he stretched the thin cloth over his body.

Harold rolled his eyes and swung the truck south onto
Van Ness. One of the city's main thoroughfares, the street
was a mixture of commercial warehouses and residential
apartment blocks. A line of tightly packed cars filled in
both curbs; every possible parking space had been con-
sumed for the night.

Several blocks down, the gilded detailing on City Hall's
enormous dome picked up the first glints of the arriving
sun. Harold squinted at the building and muttered to himself.

"Sorry?" Monty piped up from the passenger side. "I
didn't catch that."

Harold gripped the steering wheel and did not respond
as the rusted-out truck lumbered further down Van Ness,

turning right a few minutes later. Harold navigated a nest of one-way streets with the reckless confidence of a seasoned cab driver; then he proceeded up Fell Street toward Golden Gate Park.

A procession of low-rise apartments crowded the landscape, each unit designed as a rectangular cube, closed in on at least two of its sides to accommodate the tightest possible packing within the uninterrupted flow of buildings. Row after row of bulging bay windows lined the street, designed to snag every available ray of sunlight for the units' otherwise dark boxes.

Neighborhood sifted into neighborhood, becoming increasingly residential as more and more full-sized houses squeezed into the dime-sized lots. Occasional clumps of grass popped up into the gaps between residences. This, combined with a denser population of trees, signaled the truck's approach to the entrance of Golden Gate Park.

The roadway angled, feeding the truck into a narrow two-lane street, which was banked on either side by a dense thicket of forest. All evidence of the surrounding city immediately slipped away.

"So, uh, hmmm." Monty cautiously cleared his throat. "When Dilla recruited me into your little group, she was a bit *light* on the specifics."

"I would have hoped so," Harold replied tersely, without elaboration.

"Did Oscar really know where Sutro's stash is hidden?" Monty asked, his eyes glittering with speculation.

"Don't push your luck, Carmichael," Harold replied curtly.

The truck continued to roll across the smooth black tarmac of the park road. A pair of early-rising joggers braved the brisk, cool breeze on a running path cut parallel to the street. Every so often, the trees parted for an open field, the entrance to a museum, or an improbable herd of buffalo. The close proximity of the encircling city was lost completely.

About ten minutes later, the Pacific Ocean loomed up

ahead, its presence palpable long before its churning waters could be seen. A briny zest fogged the air as the bank of trees thinned and fell away. The dilapidated shadow of Harold's truck emerged from the western thicket of Golden Gate Park to face the ocean's wild, foaming edge.

Monty shuddered deeper into the dingy blanket as the truck turned onto a highway that skirted the coast's wide, sandy beach. The vehicle rounded a curve beneath the scraggly outcropping of Sutro Heights and pulled into an empty parking lot next to the darkened, windswept Cliff House.

Monty yawned pointedly as he glanced around. "There's no one here."

"Just wait," Harold growled. He pulled the gear lever into park and turned off the headlights. The sputtering engine expired with the weariness of a spent horse.

The unlikely pair waited in uncomfortable silence. Monty picked up the grimy edge of his covering and offered it to Harold.

"Blanket?"

Chapter 11

A TRIANGULAR-SHAPED SMUDGE

THE BLINDS WERE pulled down tight, but the first cracks of Thursday morning had begun to weave their way through the slats and into the third floor bedroom above the Green Vase. I rolled over, groaning at the intrusion, but a slight disturbance in the far corner of the room caught my attention. Something was moving—something small and amphibian in nature.

Plunk.

I sat up, propping my head against the pillow, blinking my eyes in disbelief at the tiny figure shuffling timidly across the room toward me. It was a green frog wearing a feathery orange mustache.

He hopped in the direction of my bed, his progress seemingly unimpeded by the hairpiece attached to the stubby, blunt end of his nose. The pointed corners of his tiny, well-groomed whiskers curved upward in a perky, almost stylish fashion.

The little frog tilted his head, studying me as if he were intrigued by my presence. The red ribbon of his tongue zipped out of his mouth and lightly tapped the mustache perched on top of his upper lip.

"Ribbit."

As if summoned by the sound, a second frog appeared. This one was heavier set with a pouchy, rolling stomach and rounded, fat-cushioned shoulders. His mustache was thicker, each side of it drooping down to the floor, the mammoth hairpiece nearly collapsing under its own weight.

"What is going on here?" I murmured drowsily as Isabella cracked open a sleep-crusted eye. The frogs' arrival appeared to have gone unnoticed by the orange and white feline heap on the bed beside me.

"Izzy, do you see them?" I asked, groggily glancing at the spot on the covers where she and Rupert were tightly wound around one another.

With slow, exaggerated movements, Isabella extracted herself from the curling cat cocoon. She stretched her mouth open into a wide yawn and rolled her rough pink tongue out at me. She gave me a skeptical look as I pointed emphatically at the floor beside the bed.

We both leaned to peer down over the edge, but the frogs—and their mustaches—had disappeared.

I CRAWLED OUT of bed and stumbled toward the shower, trying to dislodge the disturbing imprint of the morning's dream.

Isabella trotted ahead of me, leading the way to the bathroom. Rupert snorted sleepily as he snuggled deeper into the blankets. It was far too early, in his opinion, to be up and about.

Frogs, I thought, puzzling as I twisted on the shower nozzle and waited for the water to heat up. They were making a strange convergence in my life—first at City Hall, now in the Green Vase. Both locations seemed unlikely amphibian habitats. The pair from my bedroom, I decided, must have been imagined.

I waited until the hot water began to steam up the mirror over the sink, then I pulled back the curtain and, after carefully inspecting the bottom of the tub for any froggy green interlopers, I climbed in.

My thoughts traveled to the frog essay in the shiny green Mark Twain books, the first one dropped off by Harold, the second one, indirectly, by Dilla.

The Celebrated Jumping Frog of Calaveras County had swept the country when it was first published in 1867; it was one of Twain's earliest writing successes.

The tale was a bit harsh for modern, more sensitized, readers. The poor, hapless frog referenced in the title suffers the brunt of a cruel practical joke. In order to sabotage the frog's chances in a jumping competition, the antagonist of the story pours buckshot down the frog's throat to weigh it down. Even though the frog is eventually relieved of its stomachful of iron, I couldn't really see the humor that had so delighted Twain's early fans.

I began sudsing up my hair with shampoo, drowsily contemplating the ethical implications of frog torture as I began to search for a connection between the *Calaveras County* frog and the pair who had hopped into my early morning dream with their feathery orange mustaches.

TWENTY-FIVE MINUTES LATER, I stepped out of the shower, feeling refreshed and fully awake. After slipping on my clothes, I grabbed a small handheld vacuum cleaner and used it to suck up the telltale sprinkling of litter in front of the red igloo. Rupert, clearly, had begun his day.

The cats were probably in the kitchen waiting for their breakfast, I thought, as I plodded down the steps to the second floor.

"Rupert, Isabella," I called out. The apartment seemed almost unnaturally quiet, but I didn't think anything of it.

I rubbed the back of my neck, still supple from the massage of the hot water, and flipped on a switch for the kitchen's main light on the wall just inside the entrance.

I was utterly unprepared for the mess that greeted me.

Dishes that had been left to dry the night before in a rack by the sink were now strewn across the kitchen floor, several of them cracked, chipped, or shattered into pieces. Joining the pottery were several of Oscar's cookbooks that had been knocked off of their shelf, their spines spread wide, loose pages fluttering out.

A spinning spice rack from the counter by the sink had been upended. Tiny individual flakes, dried seeds, and a mixed dusting of spices were spread across the kitchen. Some of the finer particulates still hung in the air, creating a heavily scented haze.

Isabella sat in the basin of the kitchen sink, stealthily licking her front paws. They were covered in a sticky, yellow substance—all that remained of the contents of a small jar of honey that had previously resided on the kitchen table. The accompanying dispensers of cream, sugar, salt, and pepper had all been emptied, contributing to the room's overall spice mixture.

Isabella hunched her head into her shoulders apologetically as I scanned the room, stunned by the muddled disarray.

Rupert, on the other hand, stood proudly on the kitchen table, feet firmly planted in a defiant stance, his tail swinging wildly back and forth, as if he had just protected me from a vicious intruder. A fine white powdery substance, probably flour, covered his head and shoulders, creating a comically aged look to his whiskers.

"What . . . happened . . . in here?" I murmured, reeling from the extent of the mess.

"Wra-oooo," Rupert yodeled in response, the white ruff of his chest puffed out like a lion's.

I shook my head, mystified, and grabbed a bottle of kitchen cleanser and a roll of paper towels. I began wiping down the trail of sticky paw prints that tracked across the counters, table, and floor, stopping—in disbelief—when I came to a small triangular-shaped smudge.

It looked as if it had been left by a frog's webbed foot.

Chapter 12

A PERFECT OUT-OF-EYE SPACE

PARKED ABOUT A hundred yards down the beach from the Cliff House, the faint outline of Harold Wombler's rusted-out pickup truck could barely be distinguished in the misty premorning haze of sand and ocean. Inside the cold, damp cab of the truck, its occupants had been listening to the full, battering roar of the Pacific for the last half hour.

Montgomery Carmichael shifted his body beneath the dingy brown blanket. The cloth reeked of motor oil and engine fluid, but it appeared to be warding off some of the chill. Harold Wombler sat in the truck beside Monty, stolidly silent and hunched behind the steering wheel.

"Maybe you've got the wrong place," Monty mumbled sleepily, but Harold did not acknowledge this expression of doubt.

Harold's runny, bloodshot eyes glanced out across the choppy surface of the ocean, and then back up to the square pillbox edifice of the Cliff House. The pounding sea dominated the small building huddled up against the rocks; the barren scene lacked any of the bustling hallmarks of human activity. It was, as yet, too early for the tour buses to begin making their obligatory stops at this bygone hub of old-time San Francisco's social oasis.

This area hadn't always been so desolate, Harold reflected as he stared up the beach toward the Cliff House's solid bunker.

Back in the late 1800s, almost all of the land visible from the pickup truck's beachside parking spot had been owned by one man—mining millionaire, philanthropist, and eventual San Francisco Mayor Adolph Sutro. Sutro's property holdings had extended up and down the beach, including the battered bluff that ran alongside it.

Sutro had invested heavily in the land's development, turning his oceanfront acres into a recreational weekend destination for San Francisco's working-class families. Lands End, as the area became known, included the Sutro Baths, the Sutro Gardens, a collection of privately run amusement park rides, and, of course, the Sutro-era Cliff House.

If Harold stretched his neck so that he could see above the rim of the steering wheel, he could just make out the rocky outcropping abutting the opposite side of the Cliff House where the Baths had been located. In addition to numerous seawater swimming pools, the aquatic center had featured a theater, several restaurants, a large gymnasium, and a museum. During its heyday, the complex could accommodate up to twenty-five thousand visitors on any given weekend.

The Baths' water collection system was a tribute to Sutro's engineering genius—a trait which had earned him his first fortune in the Comstock mines. For the Baths, Sutro designed a seawall along the shoreline's rocky embankment. Strategically placed tunnels beneath the wall trapped incoming seawater during high tide. The captured water was then filtered and used to fill several large bathing pools. The collection of pools were all covered by an enormous glass-paned solarium and warmed to a range of temperatures to provide the optimal swimming experience.

Harold's weary eyes continued their scan across the highway to the craggy bluff overlooking the beach, where Sutro had built his mammoth mansion. While the living quarters remained private, Sutro had opened up the estate's elaborate Italianate gardens to Lands End picnickers.

Of course, if picnicking wasn't your cup of tea, Harold mused, you could have ventured across the road to Sutro's recently rebuilt Cliff House for a more refined dining experience.

The Cliff House was already a well-established San Francisco institution when Sutro built the Baths—but not one known for family friendly entertainment. It had been a favorite haunt of the Barbary Coast crowd and had acquired a scurrilous reputation for the shady activities allegedly conducted in its back rooms.

Sutro purchased the Cliff House, determined to clean the place up to meet the standards of the surrounding Lands End attractions. His efforts were facilitated by the early-era Cliff House's complete destruction, not long after ownership was transferred to him. The building imploded when a schooner carrying a load of dynamite wrecked on the hazardous rocks below.

Sutro designed a new Cliff House that was far more grand and elegant than the one that had preceded it. His Cliff House was styled as a fanciful eight-story French castle. The towering building's foundation exceeded the horizontal space provided by the rocks beneath it, so that it appeared as if the whole structure might fall into the ocean at any moment. Inside, the glamorous establishment provided fine dining for both the high society who arrived at Lands End in horse-drawn carriages as well as the swimmers who walked up from the Baths.

It was important to Sutro that the Lands End amenities

be both affordable and accessible for San Francisco's working-class families. He ensured that the entrance fees for both the Baths and the Gardens were kept at a low, nominal rate. Then, to prevent the local railroad barons from gouging Lands End travelers, Sutro constructed his own passenger rail line to transport visitors to the site from downtown San Francisco.

Harold sighed grouchily as he surveyed the near-empty coastline. Time and neglect had erased almost all evidence of this earlier-era grandeur. Sutro's palatial Cliff House was destroyed by fire in 1907. The building that replaced it introduced the current shoebox-shaped structure, which, over the years of subsequent renovations, gradually shrank down to its current size.

Sutro's elaborate gardens and estate were torn down in 1938 when his heirs donated the land to the city. The rail line succumbed to earthquakes and frequent mudslides. The Baths fell into disrepair and were eventually closed. An ill-fated condo development was planned for the Baths' property in the 1960s, but the project never commenced construction. The structures above the Baths later burned to the ground, leaving a series of exposed ponds inside the ruins of the deteriorating seawall.

The once heavily trafficked stretch of beach was now an abandoned afterthought of the city's history. While a stop at the Cliff House remained a must-see on many tourists' checklists, Lands End had long since lost its niche as a regular destination for San Franciscans.

"A perfect out-of-eye space for this morning's meeting," Harold thought as Monty began to snore beneath the blanket. "Shielded from the influence and speculations of the other political power brokers."

A moment later, the headlights of a shiny black Lincoln Town Car swept into a parking space close to the entrance of the Cliff House. A uniformed driver leapt out to open the passenger door for a slim, black-coated figure.

Monty winced from the sudden glare of the car's lights and noisily roused himself. "Well, I'll be," he murmured, giving Harold an impressed look as they watched the man unfold his long limbs and climb out of the Town Car's leather-seated interior.

The occupants of the truck watched closely as the slim man paced toward the steps that led down the embankment to the Cliff House's front door. The man's knee-length unbuttoned overcoat flapped loosely in the breeze, revealing a dark double-breasted suit and pencil-thin baby blue tie. His brown hair was slicked back, exposing the bulbing crest of his wide forehead.

Monty sat entranced, his slender fingers absentmindedly trying to brush down his own tight, towering curls, which were springing with even more vigor than usual in the ocean air's high humidity.

The Mayor paused briefly in front of the Cliff House entrance. His posture slumped apprehensively, as if he were reconsidering his decision. He wiped his left hand over the bottom half of his face, rubbed his fingers into the narrow corners of his mouth, and thoughtfully flicked his thumb against the pointed stub of his chin.

After a moment's reflection, the Mayor smiled to himself, seemingly convinced of the appropriateness of his action. He flashed a solid fence of chalky white teeth and walked inside.

The front doors of the Cliff House were still swishing shut behind the Mayor when a neon green hybrid-electric compact slid confidently into a slot next to the Town Car. The driver secured the parking brake and stepped briskly out onto the tarmac. With a flick of his wrist, the man beeped the little car's electronic security system and strutted confidently toward the entrance.

The Cliff House's second arrival wore no overcoat; he appeared not to notice the morning's chill. His grayish brown suit matched the flat color of his limp, floppy hair. Parted just off center, his mousy brown locks curved gently in toward his soft, unaging baby face. Despite its tailored cut, the man's suit wrinkled around the slight pudging of his middle.

"Is that . . . ?" Monty gawked, first at the man walking through the parking lot and then at Harold.

"President of the Board of Supervisors," Harold confirmed tetchily.

The Supervisor hopped down the front steps, casually brushing back his loose bangs before firmly gripping the door's handle and pulling it open.

Back in the pickup truck, Monty shuddered off the blanket and fumbled with the rusted latch to release his door.

"Wait," Harold grunted brusquely.

"Aren't we going in?" Monty protested, a confused look muddling the still sleepy lines of his face.

"Wait," Harold repeated tersely.

A third car swept in from the highway. This time, the graceful, sliding curves of a creamy pearl-colored Bentley pulled into a Cliff House parking space, a few slots down from the first two vehicles.

Monty's jaw dropped as he recognized the showy car's driver.

The man removed his black felt bowler and carefully ran his hands along its curling sides, smoothing the veins of a stylish feather neatly tucked into its brim. A closely barbered rim of gray hair circled the smooth brown skin of the man's balding crown. Above his lips, another patch of gray hair had been expertly shaved into the outline of a tightly cropped mustache.

The man's face beamed widely as he replaced the bowler on his head and tipped it toward Harold's dilapidated pickup truck.

Harold nodded, almost imperceptibly, back at the Former Mayor who stepped out of the Bentley with a dignified, debonair ease.

As the Former Mayor entered the Cliff House, Harold inserted his corroded key into the stem of the steering wheel and cranked the engine.

"But, but, but—" Monty's sputtering protest was quickly drowned out by that of the motor.

"We've got work to do," Harold explained enigmatically as the truck pulled back onto the highway and started its return trip to the Green Vase.

Chapter 13

THE LAVENDER LADY

BACK IN THE Green Vase showroom, I collapsed onto the stool behind the cashier counter, feeling far more weary and decidedly less clean than I had when I'd stepped out of the shower earlier that morning. After several hours of work, the kitchen was finally back in serviceable condition, all of the scattered spices swept up, the sticky smears of honey wiped away.

Two freshly bathed cats sat on the floor next to the counter, their tongues loudly grooming through their clean, damp fur. Despite the webbed footprints I'd discovered upstairs, I still couldn't believe that a frog had been the instigator of all of that feline mischief. Rupert and Isabella continued their grooming, both of them refusing to comment on my frog-chase speculations.

I grabbed the corner of the counter and leaned back in my seat, trying to imagine the scene that had played out in the kitchen during my shower. Perhaps I had developed a frog fixation, but all of my scenarios inevitably implicated an amphibian intruder.

Frogs in the Green Vase—were they real or just the product of my imagination? How on earth would they have found their way inside? Even more importantly, I pondered as I sucked in on my lower lip, where were they now?

My frog-focused thoughts were interrupted by the unmistakable pounding of stiletto heels approaching on the pavement outside. Rupert looked up, midlick through a patch of thick, fluffy hair, and emitted a startled half snork. Each of us instantly recognized the step of Miranda Richards. The increasing volume of stiletto smacking against concrete advertised her imminent arrival.

With a shuffling whump, Rupert bunny-hopped into his hiding place behind the row of books on the first shelf of the nearest bookcase. A moment later, Miranda's curvy figure swiveled on the threshold as she pulled open the front door and swung herself inside.

Miranda's ensemble this morning revolved around the color purple. She wore a pale lavender dress, the folds of which were tightly tucked around every rounded inch of her voluptuous figure. Dark plum high-heeled shoes on her feet complemented the dress and matched the large, chunky stones strung around her neck.

Isabella stood up and strolled toward Miranda, alone in her unbothered nonchalance. I watched, tension twitching across the back of my neck, as Miranda dropped the sharp edge of one of her plum-painted nails into the smooth fur on the top of Isabella's head.

Miranda's face, as always, was heavily made up. Her lips scrunched together under a deep violet layer of lipstick. Purple-hued eye shadow spread across her eyelids; a purple-tinged mascara thickened her lashes. I guess she might have been pretty if she weren't so scary—if there'd been Dalmatian puppies on the premises, I would have hidden them in the basement.

"Hello, Miranda," I managed to breathe out as I waited for my intimidating visitor to resume her full commanding height.

"Your cat's wet," Miranda muttered crossly, agitatedly brushing her fingers together as she looked up at me.

"I had to give her a bath," I explained meekly.

Miranda gave me a harsh, skeptical look. "I've never understood why you're always washing your cats. Surely that's not healthy for them?"

I shrugged my shoulders. It was the best response I could come up with. There was no point trying to explain to Miranda that both cats had covered themselves in a spicy goop while chasing mustached frogs through the upstairs kitchen.

Miranda leaned toward me, scrunching her eyes together as she stared at the shiny green cover of one of the Mark Twain anthologies laying on the counter in front of me. I'd brought them downstairs for further comparison.

Miranda's pouty plum lips pursed together. "I'm here about the Vigilance Committee."

I was momentarily thrown by this unexpected statement of purpose. Miranda was an unlikely candidate for my first official antique-purchasing customer.

"Vigilance Committee?" I asked, recovering my voice as I swung into sales pitch mode. "From the 1850s? Those items are over here."

Miranda glowered at me as I slipped uneasily around the cashier counter. She appeared oddly irritated at my response. I paced into the showroom toward a glass-topped display case, glancing nervously over my shoulder at her sharp, withering stare.

"Oscar collected several items from both the first and second Vigilance Committees," I said, my back now to Miranda. Brow furrowed, I tried to coax the historical details from the recesses of my memory.

In fortune-crazed, Gold Rush-era San Francisco, law and order had quickly fallen by the wayside. The city's sudden population surge overwhelmed the meager social services of the previously isolated outpost. Before long, San Francisco descended into a state of lawlessness, her streets ruled by ruthless gangs and thugs.

The city was particularly dangerous for the newly arrived and uninitiated. Any drink purchased at one of the Barbary Coast taverns along Pacific and Jackson streets was likely to be spiked with a cocktail of drugs that would knock the drinker unconscious for several hours.

If he were lucky, the victim would wake up facedown in a gutter, stripped of all of his valuables, perhaps even his clothes. In the worst-case scenario, he would wake up on the floor of a ship, bound for the port city of Shanghai on the eastern edge of China, to the sound of a whip being swung by the captain he'd been indentured to during his period of incapacitation.

Such individual crimes were the least of the city's problems. Drunken gangs routinely went on late-night rampages, raping and pillaging their way through the tent communities on the outskirts of town. Arson-set fires regularly swept through the rows of San Francisco's tightly packed and hastily constructed buildings. Many citizens believed that the city's beleaguered law enforcement entities were either inept or complicit in the mayhem.

In 1851, fed up with the rampant crime and overt corruption that seemed to have taken over the city, a group of local citizens decided to take matters into their own hands. Led by Mormon businessman Samuel Brannan, they formed a group called the Vigilance Committee. Armed with rifles, they marched through town, rounding up alleged criminals. The suspects were subjected to a brief trial and, if found guilty, immediately hanged in a public square. After three months of work, the Committee succeeded in terrorizing the city's most blatant criminals into hiding, and it disbanded. A second, similarly short-lived, Vigilance Committee was formed in 1856.

All of these events were well-known among local historians, as the vigilantes had left behind a sizeable collection of memorabilia.

I reached the display case holding the items Oscar had collected from the Vigilance Committees or "VCs" as they were informally called in the antique trade. On a tray beneath a protective glass covering lay several silver and bronze medallions. I ran my thumbs along the edge of the display lid and pressed in a recessed latch to raise the glass. I scooped up a couple of the metal medallions from the tray and carried them back to the front of the store where Miranda still stood, the lines of her face hardening with displeasure.

"Here are some of the items from the VC collection," I offered tentatively, my hand outstretched. "The members of the Committees made these to commemorate their participation."

Miranda glared at me, her heavily mascaraed eyes fuming. I dropped the medallions on the cashier counter next to the green-covered Mark Twain books. The metal coins clattered against one another in an otherwise stony silence.

"I'm not talking about the Gold Rush-era VCs," she spit out, never once glancing at the coins.

"I'm sorry," my voice muffled diffidently. "I don't think I—"

"There was another group," she prompted brusquely. "One that came together in much more recent times."

Miranda studied my baffled expression as if she were expecting a light to go on inside my head. For some reason, she thought her clarification would elicit a response of recognition.

"I'm not sure . . . I just don't know what you're getting at," I replied meekly after a long moment of uncomfortable silence.

Miranda's plum-painted lips breathed out a whoosh of pent-up frustration.

I was completely unprepared for her testy explanation.

"The VC group from the late 1970s," she hissed as she shoved her heavily painted face toward my puzzled one. "The one Oscar helped form."

Chapter 14

THE VIGILANCE COMMITTEE

"OSCAR?" I SAID, sputtering with surprise. "*My* Uncle Oscar . . . formed a Vigilance Committee?"

Miranda slid the long curve of her fingernail under one of the medallions and flicked it up into her hand.

"Yes, *your* Uncle Oscar," she replied, her voice sniping bitterly. "As if you didn't know."

The sculpted surface of the medallion lay flat on Miranda's palm, fenced in by the spiked barrier of her upturned fingers. Her purple-coated eyelids sank to half-mast as she stared down at the coin.

I shook my head. Despite the tension, I had to stifle a laugh. "I have a hard time imagining Oscar running around town rounding up criminals."

"Don't be silly. It wasn't that kind of a group," Miranda said condescendingly. "It was a political organization—of sorts."

Miranda turned away from me and paced into the show-room. From the sharp thunking of her shoes against the floorboards, she was clearly annoyed at my lack of knowledge on this subject.

"Seriously, Miranda," I said apologetically. "I don't know what you're talking about."

Miranda sighed loudly, clearly unconvinced. "Let me see if I can refresh your recollection."

She spun around to face me. Her posture stiffened as if she were preparing to enter a courtroom. I could tell that I was about to be put on trial, but I didn't as yet know the charges.

"Since its founding, San Francisco has attracted people from across America and around the world," Miranda began, her voice resonating in the showroom. "Today, you can find representatives of almost every ethnicity or nationality imaginable here. Chinese, Japanese, Mexican, Italian, Irish, French, Indian, Vietnamese, Thai, Korean"—Miranda fluttered her dark plum nails in the air—"and countless others." She brought her manicured hand back to her hip. "But the city is far from a melting pot. As wave after wave of immigrants moved in, they tended to locate themselves with others of their own ethnic background, sometimes by choice, sometimes by necessity, and, unfortunately, sometimes under duress or legal restriction.

"This led to the creation of distinct, inward-looking neighborhoods, isolated communities that could range from a single block to several streets, but each one with its own cultural identity. The divisions are less marked now than they were earlier in the 1900s, but San Francisco is still heavily balkanized."

I nodded silently in agreement as I slid around the corner of the cashier counter and eased back onto the stool.

"All of this plays out in city politics. San Francisco is governed jointly by both a Mayor and a Board of Supervisors. In many respects, the Board is as powerful if not more so than the Mayor."

Miranda circled the Gold Rush-era dental recliner positioned at the back of the room near the stairs. She ran the edge of her nail along the top of its worn leather cushion.

"Historically, the seats for the Board of Supervisors were selected in at-large elections. A candidate needed a great deal of money, organization, and clout in order to garner enough votes from across the city to win a seat. No one neighborhood or ethnic group had enough voting power on its own to elect a Supervisor."

Miranda raised the purple prong of her nail to emphasize her point.

"While this system was meant to elect candidates with broad, citywide appeal, traditionally, there was little cooperation or interaction between the more disparate neighborhoods. Repeatedly throughout San Francisco's history, powerful business interests have taken advantage of this political vacuum. Critics of the at-large election system often cite the city's pro-growth, big-business policies of the 1960s as evidence of this structural flaw in San Francisco's government."

Miranda left the recliner and strolled toward the glass-covered display case. Her footsteps were starting to sound slightly less irritated as she focused her attention on the story instead of me.

"During that time frame, many members of the Board of Supervisors were supported—that is to say, their campaigns funded—by a group of businessmen who wanted to develop San Francisco into more of a tourist destination. They had plans to build convention centers, hotels, and other infrastructure that would earn a much higher rate of return on investment than, say, affordable family housing. Some began to complain that the Supervisors were more beholden to the moneyed interests that funded their campaigns than the varied and diverse neighborhoods of their constituents."

Miranda paused in front of the display case and scanned the remaining Vigilance Committee artifacts, comparing them to the medallion she still carried in her palm.

"As more and more of these projects were implemented, higher rents began to push out the city's blue-collar industrial employers. They were gradually replaced by legal and financial institutions, who hired more higher educated, service-oriented employees like lawyers, accountants, and stockbrokers.

"The labor unions, the unemployed workers, and the neighborhoods where their working-class families lived—they finally started to push back. They took the fight to City Hall. They began to protest the easing of zoning restrictions, the granting of licenses for new office buildings, and the revisions to the housing codes, but with at-large elections for both the Mayor and each of the eleven Supervisor seats, the real estate and big-business interests were still easily winning the battle."

Miranda raised the glass-covered lid and dropped her medallion inside. Her voice grew quieter, more introspective, as her narrative switched from an abstract history lesson to a reflection of her own personal knowledge.

"Oscar was"—she cleared her throat—"well positioned to observe all of this."

Miranda noticed my puzzled expression and clarified. "He used to work at City Hall."

I couldn't really picture Oscar sitting behind a desk, wearing a suit and tie, but Miranda didn't elaborate on the nature of his City Hall employment, and I was afraid to interrupt her to ask. She brushed a stray strand of hair away from her face and continued.

"He and a couple of his colleagues began discussing ways to combat the business interests who were setting the agenda in the city's government. They didn't want to draw attention to themselves, so they kept their activities secret. Oscar came up with their code name, the Vigilance Committee." Miranda smiled wryly. "He thought it made a humorous play on history."

Miranda cleared her throat, resuming her serious demeanor. "They first targeted their efforts at a grassroots campaign that was working to support a referendum to change the way the Board of Supervisors were elected—from the old at-large seating system to a new regime that allocated seats on a district-by-district basis. Oscar's VC secretly funneled money into the effort that helped publicize the initiative."

Miranda arched one of her perfectly plucked eyebrows. "There were a lot of surprised faces in the city's political circles when that referendum passed. While some of the political heavy hitters survived the next election and the switch to district seating, several new Supervisors managed to win positions on the Board. Many of these freshmen Supervisors were critical of the previous administration's big-business, pro-growth agenda.

"One of the most vocal in that group of new Supervisors was Harvey Milk, who was elected from the district that included the Castro. While he was primarily concerned with gay rights issues, his populist, progressive stance struck a chord with a wide cross section of San Francisco voters, particularly those that felt they had been shut out by the big-business interests. Milk garnered support from both the Irish working-class unions and the traditionally under-represented Chinese community—groups that previously wouldn't have been caught dead in the same room together, much less one that was headlined by an openly gay man like Harvey."

Miranda began walking back toward the front of the room. I felt myself shrink behind the counter as she approached.

"A general alignment of interests framed the battle lines in City Hall. On one side were Milk and four other progressive Supervisors; they were supported by the recently elected populist Mayor George Moscone. The opposing side comprised the President of the Board and the five remaining Supervisors."

Miranda was now standing across the counter from me. Her piercing gaze fixed on my feeble one.

"On vote after vote, the slim majority of conservatives thwarted Mayor Moscone's antidevelopment initiatives. Not having a vote himself, the Mayor was powerless to pursue his populist agenda without the support of the Board."

Miranda lightly tapped the counter. "But change was in the air. It seemed clear to most observers that Harvey Milk would gain enough clout by the next election to take the Board presidency. Tensions were high; some of the city's most powerful people risked losing a lot of their wealth and influence. Oscar's Vigilance Committee geared up their resources to support Milk in the next Supervisor's election."

Miranda stopped speaking and issued a pointed glance in my direction, as if she expected me to fill in the next event.

"Then, they were murdered," I offered slowly. "Milk and Moscone were shot dead in City Hall."

Miranda nodded, pursing her lips. "By one of the conservative Supervisors, Dan White." She leaned over the counter, halving the distance between us.

"Citywide seating was reinstated the following year. In the aftermath of the riots and protests that followed the manslaughter verdict of Dan White's trial, district elections were deemed too divisive. Everything the VC thought they had accomplished was wiped out in a single blow. Disillusioned, they disbanded. District elections made a comeback in the 1990s, but the murders of Milk and Moscone forever changed the course of San Francisco politics—and the face of the city itself."

I had been listening, raptly, to the entire background lecture, but I still had no idea why Miranda Richards, of all people, had come to the Green Vase to speak to me about it.

"I just don't—" I began, but she cut me off.

"It seems that the Vigilance Committee, *Oscar's* Vigilance Committee, has been reconstituted," Miranda said bluntly. She bit her lip, as if she were holding something back.

"Oscar's dead, Miranda," I said tentatively, more perplexed than at the start of the conversation. "Who's leading the group now? And what does this have to do with me?"

Miranda stared at me from across the counter, her dark eyes throwing bullets in my direction. "You know exactly who's in charge of it," she said curtly. "My mother."

"Dilla?" I replied, immediately thinking of the strange trip she'd sent me on to City Hall.

"Don't play games with me," Miranda said bluntly. "I know you're in on it. You would have been one of the first people she turned to."

"No, no," I stuttered. "Honestly . . ."

Miranda was hearing nothing of my protest.

"I know you're involved," she repeated stiffly as she speared the shiny green cover of the nearest Mark Twain book with the curve of her plum-painted nail. She flicked her finger to spin the book across the counter toward me. "Because you've got *this*."

The tip of her nail slowly rose toward my stunned face. "Tell my mother that I need to speak with her."

And without further explanation Miranda turned and stormed out of the Green Vase.

Chapter 15

THE LITTLE GREEN BOOKS

RUPERT'S FURRY ORANGE ears rose tentatively up from his hiding place behind the row of books on the bottom shelf of the bookcase. His blue eyes slid back and forth, seeking confirmation that Miranda Richards had truly vacated the premises.

I placed the two Mark Twain books that Miranda had so accusingly fingered next to each other on the counter. Isabella hopped down from the top of the bookcase to assist in my comparison as I stared down at the emerald green covers, trying to understand their significance to the apparent resurgence of my Uncle Oscar's Vigilance Committee.

Isabella's slender tail curved up in the air as she sniffed at the books, drinking in their scent. She looked up at me, a curious expression on her face.

"Wrao," she announced as if she'd made a profound discovery.

Rupert apparently interpreted her commentary, even if I could not. There was a brief shuffling from the bottom of the bookcase as, having satisfied himself that the coast was clear, he prepared to make his exit. With an announcing "Merooo," Rupert hopped out from behind the shield of books and bounced around the counter to my stool.

His fluffy tail wiggled as he prepared to leap up onto the cashier counter. I knew, from hard-learned experience, that he was unlikely to successfully complete this endeavor.

"Wait," I called out urgently, trying to disrupt his internal countdown clock.

But the Rupert-rocket had, unfortunately, already ignited, and his furry, round body burst up into the air. I managed to catch him midleap—receiving a few unintended scratches in the process—and dump him onto the surface of the counter. Unruffled, Rupert quickly joined Isabella in the inspection of the green books.

I dodged two swishing, upstretched tails as the cats maneuvered back and forth around the books. Rupert paused with his head bent down toward the nearest green cover and took in a long, snorkeling sniff. Then, he dropped his left shoulder to the book and began rubbing the side of his body against it.

"Hey, hey, hey," I said, reaching beneath Rupert's rolling belly to rescue the book. "That's not necessary."

I pulled the book back from the counter and tried to brush off the layer of long white Rupert fuzz that now coated it. Rupert stood up and leaned toward me with a deep, rumbling purr as he tried to rub his cheek against the binding edge of the book.

"What are you—doing?" I protested, yanking the book farther away from Rupert's amorous attentions, bringing it closer to my face.

And then, I smelled it. Strange that I hadn't noticed before. In the atmosphere of the Green Vase, particularly the upstairs kitchen, the faint smell emanating from the book's pages had mixed with the permanent scent left over from the decades of Uncle Oscar's cooking. I sniffed again, trying to be sure, but there was no mistaking its source.

The book had the distinct smell of fried chicken.

I picked up the second Twain book and found the same fragrance wafting from its pages.

It wasn't just any fried chicken odor, I confirmed with another concentrated whiff. Both of the Mark Twain books bore the distinct scent of my Uncle Oscar's special fried chicken recipe.

I glanced down at Rupert, who was now sitting on the counter, his pudgy, round belly spilling out around his feet. He looked hungrily back at me and licked his lips. Rupert had always been particularly fond of Oscar's fried chicken.

Slowly, I walked around the showroom, studying the displays of Oscar's antiques. I carried the pair of green chicken-smelling books in my left hand, drumming them against my leg as I pondered. Rupert trailed closely behind, loudly smacking his lips.

Burnished gold artifacts glimmered from every corner of the room. There were displays of lockets, canes, cufflinks, and other forms of Gold Rush-era ornamentation along with several bookshelves holding traditional mining equipment.

I'd been through every item currently in the showroom; I'd examined and cleaned each piece thoroughly and completely. Other than the medallions from the 1800-era VCs, there was nothing in the antique shop that could be even remotely connected to the modern-day Vigilance Committee that Miranda had described. Surely there was something else in Oscar's possessions that gave some clue of his connection with the group.

My eyes sank reluctantly down to the floorboards. The most obvious location lay beneath me. I'd stuffed boxes and boxes of Oscar's belongings into the basement.

I tucked the pair of Twain books behind the cashier counter and grabbed my Uncle's trusty broad-beam flashlight. At the back of the showroom near the stairs, I bent down to open the basement's trapdoor.

That a basement existed beneath the Green Vase showroom had been a complete surprise to me when I first moved in. I'd discovered it by accident after Oscar's death. Many of Oscar's most intriguing secrets had been hidden down there—including the entrance to the sewage tunnels that ran beneath the financial district.

I shuddered, trying not to remember my last basement encounter with Frank Napis. The place still gave me the creeps.

I inserted my finger into a small hole in the floor that was fashioned to look like a knot in the wood paneling. Hooking the tip end of my finger, I tugged gently upwards, releasing an oval cover that popped out of the floorboards. I could now reach a retractable handle that was mounted into a recessed cavity beneath the cover. I flipped a small lever that extended the handle to a position where I could wrap my hand around it, stepped back off of the hatch, and lifted it open.

The trapdoor swung up toward me, at the same time releasing a short flight of rickety steps that unfolded down into the basement. The steps slapped against each other as they unwound, the bottom one slamming with a loud clap as it landed on the basement's rough concrete floor.

Rupert peered over the edge of the hatch, his tail whirling hungrily in the air. His expression grew more and more concerned as I started down the steps. He had never known fried chicken to originate from the basement.

"Wao?" he asked, disappointment filling his voice.

A moment later, I stood on the basement's concrete floor. A bare lightbulb next to the stairs provided the only light for the entire room. I flipped on the flashlight and swung it into the dark, cavernous space.

The basement stretched the full length of the showroom above. It was dank and musty; anything that spent any amount of time down here was soon crusted with a layer of congealed dust. The walls were formed of crumbling red bricks, most of whose interlocking mortar had chipped and fallen out over the years.

Between the brick walls lay several decades' worth of Oscar's treasured possessions, a disorganized clutter of cardboard boxes, sheeted furniture, and wooden shipping crates.

Isabella, followed by an extremely hesitant Rupert, joined me at the bottom of the stairs. Rupert huddled nervously near my feet. He had never been a fan of the basement, but he refused to be left behind.

Gingerly, I stepped forward into the room, flicking the wide beam of the flashlight into the basement's shadowed corners, trying to shake off a growing sense of creeping uneasiness. The terrain quickly became impassable, blocked by haphazardly stacked boxes and crates. I stretched my legs to straddle the impediments, reaching to plant the balls of my feet on the few open spaces of grungy concrete floor.

Isabella hopped a trail ahead while Rupert and I struggled to follow in her wake. Slowly, the three of us traversed the length of the basement. I stopped every so often to open a box and rifle through its contents, but I reached the far wall without finding anything of interest. There was nothing in the basement, it seemed, that could shed light on Oscar's involvement with the Vigilance Committee.

I was about to give up when I heard Rupert issue a snuffle of surprise from his position a couple of feet to my right. It took me a minute to find him with the flashlight—all that was visible was the orange-tipped two inches of his tail. The rest of Rupert was a humped shadow beneath the cloaked sheeting of a wardrobe.

I wiped my hand across my brow, a clammy feeling seeping over me. This was the same wardrobe Rupert, Isabella, and I had hidden in two months earlier on the night of the cat auction. From the wardrobe's main compartment, I had watched Frank Napis emerge from the basement's tunnel entrance—just as the delusional effects of his toxin were about to take hold of me. A few minutes later, I was convinced that the basement was filled with water and that I was drowning, without air, beneath the water's surface.

Rupert rustled beneath the sheet, cooing hungrily. Cautiously, I slid my way over to the wardrobe, my heart pounding uncomfortably in my chest as I lifted up the corner of the sheet.

Rupert was standing on his back legs, his front paws and his nose crammed into the half-inch opening of a lower drawer that was situated below the large clothes-hanging cupboard of the wardrobe.

With difficulty, I removed a squirming Rupert from in front of the drawer. My hand shook as I wrapped my trembling fingers around the knob. The drawer slid open with a slight pull, and I shone the flashlight down on the single item that lay inside.

It was a faded black-and-white photo. Carefully, I picked it up and brought the photo toward my face. Its scent was unmistakable; it was the same fried chicken odor carried by the Mark Twain books. Rupert looked up at me hopefully.

"It's not like I don't feed you," I sighed, shaking my head at him.

Rupert replied with a withering look as I trained the flashlight's beam on the faces in the photo.

A middle-aged but much younger-looking Dilla smiled slyly on the film. Her face wore an almost naive confidence, the shining gleam of self-conceived invincibility.

Next to her stood a slim Asian man, whose skin still retained a youthful plumpness and firmness. It took me a moment to identify the pre-raisined, pre-emphysema Mr. Wang.

On the far end of the line, a middle-aged man in a wrinkled linen suit hid behind an overtly false hanging of white hair, fashioned into an oversized mustache and beard. The scraggly eyebrows above his sparkling eyes were naturally grown—and instantly recognizable.

It was my Uncle Oscar, humorously costumed, I realized, as the writer Mark Twain.

Between Oscar and Mr. Wang stood a figure that made my whole body chill in anger.

The man's left arm stretched amicably over Oscar's

shoulders. A pair of wire rim glasses drew attention away from his flat face and thin, almost indiscernible lips. Perhaps I wouldn't have recognized the man if I hadn't subconsciously been looking for him. If I squinted my eyes, I could almost imagine a fluttering carrot-colored mustache perched on the stretch of skin beneath his nose.

A jovial Uncle Oscar was chuckling next to an earlier-era Frank Napis.

Chapter 16

AN INTRUDER IN THE BASEMENT

THE PHOTOGRAPH SHOOK in my hand as I stared down at the loathsome face of Frank Napis. My eyes fixed on the arm embracing my late uncle's shoulder, my stomach sickening at the sight. The Napis in the photo, I felt certain, was up to no good.

I tried to read into the eyes of my uncle, the small sliver of them that was visible beneath his wild, bushy eyebrows. Had Oscar known then that Napis was a fake and a fraud? Had he any inkling of the danger residing within the man standing next to him?

The dark corners of the room expanded around me, blooming into blackened flowers whose petals snuffed out the meager lightbulb on the opposite end of the basement. I was left alone with my flashlight, the dreary fascination of the photo—and the eerie sensation that my cats and I were not alone.

The surface of my cheeks dropped in temperature; my forehead became a damp sponge of sweat. I spun around in a frantic circle, wildly waving the flashlight across the crowded basement, spanning its beam along the crumbling brick walls, trying to squelch my panicked imagination.

Isabella and Rupert looked up at me, startled by my actions. I grabbed hold of the side of the wardrobe and took in a deep breath, trying to calm the pounding in my chest.

But as my racing pulse began to slow, a slight shuffling sound issued from the opposite side of the basement. The suctioned underside of a set of tiny webbed feet were inching across the cold, grimy concrete floor.

Plunk.

Two fuzzy white blurs leapt up into the air, bolting off on an instant hunt. I nearly dropped the flashlight in my effort to jump out of the cats' way.

It was impossible for me to keep up as Rupert and Isabella took off on their pursuit. Several feet ahead of me, Isabella's sleek form soared up and over a low pile of debris before disappearing again into the crowded maze of boxes and crates. I juggled the flashlight, trying to train its beam on the path of rustling cardboard and fluttering sheets as the cats raced across the basement.

Plunk.

The thudding sound was barely audible over the crashing chase of the cats. They appeared to be headed to the far corner of the basement, near the fold-down stairs.

Brow furrowed, I crept back across the room, all the while trying to get a line of sight on the action at the front.

Plunk.

Rupert's heavy bulk leapt through the air, swatting ferociously at a green springing form that my eyes couldn't quite focus on.

I crawled over an upended box, scraping my elbows against the rough edge of a crate as I eased myself closer. Brandishing my flashlight like a sword, I slowly cut its beam into the dark corner behind the steps where the cats appeared to have trapped the basement's intruder.

This corner of the basement was the current home of one of the more intriguing items from Oscar's eclectic collection—the stuffed carcass of a large kangaroo. I had found it packed into a shipping crate shortly after Oscar's death. The product of an ill-fated attempt at amateur taxidermy, the kangaroo was posed in an upright position with its right arm crooked out to rest on its hip.

I still had no idea how the kangaroo fit in with Oscar's Gold Rush interests. The beast's crate had been marked with an Australian shipping address and lodged over the top of the trapdoor to the basement. Oscar had used the kangaroo's mouth cavity to hide a clue related to Napis's poison—one that I had unfortunately failed to appreciate until it was too late.

The kangaroo had stood for a time in the showroom next to the cashier counter, but the dead animal was too gruesome to look at on a daily basis, and I didn't need any help scaring off potential customers, so I had moved it down to the basement.

Isabella inched up on the kangaroo, stalking a silent circle around it as Rupert climbed up the drop-down steps to get a higher level view. Rupert poked his head through the opening between the slats, pushing his face toward that of the kangaroo, his pink nose percolating with interest.

Isabella made a long trilling sound at my feet as I trained the flashlight on the stuffed kangaroo's head. Slowly, I slid the light upward from the curious expression of the kangaroo's crudely sewn-together mouth, past its bewitching glass eyes, to the furry, curved crown of its head.

A small frog blinked in the direct light of the beam.

"Ooh!" I exclaimed, shocked to finally meet the froggy interloper face-to-face. I have to admit, I was greatly relieved to see that this frog wasn't wearing a mustache.

I leaned forward to study the creature more closely. It appeared to be a small garden-variety frog, similar in color and size to the one that had landed on Monty's head in City Hall the previous afternoon.

The frog's webbed feet stretched out, nervously gripping the stuffed kangaroo's mottled fur. The shiny film of its thin, membranous skin glistened in the illumination of the flashlight.

"Ribbit."

I jumped back, startled by the noise. The flashlight bounced out of my hands and flipped up into the air, the arc of its beam flashing momentarily on Rupert's furry, round, midair figure, hurtling from the back of the steps toward the head of the kangaroo.

There was a muffled crash in the darkness behind the stairs as I scrambled after the tumbling flashlight.

When my fingers finally wrapped around the handle and swung the flashlight back into the corner behind the stairs, the scene had changed completely.

A wobbling Rupert was shakily wrapped around the kangaroo's shoulders while his blue eyes rapidly searched the room for the escaped prey. Isabella sat serenely on the floor next to the kangaroo's feet, placidly licking one of her front paws. There was no sign of the frog.

A man's curly brown head popped down from the hatch.

"Hello! What's going on down here?" he called out inquisitively.

I flipped the light up at his face, blinding him in its beam.

"Front door was unlocked," he explained, squinting his eyes in the glare.

"Hmmnh," I replied, not entirely satisfied. Montgomery Carmichael had a disturbing habit of making unauthorized visits to the Green Vase showroom.

I was at least relieved to see that he had resumed his regular attire and hairstyle. I focused the flashlight on the edge of the hatch where the sleeve of Monty's white cuff emerged from his gray sweater.

A bright green frog-shaped cufflink hung from the cuff.

It was too much of a coincidence. Monty had a vast collection of whimsical cufflinks, and he took great care in making each day's selection. Whatever frog-related scheme Dilla was cooking up with the Vigilance Committee, it was a safe bet Monty was chin deep in it, too.

I returned the light to Monty's face, focusing the full force of its interrogating beam directly into his eyes.

"What's with the frogs?" I demanded.

Chapter 17

REDWOOD PARK—REVISITED

HAROLD WOMBLER'S RAGGED construction boots shuffled past the massive concrete struts that formed the base of the TransAmerica Pyramid building. The shadows fell on his hunched shoulders, darkening the rough patches of stubble on his face, as he turned onto the sidewalk leading into Redwood Park.

The Thursday lunch crowd had begun to trickle in, their numbers migrating to the park's center where a small, un-shaded circle was receiving an unusual boost of solar energy. Harold watched as a group of office workers mingled around the flat wooden benches, unpacking their bundles of portable food. A few stripped off their suit jackets to revel in the unseasonably warm temperature.

The sunny weather did little to brighten Harold's dark mood. He was still out of sorts from his morning trip to the Cliff House. He didn't mind the early hour or the drive out to the far side of town—it was the company he objected to. There were few people in the world Harold loathed more than Montgomery Carmichael.

Harold gimped along beside a line of redwood trunks

and headed toward the fountain. Mark Twain's bronze frogs were enjoying their perpetual splash, their frozen, outstretched flippers forever reaching for the next stone lily pad.

Harold's bloodshot eyes studied the mossy rocks beneath the surface of the pooling water. The roar of the fountain drowned out the conversation of the nearest lunchers, allowing him to collect his thoughts.

After a moment's meditation, Harold pulled his faded baseball cap down over his eyes and grumpily hobbled over to a bench on the edge of the park that was occupied by an elderly Asian woman. The woman's face was shadowed by the ring of redwoods skirting the backside of her bench, but Harold had no trouble identifying her. The bright green go-go boots on her feet gave her away.

Dilla tucked her scarf around her neck as Harold collapsed down onto the opposite side of the bench. With a nod, she handed him a bundle wrapped up in paper emblazoned with the name of a nearby deli.

Harold tore hungrily into the package. The pricey gourmet sandwich inside promised a hearty meal. The thick slices of fresh bread had been baked that morning. In between the slices lay a substantial pile of cheddar cheese, smoked ham, crisp lettuce, and juicy tomatoes; a generous smear of Dijon mustard seasoned the tasty heap. Harold savored the first bite before turning his head toward his bench companion.

"Thanks, Dilla," Harold said as he pulled a sour dill pickle out of its separate wax paper wrapping. He was still cranky, but the sustenance of the sandwich made up, in part, for the unpleasantries of the morning.

Dilla tapped the toes of her boots against the pebbled pavement as Harold continued to munch. "How did it go at the Cliff House?" she asked cheerily.

Harold muttered bitterly into his sandwich. The only interpretable word was "Carmichael."

Dilla giggled. "Did everybody show up?"

Harold nodded and wiped his mouth with his sleeve.

"The PM gave me a wave. Pleased as punch to be running the show."

"The PM?" Dilla repeated, her voice briefly puzzled. "Oh, the Previous Mayor," she added quickly, breaking the code. "Yes, he loves to be involved," she said, laughing. "I think he's enjoying this little project. He says he'll support anything that might get those two stubborn men working together again."

Dilla stretched out her legs to reach into one of her pants' pockets. "He'll be looking for you at this restaurant tomorrow at noon," she said, handing Harold a piece of paper.

Harold unfolded it and scanned the information. "Not a very discreet location," he said skeptically. "I thought the point was to keep this hush-hush until you get everyone on board."

"The PM has a busy schedule. It was the only time I could get," Dilla replied with a harried sigh. She pointed at the piece of paper. "That's his regular spot. He eats there every Friday."

Harold's wrinkled face curdled sourly. "Isn't this French? You know I hate foreign food."

"I'm sure they buy all of their ingredients locally," Dilla replied tartly.

Harold grumbled into another bite of his sandwich. "So where are we with the Mayor and the Board?"

Dilla tugged on her scarf again. "The PBS—that's President of the Board of Supervisors," she translated with a smile. "He's a member of the *Green* Party, so there shouldn't be any problems there. He seems quite keen on the idea actually."

She sighed with a slight air of frustration. "But the Mayor is going to be a much bigger challenge than I thought. He harbors some, er, misconceptions about our little friends." She tossed her hands into the air. "I think it's just that he's never really got to *know* one of them. For some reason, he's intimidated by them."

Harold snorted his disapproval. "You know, I never voted for the man myself."

Dilla tutted her finger admonishingly at Harold. "The PM," she winked, "has a plan. He'll discuss it with you at the meeting."

Harold grimaced. "At the *French* restaurant." He finished off his sandwich and began gathering up the remaining refuse.

"This new Vigilance Committee you're putting together," Harold said thoughtfully as he wrapped up his half-eaten pickle. "It's a worthy cause you're promoting, don't get me wrong. But you didn't need to bring back the VC to pursue this project. Are you sure there isn't some other *alternative* reason for stirring all of this up again?"

Dilla swung her feet out from the bench, grateful for the protection of the mask. It made it much easier to hide her facial expressions. "I can't imagine what you're getting at, Harold."

Harold crimped his wrinkled face skeptically as he crunched the paper wrapping into a ball and tossed it through the air to the nearest trash bin. "I guess you'll need some of the Sutro money to make all of this work," he said with a shrug. "Are you certain it's still hidden in the same place?"

Dilla leaned back on the bench, tilting her head skyward. "As certain as one can be about this sort of thing," she replied, the slight wavering in her voice belying a trace of doubt. "It was a long time ago, you know. There's always a chance Oscar moved it, but I doubt it. That wasn't his style."

Harold rubbed the stubble on the end of his chin. "You're not worried about . . ."

"Old what's his name?" she asked, her voice brittle despite her attempt at breeziness. "I'm not afraid of Frank."

"No, no, of course not," Harold said wryly. "That's why you're running around in this"—he waved his hands at her costume—"*outfit*."

"Ah, for strategy, dear," Dilla replied, wagging her finger at him. "For strategic advantage." She tugged self-consciously on the hem of the baggy sweater before lifting her chin and straightening her shoulders defiantly. "Anyway, I'm heading over to the site this afternoon to check it out—we're getting close enough now. We need to be sure."

Harold chuckled and said teasingly, "Don't you think you're a little too old to be riding on a merry-go-round?"

"Absolutely not," Dilla huffed her rebuke. "And don't you tell anyone any different."

Harold stood up and brushed a few crumbs from the folds of his ragged overalls. "One last word about Carmichael," he said, taking a step toward Dilla. "I picked him up this morning—as you requested," he added pointedly. "But I still don't know why you wanted to get him involved."

Harold waved his fingers in the air in front of Dilla's face. "He's got loose lips. Bound to spill the beans."

The serenity of Dilla's smile permeated even the thick rubber of the mask. "I'm rather counting on him for that."

Harold grunted. "You're sure he's not collaborating with . . ."

Dilla's voice grew more serious. "I've never been completely certain which team he's on," she admitted. She reflected, internally, that she could say the same of her lunch companion. "But this should be a good way to find out."

Chapter 18

"WHAT'S WITH THE FROGS?"

"FROGS, YOU SAY?" Monty asked with exaggerated puzzlement as he pushed back from the hatch. He sat on the floor of the Green Vase showroom, nervously brushing his hand through the thick, bouncing curls springing from the top of his head.

"Frogs," I replied suspiciously, swinging the flashlight in front of me as I marched up the stairs from the basement. My feet stomped against the shaky steps as I held the flashlight in front of me, flourishing it at the green frog-shaped cufflinks on the wrists of the white collared shirt Monty wore beneath his gray sweater.

"I'm sure I don't know what you mean," Monty demurred, but the tone of his voice lacked sincerity. He scooted back from the hatch's open hole, crab-walking on his hands and feet in hasty retreat.

Rupert and Isabella followed me up out of the basement as Monty slid his feet underneath his bony frame and popped up to full height. He sidestepped around the leather dental chair, swiveling it like a shield between us.

His thin lips spread into a rigid grin, but the forced effort made his narrow face seem strangely contorted.

I tried to effect my most intimidating stare, but a pungent whiff of engine oil tripped up my concentration. I bent over the chair toward Monty, sniffing as I confirmed the source of the smell. Rupert hopped up onto the leather seat cushion of the dental chair and added his own loud, snuffling sounds.

I pulled back from the chair and delivered my verdict. "You smell like an auto repair shop," I said, crinkling my nose.

Monty's lips tensed tightly. "New aftershave," he replied pertly.

Rupert issued a disapproving sniff and bounced off of the chair.

"Let's get back to the frogs," I repeated accusingly, trying to redirect the conversation as I returned the point of my flashlight to Monty's frog-shaped cufflinks. "I just found a frog in my basement."

I intentionally omitted mention of the frog-sighting from the upstairs apartment. Not in a million years would I confess to Montgomery Carmichael that I had seen two mustache-wearing amphibians in my bedroom.

"A frog . . . in your basement?" Monty raised his eyebrows as he stretched his long neck to look into the dark hole of the hatch. "You don't say."

"Just like the one from City Hall," I pressed, squinting my eyes at Monty.

My mind scrambled to pull the scattered pieces together. There had to be some connection between Mark Twain's famous frog story and the inexplicable frog invasion of both City Hall and the Green Vase. I felt certain that Monty knew more than he was letting on.

Monty stroked the point of his chin as he continued to peer curiously down into the hatch.

"What a strange ecological coincidence," he said before turning away. With a skip of his leather loafers, Monty danced around to the front of the dental chair and dropped lightly onto its seat. He pulled the recline lever to extend the seat to a flattened position and leaned back, closing his eyes.

I rolled my upper lip inward, contemplating Monty's unconvincing bluff. I needed a bigger stick to prod him with.

I walked up to the cashier counter and pulled out one of the Mark Twain books. Slowly, I returned to the back of the showroom and circled around to the front of the dental chair. All along the way, Rupert trotted on the floor near my feet, his eyes hopefully following the book, as if it might suddenly transform into a plate of fried chicken.

With a stiff outstretched arm, I waved the green book in front of Monty's possumed face.

"So, you've got one of these, too," Monty said assessingly, cracking open one eye.

"*Too*?" I pressed. "How many are there?"

"What else have you got?" Monty asked loftily, ignoring my question.

I crunched my lips together, pushing out a sigh of frustration as I crossed my arms over my chest.

Monty reclosed his eyes and mimicked a snore, but a confident, knowing smile was now spreading across his face.

Ruefully, I reached into my back pocket. Monty's eyes slanted open, watching as I pulled out the black-and-white photo and laid it on the wide armrest of the dentist recliner.

Monty's eyes popped fully open. "Aha!" he said, quickly snatching up the photo. He slammed the recliner into reverse and sprang up from the chair.

"Do you see them?" I asked as he paced toward the front of the store, closely studying the photo as he walked. "Dilla, Wang, Oscar, and . . ."

"Your good friend Frank," Monty filled in sarcastically. Once more, his long, bony fingers pulled through the curls on the top of his head, this time conveying the reflexive action of a person deep in thought.

"Is this . . . the Vigilance Committee?" I asked tentatively.

Monty glanced back at me, his superior smirk my confirmation.

"I . . . just don't . . . understand," I stuttered in protest as I trailed behind him. "What is . . . what is . . . Frank Napis doing in the photo?"

Monty looked up at me, his expression brashly confident. "You don't know very much about all of this do you?"

I wiped a hand across my forehead. The little bit I knew about Oscar's Vigilance Committee days still didn't make much sense to me.

The Uncle Oscar I had known was a gruff, isolated hermit of a man. He'd never once mentioned city politics or given any hint of the populist aspirations purportedly espoused by the Vigilance Committee. Oscar had been an island, self-sufficient and inaccessible. It was difficult to imagine him mixed up with an antiestablishment movement, particularly one that had apparently threatened the power structure of City Hall.

"Oscar just didn't seem like the type," I sighed.

Monty leaned up against the cashier counter as he stared into the black-and-white photo. "I never would have guessed it myself," he acknowledged frankly. "Old Oscar, fighting for the common man, wrangling with the octopus, so to speak."

"Wrangling with the—what?" I asked.

"The octopus," Monty nodded smugly. "That's old-time slang for the many-armed monster of big business." He squiggled his arms in the air to illustrate the reference. "Weaving its tentacles into every aspect of life and politics."

I stepped back to avoid Monty's wildly swinging arms, shaking my head skeptically.

Monty shrugged his narrow shoulders. "The phrase goes back to Adolph Sutro, you know, the millionaire populist. He ran for Mayor back in the late 1800s. All of his campaign literature talked about chopping the arms off of the octopus."

I scrunched up my face, unconvinced. "Are you sure we're talking about *my* uncle? He just wasn't . . ."

Monty pumped his eyebrows at me. "Don't think of him as your dear old Uncle Oscar. Try to picture him more as—the Lone Ranger."

I put my hand on my hips. "My Uncle Oscar? The man who threw you out on your ear every chance he got?"

"Ah yes." Monty rubbed his right earlobe, remembering. "The Lone Ranger—with a dark side." Monty's face suddenly brightened. "Able to fake his own death with the use of a special spider toxin and tulip extract antidote . . ."

Groaning, I leaned over Monty's shoulder to take another look at the black-and-white photo.

"Why is Oscar dressed up like Mark Twain?" I asked, still thrown by his strange costume.

Monty let out a spurt of laughter. "You really don't know about the frogs, then?" he asked, shaking his head with a giggle.

I glared sternly at Monty; I was growing irritated by his antics. "How do *you* know so much about this?"

Monty thunked his finger against the pointed tip of his nose, causing the cartilage to quiver in vibration. Then, he swung his hand toward me, palm facing outward.

"Wait," he said as I gripped the edge of the counter in frustration.

Monty placed the green Twain book on the cashier counter next to the photo and flipped it open to the featured essay, *The Celebrated Jumping Frog of Calaveras County*. He motioned his hand between the essay and the Twain-impersonating Oscar.

I stared at the two items, trying to understand the meaning Monty apparently deemed so obvious. Nothing came to me.

"Why is there a frog in my basement?" I finally demanded testily.

"It probably came in through that nasty tunnel of yours,"

Monty said with a dismissive shudder. He raised his finger professorially. "I'm far more interested in the frog at City Hall." He winked encouragingly. "That's the one you should be asking me about."

I sighed, trying to draw on my last reserves of patience. "Okay, fine. What was the frog doing at City Hall?"

Monty clapped his hands together gleefully. "It's the VC's calling card. The sudden appearance of frogs, that is." Monty's eyes were now gleaming with excitement. He pointed enthusiastically at the photo. "Back then, back when the Vigilance Committee was active, that was their code, their symbol—their mark."

Monty stepped back from the counter and slashed his right arm through the air as if he were holding a sword, making three wide strokes in the shape of a Z.

"Perhaps less of a Lone Ranger," Monty said slyly, pinching his fingers over his lips and drawing out a long, curving mustache. "Your Uncle Oscar had more panache than that. He was more like . . . *Zorro!*"

I pursed my lips to stifle a retort as my eyes focused back in on the photo where Frank Napis and my uncle stood, shoulder to shoulder, smiling in a friendship I knew to be fake. The sight made me cringe.

"And, now?" I asked, afraid I already knew the answer. "What is the significance of a frog appearing now?"

"It means they're back!" Monty announced exuberantly. "The VC is back in action!"

He started jumping up and down on the squeaky floorboards, triumphantly throwing his hands in the air before finally bubbling out.

"And the best part is—*I*'ve been recruited!"

Chapter 19

THE BUS RIDE

MONTY BEGAN RUNNING celebratory victory laps around the Green Vase showroom as he reveled in his pronouncement. I picked up the photo from the cashier counter, this time focusing on the background of the scene.

Dilla, Mr. Wang, Frank Napis, and Oscar appeared to be standing outside of a small storefront on a busy neighborhood street. The number for the store's street address was painted on a glass door behind the group. Squinting through my glasses, I could just make it out: 575.

"Do you know where this was taken?" I asked, pointing at the photo. "It looks like it's in San Francisco?"

Monty spun around, flipping his head toward me in surprise. "You really don't know?"

I shook my head. I was growing weary of feeling so uninformed.

The shadow of an orange and white MUNI bus lumbered past the window, and Monty's eyes brightened with the flicker of an idea.

"Grab your coat. I'll take you there," he said brightly,

picking up the photo. "If we hurry, we can catch the bus at the corner."

"Oh no," I moaned as Monty grabbed my wrist and pulled me toward the front door. "Not the bus."

I snatched my jacket from a peg near the cashier counter as Monty yanked me outside of the Green Vase.

"It's unhealthy, this phobia you've developed about buses," Monty opined as he dragged me down Jackson Street. "I'm staging an intervention. Come on, it'll take us right there."

Monty waved frantically at the driver who downshifted the bus to an idle, holding it at the corner. Monty sprinted ahead of me as the side doors of the bus unfolded. With a flourish to indicate his thanks to the driver, he bounded up into the carriage.

I hung back, balking from an overwhelming sense of dread, but Monty waved urgently for me to follow him inside. Monty paid my fare as I reluctantly started off after him.

I should have trusted my instincts. I should have resisted Monty's persistent hand gestures. I should have known better than to get on that bus.

I BROKE INTO a sprint to catch up to the front door of the bus before it took off. As I climbed up the steps, I glanced briefly at the driver. His face was turned away from me; he appeared to be adjusting the driver's side mirror. Something struck me funny about the way he stuck his arm out over the back of his shoulder to wave me past, but I thought nothing of it until later in the ride.

Even though the bus was practically empty of riders, Monty strode purposefully toward the rear seats, plopping himself down onto a bench near the back.

Monty reached his seat just before the bus lurched forward, but I was still walking, midway down the aisle. The momentum of the sudden acceleration nearly knocked me off my feet. I had no chance to regain my footing. The bus immediately swung into a sharp right turn, causing my hips to bang against the metal framing of the nearest seat.

Gripping onto a seat back, I hauled my wobbly legs down the remaining length of the bus, finally landing with a hard bump on the bench across the aisle from Monty.

"So, where are we going?" I asked weakly, my stomach already protesting from the roughness of the ride.

Monty smiled, preening in his knowledge advantage. "The Castro, of course."

"The Castro?" I repeated, thinking back to my conversation with Miranda. "Does this relate to the slain Supervisor, Harvey Milk?" I asked, trying to make the connection.

Monty nodded his head. "The members of the Vigilance Committee were big supporters of Harvey. He was a perfect fit for them, really. He epitomized many of the goals they were trying to accomplish."

Monty threw his right arm casually over the back of his bench seat. "You see, when the VC first got together, they focused their efforts on helping pass a grassroots initiative that was aimed at changing the seat allocations for the city's Board of Supervisors—from citywide to district-by-district. The VC felt that district seating would give cash-poor candidates a better chance of winning since they would have a much smaller area to canvass and solicit voters. The VC reasoned that Supervisors elected under a district-by-district system would be more connected to the concerns of their respective neighborhoods and less likely to be influenced by the political power of the pro-growth real estate interests."

Monty spread his hands wide. "It was a huge coup when the referendum passed. San Francisco's political power-houses were completely blindsided. The VC had their appetite whetted by that first taste of success, so they set about picking Supervisor candidates to support in the newly outlined districts. There were several contenders that caught the VC's attention, but Harvey Milk stood out from the crowd."

I stared up at the exposed metal roof of the bus as I listened to Monty's speech, desperately trying to calm the queasiness in my stomach. My aversion to public bus transport was growing by the second. I must not have been alone in my dim opinion of the city's bus system. We'd made only one stop since Monty and I got on, and no other passengers remained on board.

"Harvey had run several times for a citywide Supervisor seat, but he'd never garnered enough votes to make the cutoff," Monty chattered on. "Even after the switch to district seating, no one took him seriously. He was even shunned by the established leaders within the gay community. They saw him as an upstart, someone who was pushing too hard and who hadn't yet paid his dues. Harvey ruffled a lot of feathers when he signed up to run for the Castro district's new Supervisor seat."

I was trying to listen to Monty's discourse, but our bus driver seemed bent on plowing through each and every bumper-scraping pothole he came across. Each dipping whomp caused a jarring recoil in the back end of the bus. The spring beneath my seat, I was convinced, had been permanently rearranged to its most uncomfortable conformation.

"Harvey refused to listen to the naysayers," Monty continued. "He was relentless. He canvassed street corners, bus stops, anywhere he might get ten seconds with a potential voter. He campaigned nonstop during the day, and then returned to his camera shop on Castro Street—his campaign headquarters—to work late into the night on fliers, posters, all of the nuts and bolts that a political campaign needs to get its message out."

Monty clamped his hand back down on the seat as we rode out another roller-coaster bump.

"More importantly, Harvey's political message began to resonate across the city. In addition to promoting gay rights, Harvey had a broad populist agenda. He talked about promoting small businesses and protecting San Francisco's eclectic neighborhoods from rampant real estate development." Monty tilted his head toward me. "And, of course, it didn't hurt that Harvey was extremely charismatic. The way I hear it, he could charm the wool socks off of an Eskimo."

Monty grinned, waiting for me to appreciate his joke. I was too green to offer more than a weak smile.

"As Harvey's campaign took off, his volunteer base expanded. He gained the support of the city's unions and the Chinese American community, both of whom sent workers to his campaign headquarters. The Vigilance Committee easily slipped themselves—and their money—into the mix."

Monty pulled the black-and-white photo I'd found in the basement wardrobe out of his back pocket and handed it to me. "This picture was taken outside of Milk's camera shop, 575 Castro Street, the site of the Harvey Milk campaign headquarters."

I slipped the photo into my jacket pocket, pondering Monty's VC story. Both he and Miranda had mentioned the importance of the VC's money to its political endeavors, I reflected, but it struck me as odd that neither one had said where that money had come from. Before I could ask Monty about the source of the VC's financing, he switched topics.

"People often wonder why San Francisco became so closely associated with the gay movement," Monty said conversationally, his stomach apparently unaffected by the nonstop bouncing of the bus.

"It goes back to the city's history as a naval port. Throughout most of the nineteenth century, if a sailor were suspected of being a homosexual, he would be kicked out of the Navy and decommissioned, usually here in San Francisco. Many men decided to stay in California rather than return to their hometowns and face the stigma of that label. It's not that San Francisco was all that amenable to the gay lifestyle—many citizens were openly hostile to gays, and the police were constantly conducting late-night raids targeted at homosexuals—but gay life here was better than, say, small-town America."

Monty paused briefly to look out his window as the bus slowed to a halt in front of the 17th Street stoplight, cueing up for the sweeping left-hand turn from Market onto Castro. Seeing our location, Monty pulled down on the signal rope by his window, indicating we would be getting off at the next stop. The driver's head nodded, acknowledging receipt of our request. Monty leaned back in his seat and resumed his history lesson.

"Just as San Francisco's gay movement began to build, the historically Irish Catholic, blue-collar neighborhood of the Castro fell into decline. The area was filled with rotting, peeling Victorians. The local grocery store was falling into bankruptcy, and a crime syndicate had taken over the streets. The few working-class families that remained were horrified when the city's growing gay population began to move in. Many of the older residents sold their property at a discount; they were convinced that the presence of gays in the neighborhood would cause property values to tank further."

Monty waved his hands at the busy street-life surrounding the intersection where the bus idled, waiting for the light to change. "What happened, of course, was just the opposite. Gay men from across the country began flocking to the Castro. They bought many of the old, rundown Victorians and began fixing them up. Property values skyrocketed, increasing four or fivefold over the next ten to twenty years."

The light turned, releasing the bus for its wide left turn. The gentle down slope of Castro Street spread out below us as the iconic Castro Movie Theater sign loomed into view. The bus began to pick up speed as it accelerated down the crowded street—and barreled straight past the next bus stop.

Waiting passengers yelled, angrily waving their hands in the air as the bus zoomed past.

"Hey!" Monty yelled at the driver, but he merely hunched deeper into his seat. "Well, that *was* Milk's old place," Monty said, annoyed as he pointed at the storefront of one of the many renovated Victorians we were now zipping by.

Irate car horns honked from every direction as the bus blasted through the next intersection. We hit Castro's valley floor and began driving up the ascent of a steep, city-topping hill. Monty lifted himself off of his bench seat and staggered up the aisle toward the driver.

I could hear the gears grinding in the engine beneath me as the bus sped up the incline. The driver had committed the full resources of the gas pedal to the climb.

Monty was striding forward now, gripping the metal handles that hung down from the ceiling. He was working against gravity and momentum, but he would soon reach the front of the bus.

In the rearview mirror, I saw the top half of the driver's face as he glanced back at the carriage. The driver's hat was pulled down low over his forehead, nearly obscuring his eyes, but the reflected image struck me cold.

I'd seen those eyes just moments earlier—in the black-and-white photo tucked into my coat pocket—and, a few months ago, on a face that wore a feathery orange mustache.

"Monty!" I called out, trying to warn him, but the sound of the bus's roaring engine drowned out my voice.

The two visible slits of the driver's eyes flicked once more to the mirror, honing in on Monty's advancing figure.

"Monty!" I yelled again, but he didn't hear me. He had almost reached the front of the bus.

I rose out of my seat as the bus slowed slightly at the top of the hill to navigate a left-hand turn. Tires squealed as the bus tilted, nearly toppling over as it screeched across the intersection. I crawled back into my seat, bruised and nauseous, and caught sight of Monty's curly head poking up from the floor.

Ten seconds later, midway down the next block, the bus lurched to a sudden stop, throwing me chin first against the bench back of the seat in front of me.

Rubbing my jaw, I looked up the aisle toward the

driver's windshield. The road dropped off in front of us, rolling down toward the flatlands of the Mission. We were at the top of 22nd Street, at the crest of one of the steepest hills in the city.

I watched in horror as Monty staggered forward and reached out to tap the driver on his shoulder. Just as Monty's arm swung around, the driver cut the engine, jerked out the key, and leapt up from his seat. Monty stood, stunned, as the driver hurled himself down the steps and out the front door.

Frank Napis glanced back at the bus, a smirking sneer on his flat face, before scuttling away down a side street. As Monty and I stared at his fleeing figure, the bus began to roll, driverless, down the hill.

Chapter 20

DOWN THE HILL

THE WHEELS BENEATH the bus rolled faster and faster, picking up speed as we careened down 22nd Street. A block of Victorians flashed by my window, their bright painted colors blurring into a gabled rainbow.

The rear side exit of the bus had opened when Napis fled out the front door. I climbed across the aisle toward it and looked down at the street, measuring the pace of the asphalt. We were already moving far too fast for either one of us to jump out safely.

Monty spun his head back toward me, his mouth dropped open in surprise. "That was—"

"I know! I know!" I yelled, my voice echoing in the eerily silent, motorless bus.

"But what was he—" Monty sputtered.

"Grab the wheel!" I cried, cutting him off. "Pull the emergency brake!"

Monty nodded, acknowledging my advice with a raised finger. He crawled forward as the bus began to weave wildly back and forth. The flat, terraced square of an intersection, filled with crossing traffic, loomed in front of us.

With difficulty, Monty threaded his lanky figure into the driver's seat. His hands gripped the steering wheel as he frantically searched through the numerous levers, buttons, and switches for the brake.

I watched, heart in mouth, as the bus soared past a red stop sign, its traffic instruction unheeded. There wasn't enough time, I thought. We were accelerating toward disaster. Fearing the worst, I ducked down behind the nearest seat back and braced myself for the brunt of an inevitable collision.

The bus bottomed out on the intersection's short stretch of flattened road. The recoil bumped my rear end nearly two feet off of the seat cushion as if I were on a trampoline. From the height of my midair position, I had a brief, unimpeded view of a street full of oncoming traffic, an impenetrable net of metallic-hued mallets whose pounding path we couldn't possibly avoid.

"Ahhhhh!" Monty hollered from the driver's seat. The bus swerved as he twisted the steering wheel, and a small sedan, horn wailing in affront, narrowly dodged around us. Miraculously, we made it through the crossing without crashing into any bystanders, but, looking out at the road ahead of us, there was no respite in sight.

As we reached the opposite side of the intersection, the front end of the bus tipped forward, dropping over the edge for the next block's descent. It felt as if we were driving down the side of a cliff. My stomach sickened as we sped past a yellow sign in the shape of a triangle, warning of the steep grade.

Monty flailed at the implements surrounding the driver's seat. I could hear his feet pumping, to no avail, against the brake pedal on the floor. None of his actions seemed to be having any effect on our ever-increasing speed.

We were now in a heavily residential area; both sides of the street were lined with houses. In typical San Francisco fashion, every available inch of curb space was occupied by a parked vehicle. Due to the steep slope of the street, the parking spaces were slotted lengthwise, perpendicular to the flow of traffic.

Up ahead on the right, the rear bumper of an SUV began backing out of a narrow parking spot. Given the angle of the road's upward slope and the added visual impairments of the other parked cars, the driver wouldn't be able to see us until we were right on top of him.

"Ahhhhh!" Monty yelled again. He laid into the horn as he swerved the bus, trying to avoid the backing SUV. The horn emitted a panicked, tooth-shattering honk that echoed through the otherwise quiet neighborhood. I caught a glimpse of the other driver's terrified face, cursing us as he scrambled to reverse gears.

The bus swung wildly to the left, nearly sideswiping a line of parked cars. Monty strained against the steering wheel, trying to pull the bus back on course. The rubber treads beneath us skidded across the pavement as the bus careened from left to right, overcorrecting against a painted brick wall on the opposite side of the street. Sparks flew up as the rending sound of metal scraping against brick pierced the air.

The brief contact-friction, unfortunately, did little to slow our pace. We were fast approaching another intersection, this one wider across with more lanes, the connection point with a far busier artery of traffic.

Monty gulped visibly as he registered the danger. His right hand clamped down on a handle mounted into the floor beside the driver's seat.

"Found the hand brake!" he called out excitedly.

I closed my eyes, grimacing as I anticipated the coming jolt from the brake's application—but after thirty seconds of holding my breath, my eyes popped back open. The bus was still rolling along, as fast as ever.

I looked up the aisle toward the front of the bus. Monty was holding up the detached handle of the hand brake in his limp right hand.

We were trapped on a roller coaster without any rails, without any brakes. From the distance, a police siren sang out the promise of rescue, but there was no way it would reach us before we hit the next intersection. I was certain we were going to die.

"Horn!" I shouted up at Monty, who was still numbly staring at the sabotaged hand brake.

Monty's face paled as he dropped the brake handle and pummeled the horn button in the center of the steering wheel.

The sound was deafening, but effective. Startled motorists on either side of the intersection screeched to a rubber-burning stop, gaping in horror as the bus plowed through without slowing. We were surrounded by another interlude of streaming color and blaring horns.

If only I managed to get off of this bus alive, I swore to myself, I would never, *ever* board another one.

The road began to level out as we exited the second intersection, but the bus's built-up momentum continued to push us forward. Our speed was now gradually decreasing, but still more intersections lay ahead. Our luck couldn't hold out much longer.

A flashing red and blue light bounced against the metal walls of the bus, and I felt the first calming waves of relief. It was a miracle. The police car had caught up to us.

A bull-horned voice immediately barked instructions. "Pull the emergency brake!"

The voice was gruff, angry, irritated, and oh-so-welcome.

Monty grabbed the broken handle and waved it out the driver's side window.

There was a short, tense silence before the voice returned. "We're bringing a car around in front. He'll slow you down manually."

Monty waved cheerfully from the driver's seat. With the arrival of the police, he'd suddenly relaxed—it was as if he were now enjoying this terrifying experience.

"Manually?" I murmured, nervously gripping the seat in front of me. "What does that mean, 'manually'?"

A second police car suddenly pulled out in front of us from a side street. The vehicle slowed, immediately disappearing from my narrow, angled view out the front window.

Monty hollered toward the back of the bus, "Prepare for impaaaa—"

A jarring crunch signaled the contact of the grill of the bus with the police car's steel bumper. My fingers clenched the leather seat cushion, pushing against the momentum of the sudden deceleration. The bus shuddered in fits and starts as the police car applied more braking pressure, finally bringing us to a complete stop.

A wave of blissful, motionless silence fell over the carriage of the bus as Monty sprang energetically down the front steps and waved triumphantly at the police car.

My wobbly legs managed to carry me out the mangled rear door. I gripped the bent handle bar next to the steps, trying to steady my dizzied head as I stumbled onto the curb. All the while, the scrambled contents of my stomach threatened to make their own exit.

Monty's flat-soled footsteps pattered off down the sidewalk, in deep conversation with a growing knot of policeman. Fire trucks and ambulances appeared as if from nowhere, quickly filling the scene.

I closed my eyes and ran my hands over my clammy cheeks. I felt lost, abandoned, and exhausted. I sat down on a curb and put my head between my knees, trying to center myself.

And that's when it hit me—a strangely familiar smell—one I'd previously encountered in only two other instances.

The first was in the kitchen above the Green Vase. The second was in my growing collection of VC items—in the pages of the shiny green Mark Twain books and on the surface of the black-and-white photo I'd found in the basement wardrobe.

The air on the sidewalk was filled with the smell of sizzling herb-crusted chicken, cooked up in a wrought iron skillet, filled with several inches of deep, savory animal fat. I could hardly believe my nose, but there could be no mistake.

Someone nearby was cooking my Uncle Oscar's fried chicken.

Chapter 21

A FAMILIAR SMELL

MY NOSE SOAKED up the familiar scent, pulling it inward to meet the memory of my uncle's short, rounded shoulders bent over a skillet, grousing grumpily as he perfected his signature dish of crispy fried chicken.

As far as I knew, Oscar had never written down the exact ingredients he used to make the coating for his chicken. I had assumed that the recipe had died with him, but it appeared someone, somehow, had managed to replicate it.

I took a quick glance at the melee surrounding the disabled bus. Monty had commandeered the attention of the police, firemen, and gawking onlookers circling the scene. He stood in the middle of the crowd, his hands gesturing wildly in the air as he spun a phantom steering wheel. Knowing Monty, the story was rapidly drifting further and further from the truth.

No one appeared to notice as I edged away from the throng. I assumed a casual, nonchalant pace until I was a full block away; then I headed off in search of the source of the haunting fried chicken scent.

The succulent aroma intensified as I turned onto a narrow side street. On either side of the road, shady elm trees dug into the sandy dirt beneath the asphalt. The efforts of the roots cracked the sidewalk, pushing up the corners of the concrete. As I stumbled over the crooked pavement, an unsettled feeling crept over me—one that was completely unrelated to the turbulent bus ride.

Monty's droning voice wormed its way into my head, spouting off theory after wild, crazy theory of how my Uncle Oscar might have faked his death. Despite the niggling anomalies surrounding his passing, I had refused to consider Monty's speculations, confident in what I had seen at Oscar's funeral, in what I believed to be the truth. But now, for the first time in months, that certainty was once again tinged with doubt.

I read the name off of the nearest street sign, trying to find my location in my mind's map of San Francisco. I was fairly certain that our ill-fated bus ride had terminated on the outer edge of the Mission district.

In San Francisco's early years, this area was a wide expanse of sandy dunes, inhabited only by cowboys and the Spanish missionaries of the Mission Dolores. After the Gold Rush boom, the dunes were leveled and waves of working-class immigrants began to move in. Irish, Germans, and Poles dominated the densely populated neighborhood in the first half of the nineteenth century; Mexicans and other groups from Central and South America took over in the 1950s.

By the late 1990s, when the dot-com boom pushed Bay Area rents to astronomical heights, the Mission gained a niche status with San Francisco's young professionals. Many of its ramshackle tenements were torn down to make way for a proliferation of geometric lofts. The concentration of yuppie diners combined with comparatively lower rents to make the neighborhood one of the best addresses for new restaurants seeking to make a splash in San Francisco's ultracompetitive culinary scene.

Up ahead on the right, halfway down the block, a steady

trickle of pedestrians approached the awning-covered store-front of a small bistro. The awning's sheeting stretched out from the porch of a renovated Victorian. The bright green fabric fluttered in the breeze, making it difficult for me to read the gold-colored letters painted onto its front banner. It wasn't until I was standing flush in front of the bistro that I could make out the writing.

I read the banner several times, my stunned mind refusing to process the words—the sign identified the name of the restaurant as "Oscar's."

A petite woman with bare arms heavily inked in tattoos stood in the doorway, taking down names for table reservations.

"Number?" she asked roughly, eying me suspiciously as she barricaded the door with a forbidding stance.

"Umm," I replied vaguely, trying to peek over her head to the inside of the restaurant. The crispy smell of what I was convinced was Oscar's fried chicken overwhelmed my senses.

"Ma'am," she said sternly. "It's close quarters inside. You have to wait out here until your table's ready. How many in your party?"

A tenor voice answered from behind my right shoulder. "Two, please," Monty piped in as he stepped up next to me. "We'd like a table for two, close to the kitchen, if you can swing it."

The woman scowled at him callously. "You'll get whatever comes up next unless you want to wait out here all night."

"Of course, of course," Monty said, drumming his fingers across his chest, unabashed by her rebuff. Monty was so used to the cold shoulder treatment, its chill had absolutely no effect on him. He simply ignored it.

Monty leaned in toward the woman's tattooed arm. "Nice skull and bones," he gushed. "Did you get that done here in San Francisco?"

In his wool sweater, gray slacks, and pointed loafers, Monty looked an unlikely candidate for a tattoo parlor, but as the waitress pulled up her shirt to show Monty a large spider inked across her midriff, I took advantage of the distraction and slipped around the side of the building. I figured there had to be a service entrance in the back.

In the alley behind the restaurant, I watched as a harried busboy heaved two large garbage bags of refuse into an already loaded Dumpster. Dusting his hands together, he pushed open a small wooden door with the back of his hip and walked inside the restaurant.

I crept up to the door and looked through the mesh screen that covered its upper half. A cloud of the familiar chicken scent mushroomed out at me. I could hear the sounds of clinking silverware and muted dinner conversation, so I pushed open the door and stepped inside.

A narrow corridor led around a sharp corner, emptying out on one end of a crowded dining room. The eating space had been hollowed out from several smaller rooms; remnants of the original Victorian floor plan were still discernible, particularly in the height differential of different sections of the ceiling.

A bevy of waitstaff maneuvered through a tight tangle of wobbly wooden tables, the surfaces of each one worn and homely. The overall effect was one of closeness, walls and shoulders both within easy touching distance.

All available chairs were occupied by hungry eaters, digging into the fried concoction whose smell had drawn me from several streets over. The food was piled up, family style, in the middle of each table. But as I stared at the plates, I realized that there was something decidedly un-chicken-y about the food's appearance. The shape of each piece seemed much smaller in size than a typical cut of chicken.

I eased out from around the corner and stepped into the stream of waiter traffic winding through the tables. Phrases leapt out from the surrounding chatter.

"Read about this in the Chronicle the other week . . ."

"My friend wouldn't stop talking about the food, so I had to come try it for myself."

A waiter swung past me hefting a huge bowl of freshly pounded mashed potatoes. The consistency was visibly lumpy, made just the way my Uncle Oscar used to prepare it—but then again, I noted as a second bowl passed me, upon closer inspection, there was something about the white buttery mass that didn't seem quite right. Something was different.

My head was swirling, feverish with confusion. Perhaps it was all a coincidence. By chance, another cook had arrived at almost the same recipe as my Uncle Oscar's. How many different ways could there be to cook fried chicken, anyway? I'd been foolish, I thought, to let Monty's persistent Oscar theories get to me. If I could just take a quick look at the cooks, I could dismiss this as merely an odd fluke.

All of the waiters carrying hot food were coming from the opposite side of the dining room, which must, I reasoned, lead toward the kitchen. I pushed my way through the crowded tables until I reached a brick-framed cutout in the far wall that revealed the busy cooking area.

The front side of the kitchen was lined by a long stainless steel counter. Every few seconds, another hot plate slid across it for pickup. Pots and pans hung down from the ceiling, blocking the view to the line of stoves beyond—save for brief flashes of the white-coated chefs working on the opposite side.

I followed an empty-handed waiter through a nearby swinging door and into the chaos of the kitchen. Sizzling sounds filled the dense, greasy air.

Several of the cooks and waiters stopped and stared at me, but I didn't notice. My feet were traveling in only one direction, toward the hunched shoulders bent over the farthest stove in the back corner of the kitchen.

"Hey, what are you doing in here?" a voice called out, but it was mute to my chicken-numbed ears.

I rounded the corner of the hanging pans and took my first unobstructed look at the chef I'd been tracking since I caught the first scent of his cooking.

His back was turned to me, but the thinning white hair on the top of his head was unmistakably familiar. So, too, was the wrinkled hand that reached down to wipe the apron tied around his thick waist.

I leaned forward to tap him on the shoulder. I didn't breathe; I couldn't breathe. It had to be him. It couldn't be him.

But as the curve of the cook's stubbled face came into view, I saw a piece of meat that he was about to dunk into a deep tray of creamy white batter. The leg had just been separated from its host animal; the remains of the carcass filled a bin near the cook's left hand.

I realized what I should have known all along. The man in the chef's coat wasn't Oscar. My mind had been playing tricks on me.

My Uncle Oscar would never have been caught dead cooking up fried frog legs.

THE REST OF the encounter faded into a greasy blur. Monty's arm appeared as if from nowhere, wrapped around my shoulders, and deftly steered me out of the kitchen.

A diner's comment floated up from a table as Monty pulled me through the dining room.

"Tastes just like chicken . . ."

Chapter 22

DILLA TAKES A WALK

MIRANDA RICHARDS HID behind her menu as a tall, stringy man in a gray sweater led a dazed, bespectacled woman with long brown hair out of the kitchen and toward the front door of the trendy Mission restaurant. Neither of the pair appeared to recognize Miranda, who had just been seated in the crowded dining area.

Miranda's plum-painted nails drummed against the rough wooden surface of the table as she pretended to study the contents of her menu. She had been surprised, to say the least, to see those two in this location. The nails on her right hand rose up to her chin and dragged along the underside of her jaw as she pondered the implications.

She took a long sip of iced tea, puckering her lips so that they left a purple smudge on the rim of the glass. She stuck a long-handled spoon into the drink and swirled the ice cubes, thinking as she watched the brown liquid circulate.

Miranda caught sight of a waiter anxiously eying her table and returned her attention to the writing on the menu. Given the restaurant's limited offerings, she couldn't imagine that it would be open for long. Food fads shifted quickly in this city. What was "in" one week would be "out" the next.

The waiter paused timidly at Miranda's table. She dined out frequently and her temperament was well-known in San Francisco's culinary circles. The mere sight of her name on a reservation list generated fear and trepidation amongst the city's waitstaff. Even the tough-looking tattooed woman outside had paled when Miranda approached and asked for a table.

"Are you ready to order, ma'am?" the waiter asked cautiously.

Miranda waved him off. "I don't think I'll be staying for lunch after all," she replied curtly. "Please, just bring the bill for the iced tea."

The man sprinted away from her table, looking puzzled but relieved.

Miranda flipped open a slender cell phone and scrolled through the programmed numbers until she found the one she wanted. With the sharp curve of her fingernail, she pushed the call button.

Across town on Jackson Street, a phone began to ring in the loft apartment above a glass-fronted, seemingly abandoned antique store next door to the Green Vase.

Miranda waited as the line droned a flat, absent-sounding buzz, over and over again. She was about to hang up when a man answered the phone.

"Yes?" The voice was thin and feeble, matching the body of the speaker.

Miranda dispensed with the pleasantries used to begin most phone conversations and dove right to the point.

"Frank Napis was sighted in San Francisco today," she said tensely. "Are you sure you're safe in your current location?"

"I have a perfect view of the action from here." Although weak, the voice sounded confident and unconcerned.

Miranda pursed her lips tensely. "You're sure no one knows you're there?"

"No one outside of the immediate circle." There was a long pause. "You and, of course, your mother . . ."

Miranda slammed the glass of iced tea against the table. "Funny you should mention *my mother*." Her words sharpened harshly. "Would you happen to know where she is?"

The voice paused, hesitating. Finally, the man sighed and checked his watch. "She should be arriving at the Ferry Building in about twenty minutes. If you leave right now, you might be able to catch her."

DILLA'S GREEN GO-GO boots chugged down Market Street, weaving through the crowds of pedestrians as she headed toward the bay front Embarcadero. Her purposeful, energetic pace was easy to pick out amidst the casual, easy stroll of the surrounding office workers who had just left their desks in the financial district and were heading home for the evening.

Straddling the juncture of Market and the Embarcadero, the Ferry Building marked the main transit point for water traffic from cities on the north and east sides of the bay. A wide array of vendors took advantage of this concentrated foot traffic. Parked beneath a showy planting of palm trees, a clutter of street cart vendors tried to draw Dilla's interest to their kitschy offerings of homemade jewelry and cable car key chains, but she sped right past them without slowing.

A moment later, Dilla stepped out into a wide crosswalk, quickly traipsing to the front of a pack of commuters headed for the boats docked on the nearby pier.

It was a brisk but sunny afternoon, and Dilla was already breathing heavily through the confines of the thick mask, the sticky rubber sliding on her face as she perspired. Dilla tugged on her scarf, trying to correct the mask's position as she scampered toward the gray stone archway of the Ferry Building's south entrance.

Several food stalls were set up on the pavement leading

into the Ferry Building, previewing the offerings for the coming weekend's farmers' market. A flurry of high heels and silk ties perused the array of organic, picture-perfect produce. Samples of Northern California's finest gourmet meats, cheeses, and olive oil were on offer for tasting. The decadent leisure food displayed outside the Ferry Building was a far cry from the more functional fruits and vegetables sold in the market at the Civic Center.

Dilla kept her head tucked down into her scarf as she threaded her way through the kiosks, studiously avoiding eye contact with any passersby. She felt a rush of anxiety as she approached the designated location for her meeting. This, she felt, was the most precarious point of her day's subterfuge—to be seen and not be seen, each by the right watchers. Not all of the members of her team, she suspected, were as diligent as they should be regarding the operation's secrecy.

Dilla felt a tug on her sleeve. She froze, fearful that her carefully calculated strategy had been undermined. Slowly, she turned to see a concerned man holding out her handkerchief.

"Excuse me, ma'am," he said politely, his face muddling in confusion as he looked into the disjointed eyes of Dilla's mask.

"Thank you," she whispered hoarsely. She snatched the lost fabric from the man's outstretched hand and turned away, fleeing inside the Ferry Building.

Adrenaline pumping through her elderly body, Dilla tried to proceed as nonchalantly as possible down the building's long interior corridor, which was filled with an arcade of restaurants, gourmet eateries, and newspaper kiosks. A high-tented ceiling stretched above the length of the gallery, naturally lit by a center row of skylights.

Cautiously, Dilla approached the bustling storefront of an oyster bar, packed near capacity with the same well-heeled patrons from the farmers' market stalls.

A stand had been set up just outside the designated seating area for those customers who didn't have time to wait for a table. Fresh-shucked oysters waited on an ice-packed display to be dribbled with the purchaser's preferred sauce and dropped into an easy to carry, funnel-shaped paper bowl. A young Asian woman with long, shiny black hair manned the busy counter.

Dilla shuffled through the oyster line, keeping her scarf wrapped tightly around her neck. She drew a few questioning stares but kept her head down, waiting for her turn at the counter.

Lily Wang showed no outward sign of recognition when Dilla proffered the payment. As Lily dropped Dilla's oyster into the paper bowl, her right hand slid almost imperceptibly into her pocket. Lily tucked a slender metal key into the palm of her right hand and reached for Dilla's dollar. In the quickest flash, the key passed into Dilla's possession, the discreet action lost amongst the crowded din of the surroundings.

Lily looked up at Dilla as she handed over the oyster, her eyes smiling even though her face remained placid. Beneath the mask, Dilla returned the look before turning away and disappearing from the oyster stand.

As soon as Lily secured Dilla's cash inside of the register, she turned and walked out of the oyster bar, nodding briskly to the maitre d'. She was replaced almost immediately by the regular server.

DILLA SLURPED DOWN the slippery treat as she fled the Ferry Building, savoring the salty tang of the oyster. She tilted her head back, letting the stiff fingers of the afternoon breeze pry their way into the stifling holes of her mask, coating her lungs with its lifting spirit. She was on the last leg of her journey. Soon, all of the unpleasantness of the previous weeks would be behind her.

Dilla reversed her tracks back over the Embarcadero's crosswalk, the rubber soles of her shoes springing against the asphalt when she reached the other side. She pushed her way past the palm tree throng of street vendors, her pace quickening as the length of Market Street spread out in front of her.

The towering markers of the financial district sidled up against the sides of the thoroughfare as Dilla skipped, faster and faster, toward her destination. A traffic light threw up a temporary barrier, and a giddy impulse she couldn't dampen grabbed her feet and spun them in a dancing circle.

Midturn, her stomach dropped.

Dilla wrapped her arms instinctively around her middle, squeezing it as if she might disappear into the bracing wind. Marching straight toward her, two hundred yards and a traffic light behind, Dilla had spied the face of disaster.

Dilla pulled down hard on her scarf and reset her green boots back onto their path. An electronic traffic sign flashed a walking stick figure, and she strode forward. The brick corner of the Palace Hotel rose up on the left-hand side of the next block. If Dilla was going to change course, she would have to move quickly. She didn't have much time to decide.

A MUNI bus pulled up for a stop, releasing a stream of passengers out onto Market at New Montgomery. Dilla took advantage of the cross traffic. She slipped into the spillage of the bus's passengers, filtering in and out of the flow, working her way behind a blocking wall of square metal newspaper dispensers.

The bus pulled away from the curb, its engine burping on a guzzle of low emission fuel. The bus's departure released a pent-up burst of cabs that flooded the right-hand turn lane. Dilla sprinted the fifteen feet from the newspaper canisters to the corner of the Palace Hotel. She hugged the side of the building as she sped along New Montgomery. Her feet didn't stop pumping until she reached the cabstand in front of the hotel's entrance where a line of five un-passengered cars waited for a fare.

The bellman was easily identified in his long coat and tails. Dilla huffed heavily as she staggered up to him, holding a bill between her fingers. The man's perplexed look did not inspire confidence, but Dilla nevertheless delivered her breathless instructions with the bill.

A couple of minutes later, from a booth in the bar across the street, Dilla watched as Miranda Richards strode fiercely up to the bellman, her heavily made-up face clearly transmitting frustration.

The dark plum paint on Miranda's elongated fingernails flailed in front of the bellman's chest as she used her hands to illustrate her demands. He looked briefly amused before straightening his expression into one of informative credibility. The bellman swept his arms along the length of the cab line and then pointed down New Montgomery's one-way street.

Miranda twisted her lips into a sour plum-painted spout. The charcoal outlines of her eyes scanned furiously up and down the sidewalk in front of the Palace Hotel, but Dilla knew her daughter well. Miranda had conceded defeat—for the moment.

Dilla sank down against the wooden back of the booth, her body relaxing in relief. She would have to wait before proceeding further. There was too great a risk she might be caught out on the street right now.

She pulled the bottom lip of the rubber mask up and over her head, dropping it onto the seat beside her. No one raised an eyebrow at the action. There were only a few people in the bar, and they had observed far stranger characters on the streets of San Francisco.

Dilla ordered a cup of hot tea and lemon from the unquestioning waitress who attended her table. As the warm liquid pleasantly seared down her throat, she focused her eyes on a plaque on the wall near her booth, boasting of the bar's historical significance—as a frequent watering hole of Mark Twain.

Chapter 23

NO WAY TO TREAT A CAT

EARLY THE NEXT morning, a disgruntled Rupert stalked grumpily into the Green Vase showroom. He stomped over to the cashier counter and glowered up at the woman sitting on the stool behind it. His whiskers twitched with irritation as he angrily *thunked* his tail against the floorboards.

What kind of a person returns to the house smelling like fried chicken and doesn't bring any back for Rupert? It made no sense to him. He was deeply affronted.

He'd been up half of the night, making his concerns known to the woman sleeping in his bed. He'd bounced up and down on the blankets, swished his tail in her face, and pounced at every movement she made beneath the covers. He'd experimented with various howling sounds aimed at communicating his displeasure. But none of these efforts had produced the desired result. No fried chicken had appeared in his dinner bowl.

After all of these exertions, Rupert had finally fallen asleep, his head dug into his person's chicken-smelling hair. The scent had surrounded him, permeating his dreams—

dreams that were filled with bowls and bowls full of scrumptious fried chicken. He'd made loud smacking noises with his mouth as he slept; he could almost taste the crisp, greasy texture.

Sometime around three or four o'clock the following morning, Rupert had woken, a renewed hope in his stomach. There was a faint whiff of fried chicken in the air—he was almost certain of it—and it was emanating from a source other than his chicken-stingy person or those green chicken-smelling books. Somewhere in the apartment above the Green Vase, there must be a hidden cache of fried chicken.

Rupert began his search in the kitchen. It seemed like the most logical location. That was where Oscar had always prepared *his* fried chicken. Rupert sighed in reminiscence. He really missed Uncle Oscar.

Rupert hopped up on top of the kitchen counters, checking each one for a clue to the location of the fried chicken smell. He persistently nosed his way into each of the cabinets, meticulously inspecting the contents. He even peeked through the little window into the stove. There was no fried chicken to be found.

The refrigerator had been a bit of a challenge to break into, but he had long since learned that if he threw his body weight against the side of it, the refrigerator would rock back and forth until the door eventually popped open. Rupert diligently poked around inside the fridge, but quickly decided that such a cold environment was no place for his fried chicken.

The kitchen, he concluded, was chicken-free.

Rupert then moved on to the second floor's small living room. He plowed his way through the dust bunnies that lived beneath the couch. He crawled through the inner workings of an aged recliner, sharpening his claws on the underside of its already frayed fabric. After another thorough investigation, he felt satisfied that there was no fried chicken in the living room.

The smell, Rupert thought, appeared to be coming from

an elevated location, so he returned to the third floor where he continued his search in the bathroom.

The red igloo-shaped litter box would seem like an odd place for someone to put fried chicken, but people were always hiding things in there, taping little packages to the inside roof of its covered dome. That practice was rather irritating, Rupert thought, as he made an enjoyable dig through the sandy pile of litter. He should really institute a ban against it—unless, of course, the package contained fried chicken.

As expected, there wasn't any chicken in the litter box, but the dig had given Rupert a good opportunity to think. His little feline brain was absolutely fixated on this single pressing issue. Where was this pungent chicken smell coming from?

Still pondering, Rupert hopped up onto the sink and stared at himself in the mirror. He carefully studied the white fluff of hair that collared his neck. Yes, everything looked appropriately fluffy. He counted his whiskers and was pleased to see that they were arrayed in perfect symmetry on either side of his pink nose.

The bathroom stop had been the most fun of the whole search, Rupert reflected, but he had still not found the source of this mysterious fried chicken odor.

Rupert left the bathroom just as his person and his sister got up out of bed, both of them complaining about the racket he'd been making. His person eventually made it down to the kitchen to serve him breakfast, but she had only offered him the same old dry cat food; no chicken had been provided.

And now, here she was, back downstairs in the Green Vase showroom, reading one of those green chicken-smelling books, acting as if no slight had occurred.

Honestly, this was no way to treat a cat. Rupert sat on the floor next to the cashier counter, scowling up at his person. He could not imagine a more egregious offense.

There was a noise on the street outside as a white van pulled up in front of the studio across the way. Rupert turned toward the window and watched with interest as a tall, skinny man got out of the driver's seat.

It's Monty, Rupert thought, as the man walked into the entrance of the studio. Maybe Monty has fried chicken in the van. A chicken delivery van. That sounds like just the kind of idea that Monty might come up with.

Rupert jumped aside to dodge the whirling of his person's legs.

"I'll be right back," she whispered down to him as she sprinted out the front door.

Rupert propped the pads of his feet up against the glass paneling of the front door to get a better look. He watched his person scurry across the street and climb into the back of Monty's van.

Rupert's face crunched up in consternation. She was going to eat all of the fried chicken herself, he just knew it.

Monty emerged from the studio, climbed into the driver's seat of the van, and shifted the van into drive.

"*Et tu*, Montgomery," Rupert thought with despair as the chicken delivery van rolled off down the street.

As Rupert sat on the floor, mournfully looking out at the empty street, feeling sorely betrayed and unfairly put-upon, a long, winding creak issued from the back of the showroom. An old, rusty spring was being called into service after many years of inactivity.

His interest piqued, Rupert trotted across the showroom, listening for a follow-up to the first sound. Isabella leapt down from the top of her bookcase and stalked past him, quickly assuming the lead in the investigation.

Crrrreeeeak. The coils of the rusty spring made another vocal protest.

Rupert tensed and crouched down behind the dentist recliner. Unintimidated, Isabella sauntered toward the stairs that led up to the second floor, her ears perked, her tail stretched out behind her. She put her two front feet on the first step of the stairs. Rupert crept nervously in behind her, hunkering down below her confident frame.

Ka-thunk.

Rupert jumped back from the stairs and scooted to safety behind the nearest bookcase.

Isabella was undeterred. "Wrao," she assured him. Calmly, she climbed to the sixth step and looked up at the ceiling.

Rupert slunk back to the bottom of the stairs, surprised to see that the low-hanging beam above the sixth step had swung down to reveal the rungs of a ladder. A moment later, a man wearing a pair of worn house slippers began climbing down the steps.

Rupert's heart soared. The man was holding a plate—a special plate with a lovely, fragrant smell.

It was a plate of fried chicken.

Chapter 24

THE SUTRO BATHS RUINS

IT WAS STILL dark when I crawled out of bed the following morning. I'd given up trying to sleep with all of the racket Rupert was making.

He'd kept me up half of the night with his constant pestering—bouncing all over the bed, swatting at my hair, and howling at me with an oddly strangled caterwaul. It was no use trying to convince him that the smell on my clothes was from something altogether different than fried chicken. I'd been about ready to throw him out the bedroom window when he collapsed near my pillow and settled down to sleep.

But long before the clock hit four a.m., Rupert was back in action. At first, I tried to ignore the strange bumping sounds emanating from throughout the apartment, but after nearly half an hour of imagining the mess he might be making, I finally exited the bed and crawled into the shower.

It was Friday morning in name only when I trundled downstairs to the Green Vase showroom. Light from the streetlamp outside still shone in through the front windows. No one else in Jackson Square, it seemed, had been roused from their bed by the middle-of-the-night machinations of a chicken-obsessed cat.

With a groggy yawn, I settled onto the stool behind the cashier counter, pulled out the pair of green Mark Twain books, and began flipping through the pages to compare the contents.

After a couple minutes of side-by-side comparison, I realized that the older book, the one Harold had left on my counter, included an extra essay. *Early Rising as Regards Excursions to the Cliff House* was tucked in just after the famous frog story. I took a sip of my fresh-brewed coffee and began to read.

Before long, I found myself chuckling at Twain's exaggerated recounting of his misadventures during an early morning carriage ride to the pre-Sutro-era Cliff House. In his hallmark tongue-in-cheek rant, Twain railed against the bitter cold, the soupy fog, the offensive smell of the horse blanket he had taken refuge in, and the alleged benefits of "early rising."

I was almost at the end of the essay when a white van stopped on the street outside. I glanced up from the book as Monty jumped out of the driver's seat and sprinted into his studio. He left the van stranded, motor running, in the middle of Jackson Street.

Monty typically used the van to transport paintings and other art for his studio. The large cargo area in the back of the van provided ample storage space for even his largest picture frames. Monty was probably preparing to load some items for an out-of-town show, I told myself sleepily.

But the events of the past two days made me think again. It was an odd hour for Monty to be up, about, and moving so vigorously. Like Twain, he generally preferred to sleep in.

Monty had left the motor running, indicating his studio stop would be a quick one, unlikely to involve multiple trips to load the van. Maybe he was up to something else,

I thought—something related to his recent membership in the revitalized Vigilance Committee.

Rupert sat on the floor gazing wistfully at the van. Then, for some strange reason, he licked his lips.

I shook my head at my cat's ridiculous behavior and returned my concentration to the van. If it weren't already packed with picture frames, there would be plenty of room in the back of it for me to sneak inside and ride along undetected.

After the previous day's unplanned bus ride, I was loath to experiment with another impulsive form of transportation, but my reticence was overcome as the image of the black-and-white photo flashed into my memory. The frogs, the Mark Twain books, and the sudden reappearance of Frank Napis, I sensed, were all somehow linked to the group in the photo. I was slowly being dragged into whatever scheme this renewed Vigilance Committee was cooking up, and I had the sneaking suspicion it involved more than mere political maneuvering.

I considered my options for another half second; then I grabbed my shoulder bag, snatched up my coat, and sped around the corner of the cashier counter to the front door.

"I'll be right back," I assured Rupert, who glanced up at me with concern. He followed me to the door, a forlorn droop in his fluffy tail. He put his front paws up against the glass as I closed him in. I looked down at his sad, dejected face and vowed to prepare him some fried chicken when I returned.

A light flicked off in the second floor study above Monty's studio. I heard Monty's flat feet slapping loudly against the slats of the steps, indicating that he was returning to the first floor. If I were going to make my move, I had to do it now.

I scampered across the street to the rear of the van and snuck around the far corner of its back bumper. With a tug of the handle, I pulled open the back door and peeked inside.

The racks cinched into the floor that usually held Monty's

picture frames were all empty, and there was none of the extra padding he typically carried to safely transport his artwork. I had to decide, quickly, just how curious I was about Monty's next destination. There was a good chance, I thought with a sigh, that I would regret hitching this ride.

Without further hesitation, I hopped inside the dark metal interior and carefully secured the door behind me. A moment later, I heard Monty jangle the studio's front exterior lock.

I caught a glimpse of Monty's tall shadow circling around to the front of the van as I crouched down on my knees and hid behind the partition that separated the driving area and the cargo space. Wincing from the painful hardness of the metal floor, I listened as Monty wrenched open the driver's side door, slid into his seat, and slammed the door shut. Before I had time to second-guess my decision, Monty snapped his seat belt into the buckle and hit the accelerator.

I clutched the frame of the nearest empty rack to steady myself as the van sped smoothly forward and then swung around the corner at the end of the block.

The van rumbled swiftly through the vacant streets of the yawning city. Only the earliest of risers had begun to emerge from their slumber. Streetlights occasionally flashed into the dark cavern of the van's interior, but I quickly lost navigational track of where we were headed. There were no windows on the back or the sides of the van, and I dared not poke my head up to look out the front window for fear of being spotted.

So far, Monty appeared oblivious to his extra cargo. Several times, I nearly yelled out to alert him of my presence, but my gut instinct told me to wait. I was going to feel awfully silly if he were simply driving to Sonoma to pick up a painting.

We'd been briskly traveling through the stop and go of city streets for about twenty minutes when the road beneath us suddenly smoothed out to a quieter ride. Holding my breath, I risked a quick glimpse over the seat partition out through Monty's front windshield.

A dense net of trees had closed in around us. Painted lines on either side of the road's black tarmac demarcated bike lanes, and a chalky trail of well-maintained sidewalk snaked a running path through the grass along the curb.

Even though I'd been closed off from all visual clues in the back of the van, I was fairly certain we hadn't crossed any of the local bridges, meaning that we were still within the confines of San Francisco's peninsula. Given those parameters, there were only a few possibilities for our current location, and, from the glimpse outside, I had a good guess of where we were. I'd taken many a glorious jog through this multi-acre green zone. I was willing to bet we were driving through the long rectangular length of Golden Gate Park, heading, I suspected, toward the beach.

Before long, the van was greeted by the quiet roar of the ocean, and I chanced another peek out the front windshield. The eastern edge of the Pacific stretched out before of us; its swath of deep, churning blue lined up against the pale morning gray of the lightening sky. We had reached the ocean end of Golden Gate Park.

The van paused long enough to clear traffic, and then it turned right onto the highway that ran along the coast. I felt the curve of the road as it threaded through the narrow track between the Cliff House and the rocky bluff of Sutro Heights.

Monty slowed the engine to navigate a blind turn. After the short span of a couple hundred feet, he turned left into a parking lot. I knew from my jogging experience that this lot serviced the trailhead for the Lands End recreational area, a park that covered the water's edge from here to the Golden Gate Bridge.

Monty hummed to himself as he opened his driver's side door and stepped outside. I peered out along the top rim of the seat partition, trying to see what in the world he was doing.

Monty was not a runner, a jogger, or even a casual walker. He took great pride in maintaining a fastidious appearance at all times: dressy slacks, neatly pressed collared shirts, and leather pointed-toe loafers. As a rule, he generally avoided any situation where he might risk breaking a sweat.

I was surprised, then, to see that Monty had changed clothes when he'd stepped inside his studio earlier that morning. He was now wearing a white T-shirt, blue sweatpants, and, I noted before sliding back below the partition, a pair of shiny white tennis shoes.

I waited for the slamming crunch of the driver's side door before I poked my head back up again. I watched in awe as Monty's slim figure jogged across the parking lot to the trailhead. Beyond the edge of the lot, the trail dropped out of sight down a steep slope toward the ocean. Monty reached the trail's entrance and quickly sank from view.

The sun was just breaking its morning half-light. To the left, beneath the rise of the road, the distinctive outline of the Cliff House etched the horizon. I slowly eased out the back door, closely hugging the van's shadow.

A pair of joggers passed me, chatting with each other as they took off across the parking lot. I followed them to the trailhead and looked down the embankment.

Montgomery Carmichael off on a vigorous, early morning run—I simply refused to believe it. I scanned the hillside, trying to make sense of Monty's atypical behavior.

The trail led down a flight of stairs that had been cut into the sandy, eroding soil of the hillside's upper embankment with the use of four-by-four beams. A loose post-and-rope fencing structure lined both sides of the path to discourage visitors from trampling the hillside's carpet of freshly planted succulents. Rows and rows of tiny yellow flowers bent toward the rising sun as the plants sucked in a morning drink of dew.

Scattered across the lower roll of the hillside lay the ruins of the Sutro Baths. Occasional piles of crumbling bricks gave hints of the huge complex that had burned to the ground almost half a century earlier. At the bottom of the hill, up against a rocky interface with the ocean, the gutted remnants of Sutro's seawall still retained enough integrity to fill a large, stagnant pool with water.

A manicured running path cut off toward the Lands End trail about forty feet down from the parking lot's entrance. I watched as Monty's blue-suited figure bypassed the running route and progressed into the lower portion of the ruins.

A minute later, Monty reached the bottom of the hill, near the spot where the ocean's foaming waves broke against the seawall. He spread his long arms out for balance as his white tennis shoes trod carefully across the crumbling flat edge of the wall. At the opposite end of the wall, he stepped off into the eroded remains of the Baths' lowest foundation.

I continued my descent on the trail, puzzling on Monty's suspicious foray into the Sutro Baths ruins. This seemed far more in line with his personality than a coastline jog, but what, I wondered, was he up to?

Monty was now twenty feet past the first section of the seawall; he had begun to navigate through a maze of chipped concrete that surrounded the remnants of the Baths' semi-intact pool. The outlines of the pool's long rectangular shape stretched out parallel to the ocean. Several families of ducks circled through the brown brackish water, occasionally diving beneath its surface to chase a bottom-crawling insect or a small, briny fish.

The formal structured trail with its carefully chiseled steps and side barriers transitioned into a sandy dirt path occasionally interspersed with uneven stretches of chewed-up asphalt. It was as I reached this point that I lost sight of Monty's blue sweatpants down in the ruins.

An ominous, prominently positioned sign warned of the likelihood of sudden powerful waves and cautioned me against proceeding further. The posting included a drawing of a flailing stick-figured man being swept out to sea by an unanticipated surge of water. Grimacing, I continued on.

After I descended another forty or fifty feet, I reached the spot where I had seen Monty turn off into the ruins. I passed a second warning sign, this one offering more dire predictions for anyone foolish enough to wander so far down the cliff.

Nervously biting my lip, I crept along the top of the same seawall Monty had traversed, trying to split my concentration between the ledge's loose footing and the waves crashing on the rocks just below.

As I reached the end of the wall and hopped off, I regained sight of Monty. Oblivious to the safety warnings, he sat down on an outcropping of concrete next to the stagnant swimming pool and began taking off his tennis shoes.

I crept up behind a pile of concrete so that I could sneak in closer. Monty finished removing his shoes and stood up, barefoot, next to the edge of the swampy pool of water. He stretched his arms out over his head, as if preparing for some type of strenuous physical activity—then he stripped off his white T-shirt.

I gasped at the sight of his bony, narrow chest. A light sprinkling of curly brown hairs dotted the otherwise pale expanse of his skin.

Eeeek, I screeched internally. This was far more of Monty than I had ever hoped to see.

But he wasn't done yet. Before I could blink, he slid off his sweatpants to reveal a pair of tight-fitting baby blue swim trunks. I covered my face with my hands, trying to obliterate the shocking image now seared into my memory.

As I huddled behind the concrete pile, I heard the slapping snap of spandex on skin immediately followed by a large human-sized splash. Anxiously, I looked back up over the pile of concrete to the pool of water.

A small duffle bag that Monty must have been carrying with him sat open on the ledge next to the stack of clothing. Monty stood chest-deep in the murky water, struggling to fit a snorkel mask over his head. A pair of rubber flippers poked out of the mouth of the bag, waiting to be slipped onto Monty's feet.

I shivered, imagining how chilly the water must be. When the Baths were in operation, a system of heaters had been used to warm the water for the swimmers. No such warming device was working on the pond where Monty was now immersed. Even in the heat of San Francisco's warmest day, the seawater collected in the pool would have been a frigid, icicling temperature. At this early hour of the morning, it had to be bone-shattering cold. I couldn't imagine what would have inspired Monty to jump in.

To my surprise, Monty appeared unaffected by the freezing water. Once he had put on his snorkeling equipment, he started swimming down the length of the pool. When he reached the far end, he turned, moved over about one yard to the left, and began his return. He continued to swim back and forth, as if in formation, sweeping along the surface of the dingy water, his eyes submerged as he breathed through the air tube of the snorkel. A small family of ducks squawked angrily at him, but he paid them no heed.

After about ten minutes worth of this regimented paddling, Monty and his snorkel tube dove beneath the surface, leaving behind nothing but a stream of bubbles.

Chapter 25

IN THE MAYOR'S OFFICE

THE MAYOR'S RECEPTIONIST sat primly at her desk in the anteroom outside of his office on the second floor of City Hall, preparing to sort through the towering heap of Friday morning's mail. The receptionist stretched her arms up over her head as she surveyed the haphazard collection of envelopes, packages, and postcards spread across the surface of her desk. With a quiet sigh, she cracked her knuckles, slid on a pair of white cotton gloves, and attacked the pile.

First, she culled out all of the standard letter-sized items and placed them into a neat, even-sided stack. Meticulously, she slit open the long edge of each envelope, scanned its contents, and categorized the correspondence.

Invitations to upcoming events took the most prominent position on her desk. These represented valuable opportunities for free publicity, and the Mayor's staff tried hard to work them into his schedule. Rarely did the Mayor stay more than five minutes at these photo ops, but his personal photographer closely shadowed his every move to ensure that each brief appearance was extensively docu-

mented. The Mayor was expected to be a prime contender
in the coming year's gubernatorial race, and the volumi-
nous photo catalogue of his bright, flashing smile standing
next to constituents of every possible ethnicity, age, gen-
der, and social status would be used to create a wide array
of campaign literature.

The receptionist flipped through the stack of invitations, identified the ones the Mayor was the most likely to
accept, and set them aside for his perusal.

Next, the receptionist moved on to the large pile of
constituent mail. Some of this correspondence related to
legitimate proposals to improve life in the city: suggested
maintenance projects, modifications to traffic or safety or-
dinances, changes to sections of the housing code, and the
like. She shifted the most reasonable requests to the top of
the pile, although she doubted any of them would ever
reach the Mayor's in-box. Few constituent ideas passed
the litmus test of the Mayor's recently hired campaign
manager.

Since his arrival, the campaign manager had insisted
on personally vetting any new policy or initiative for statewide suitability. The rest of California already considered
San Francisco to be an outlying bastion of crazy, kooky
liberals. The Mayor was seen by many across the state as
a prime example of this caricature. The campaign manager had firmly clamped down on any new proposal that
might further enhance that image, severely curtailing the
Mayor's legislative agenda.

The campaign manager was a burly, forceful figure,
and the receptionist didn't much like his brash, overbear-
ing manner. But he was deemed an important cog in the
machinery that promised to propel the Mayor's nascent
political career forward, so, she resolved with an irritated
grunt, she would just have to put up with him.

The receptionist turned her attention to the remainder
of the constituent correspondence—that not containing serious proposals or complaints. Of all of the Mayor's daily

mail, this group of letters most accurately reflected the wacky, irreverent personality of San Francisco's citizenry. These missives, she knew from long experience, would include bizarre, random commentary on all manner of odd issues, including, of course, the Mayor's highly controversial sweptback hairstyle. Lately, the receptionist mused as she ran a mental tally, the volume of hair mail was far outpacing that of all other categories.

The receptionist shook her head and shoved the entire mound of constituent mail into a large interoffice envelope for the campaign manager. Wryly, she surveyed the bulging package. The campaign manager would never state such a thing out loud, but she suspected the main reason he read the constituent mail had nothing to do with the Mayor's legislative initiatives. The campaign manager was greatly concerned about the public's perception of the Mayor's hair.

The receptionist pulled the last pile of mail to the center of her desk. This collection included thank-you notes, mostly for the Mayor's numerous public appearances of the previous week. The receptionist saw no reason to burden the Mayor with this correspondence; typically she simply filed each one into the folder for the related event. But as she sifted through the cards she'd accumulated in this stack, one of the names scribbled on the signature line caught her attention.

"Surely not," the receptionist muttered to herself. She skimmed the information in the note and quickly pulled out the Mayor's calendar. There, listed at 2:45 p.m. on Wednesday afternoon, was a name on the appointment ledger that caused the receptionist's eyes to pop in panic.

She, herself, had spent the afternoon at an excruciatingly painful dentist appointment having a root canal done on one of her molars. Two days later, she was still unable to chew anything more resilient than a mound of Jell-O on the right side of her mouth.

A temp had been.brought in to handle the Mayor's affairs for the afternoon. That woman, the receptionist thought grumpily, had better not ask for a recommendation. She had returned from the dentist's office to find the reception desk a cluttered, disorganized mess. What's more, the room had been filled with a strange orange-infused scent of stale fish. And now this—an utterly and completely inappropriate appointment had somehow made its way onto the Mayor's calendar.

The receptionist leaned back in her chair and rubbed her temples, wondering if she should call the campaign manager immediately.

One of the receptionist's primary responsibilities was to screen the Mayor's appointments for any potentially embarrassing interviews that might endanger his future political prospects. As part of this duty, she scrupulously studied the credentials of each individual who requested time on his calendar. She'd caught a few unregistered lobbyists and the occasional underhanded political spy, but the bulk of her efforts were directed at far more obvious targets. The receptionist spent the vast majority of her time walling off the Mayor from the leagues of his amorous female fans.

Being young, handsome, and recently divorced, the Mayor was constantly sought out by all manner of persistent women. The groupies, as the campaign staff called them, followed the Mayor with a level of devotion typically reserved for rock stars and movie actors. These desperate women showed up, en masse, at each and every one of the Mayor's public appearances—another reason the campaign manager sought to keep those stops as brief as possible.

But among this group of obsessed admirers, one woman stood out above the rest. This well-meaning but downright loony old lady was unmatched in her creative efforts to finagle meetings with the Mayor. Never mind that he was at least thirty years her junior—or that she, herself, professed to be happily married. Somehow the old bird always managed to circumvent the receptionist's efforts to block her advances. And every time, *every time*, it seemed, the old lady managed to create an odd or embarrassing headline for the Mayor.

The campaign manager would blow his top if he knew that Dilla Eckles had been in the Mayor's office Wednesday afternoon. The receptionist shuddered, imagining his wrath. She knew full well who would be blamed for this lapse in protocol.

The receptionist tapped the thank-you note against the edge of her desk. Maybe, she thought hopefully, there was an innocent explanation. Maybe she could avoid making the call to the campaign manager. She got up from her desk and headed toward the Mayor's office.

THE MAYOR SAT behind the wide expanse of his mahogany desk staring down at a shiny green portfolio Dilla Eckles had given him during her visit the previous Wednesday afternoon.

He stroked the sides of his chin as he recalled their meeting. It had been one of their more memorable interactions—and that was saying something.

Dilla had arrived wearing a peculiar disguise. Her face had been covered by a thick rubber mask designed to make her look like an elderly Asian woman. Her clothing had been unusually drab and subdued, the only exception being the bright green go-go boots she'd worn on her feet. The Mayor had been somewhat confused by the outfit, but then, he'd seen far stranger things than that during his term as Mayor of San Francisco.

He had to admit, he had a soft spot for Dilla. She was one of the most endearing of his eccentric constituents, and the proposal she had laid out for him on Wednesday was certainly worthy of consideration.

The emerald green portfolio contained detailed plans for an amphibian preserve to be established on the grounds of the old Sutro Baths ruins. Under the proposal, the brackish water in the ruins' last remaining swimming pool would be drained and the seawall at the bottom of the ruins modified to create a desalinated habitat amenable to an endangered species of frog that was once plentiful in the Bay Area. An anonymous donor had agreed to put up the funds for the necessary renovations to the seawall and for the creation of several smaller freshwater ponds farther up the hill.

Dilla had certainly worked hard on this proposal, the Mayor reflected. The morning after she'd outlined the idea for him in his office, he had found himself at the Cliff House discussing the project with his mentor, the Previous Mayor, and his arch nemesis, the President of the Board of Supervisors. No other political operative in the city could have arranged such a gathering, he thought with an impressed grin.

The Mayor strummed his long fingers against the edge of the green folder. This seemed like a reasonable use of the land, the environment was one of his signature issues, and Dilla was awfully persuasive, but he was still wavering. It had nothing to do with the merits of the proposal, or even the fact that the President of the Board of Supervisors had decided to support it. Okay, the Mayor conceded with a brief pang of conscience, perhaps the Supervisor's involvement had a *little* bit to do with his reticence. But no, the main reason was the underlying subject matter. It was the frogs.

Frogs had always made him nervous, ever since he was a little boy. There was something about the spongy, slimy texture of their skin that was off-putting to him. The substance was so unfamiliar, so unlike that of any other creature. Simply put, the Mayor thought as he carefully ran his hand over the gel-coated crest of his sweptback hair, frogs made him extremely uncomfortable.

It was as the Mayor rifled through the documents in the portfolio, pondering his frog phobia, that he first had the sensation that he was being watched.

He looked up from his desk and scanned his surroundings. It was easy to spook oneself in this room. Every occupant of this office since the horrifying events of 1978 had routinely done so. And yet, no one had dared to change the layout or design of the room, afraid such a move might evoke accusations of cowardice or insensitivity. Almost every aspect of the office remained essentially the same as it was when the City Hall murders of Mayor Moscone and Supervisor Milk occurred.

The Supervisor-assassin had entered the Mayor's office suite through a side corridor, bypassing the bodyguards who stood at the main entrance. The man had then slipped into the reception area and convinced a secretary to arrange an impromptu meeting with the Mayor. Five minutes after the Supervisor entered the Mayor's office, shots rang out. Mayor Moscone was soon found dead, sprawled across this very floor, with multiple gunshot wounds to his head and torso.

As the Current Mayor remembered all of this grim history, his vision drifted up toward a nearby window—and locked in on a pair of bulging eyeballs that were quietly observing him from the window's ledge. The eyeballs belonged to a slender, inquisitive-looking frog.

The Mayor rubbed his eyes in disbelief. He must be hallucinating, he thought hopefully. Slowly, he removed his hands from his face and looked anxiously over at the window.

The frog tilted its head as if in greeting. Its red zipper of a tongue flipped out of its wide mouth and licked its nose.

"Ribbit."

The Mayor's mouth issued a sound halfway between that of a startled mouse and a hissing squirrel.

"Cheeeeeee," he whimpered hoarsely.

The terrified Mayor gripped the sides of his desk as the frog wiggled its back legs, preparing to jump.

"Please don't," the Mayor pleaded. "Please, please don't . . ."

The frog leapt through the air and landed on the red

plush carpet near the Mayor's desk with a muffled plunk. The Mayor scrambled to scrunch his legs up into his chair as the friendly frog waddled toward him.

"Ribbit."

THE RECEPTIONIST CARRIED the thank-you note with her as she approached the massive wooden door leading into the Mayor's office. She knocked briskly against its smooth, polished surface.

Other than a strange shuffling sound coming from the room within, there was no response. She knocked again, this time a bit more authoritatively.

The Mayor's strained voice called back, "Uh, yes?"

"Are you okay, sir?" she asked, concerned.

"Uh, yes," he replied, but he did not sound convinced.

The receptionist glanced down at the incriminating thank-you note, her eyes narrowing with suspicion.

"Sir, there's something I need to see you about," she said persistently. She wrapped her hand around the doorknob and rotated it to release the barrel from the lock. "I'm coming in, sir," she announced boldly.

The receptionist pushed open the heavy wooden door, took one look at the sight of the Mayor cowering on top of his desk, and returned to the reception area to call the campaign manager.

Chapter 26

MONTY'S MISSION

I WAS BEGINNING to worry about Monty's trail of bubbles. The open tip of the snorkel tube had followed him beneath the surface of the water and was no longer providing him with fresh air. I hadn't been counting the seconds, but it seemed as if Monty had been underwater, holding his breath, for an inordinately long amount of time.

A quick glance around the ruins revealed no one else who might be called upon to rescue him, and *I* had no intention of setting foot in that cold, algae-ridden water.

"What could be worth diving down there for?" I muttered out loud as I peeked over the pile of concrete and stared into the muddy mire of the pool.

I was willing to bet that Monty's early morning visit to the Sutro Baths ruins and his absurd swimming routine related in some way to his new role in Dilla's Vigilance Committee. I combed my memory for what I knew of Adolph Sutro—the octopus wrangler, as Monty had called him.

The Prussian engineer's first California success had come

in the silver mines. Sutro had developed a groundbreaking tunnel system that drained excess water away from the mineshaft, greatly increasing both the safety and the efficiency of the drilling process. The use of the tunnels during the silver mining boom had earned Sutro a small fortune.

While many entrepreneurs had profited from the mines, Sutro was one of the few who managed to hold on to his money. He sold his mining shares mere months before the main lodes dried up and the California silver boom collapsed.

Sutro invested a large portion of his mining proceeds in San Francisco real estate. He focused his investments on the cold, gray scrubland stretching along the coast to the west of the city. The property in this area was generally deemed worthless by many of Sutro's contemporaries, but he was undeterred.

Sutro would eventually own almost one-twelfth of the land included within the current city limits of San Francisco, including the majority of the modern-day Richmond and Sunset districts. Sutro doubled his mining fortune several times over as this once barren area was developed to provide housing for San Francisco's ever-growing population.

An ardent populist, Sutro shared a great deal of his wealth with his adopted city. The Sutro Baths, the Cliff House, and the public gardens surrounding his estate were all popular attractions. To ensure the Lands End entertainment area would be affordably accessible, Sutro built his own low-fare rail line to connect it with the city.

For this last act of benevolence, Sutro drew the ire of the railroad barons, who were widely seen as exerting an unfair monopoly over many of the city's essential goods and services. Sutro refused to cave in to the barons, a move that made him a hero among the city's working classes. He rode that wave of popularity straight into the Mayor's office.

Sutro's political success, however, was short-lived. He

served only one two-year term; his brief tenure was seen by most as a failure. Accustomed to running projects by dictate and command, without the need to build consensus, Sutro was ill equipped to adapt to the inevitable compromises necessary for success in politics.

Sutro died two years after he left office, still bitter and reeling from his disastrous term as Mayor.

Upon Sutro's death, his finances were discovered to be in unexpected disarray. While most of his land holdings remained intact, there was little cash left to manage them. To make matters worse, Sutro's surviving children sought to overturn his will and battled for years over the estate, further leading to its eventual ruin. The reason for the mismanagement of the once acute businessman's assets has never been fully explained.

I checked again on the pool. A small brown duck paddled over the last few bubbles left from Monty's dive beneath the surface, muddling their distribution. I considered the brown soupy water once more, tamping down a wave of guilt. Monty dove down into that fetid water of his own volition; he could come out of it the same way.

I scanned the hillside as I waited for Monty to emerge, trying to fill in the buildings mapped out by the crumbling mounds of rocks, bricks, and concrete. The Sutro Baths ruins were an apt reflection of the forgotten image of the once influential philanthropist. For all of Sutro's contributions to the city, there was little left to remember him by.

The rail line he'd built along the coast had been susceptible to both earthquakes and mudslides. The frequent occurrence of both made the line impossible to maintain, and it fell into disuse. All that remained today was a wide trail that ran through the woods between the Lands End parking lot and the Golden Gate Bridge.

The Sutro mansion and its surrounding Italianate gardens were torn down when the last surviving heir died and the property passed to the city. The modern-day park on the brutally windswept bluff that hung with foreboding above the Cliff House featured Sutro's name—and little else.

And here, in the ruins of the Baths, the spot where I stood looked as if it should be condemned to prevent just the type of dangerous activity Monty was now engaged in.

At the far side of the pool, twenty feet from the edge where I stood, a duck squawked in protest as a shot of bubbles poked it from underneath.

I scrambled back behind the pile of concrete to avoid being seen as Monty's snorkel pipe, followed by his curly brown head, popped up out of the pool. The rising sun had begun to reflect off the water, so I had to squint to see him, but Monty appeared hale and healthy, unaffected by all of the time spent crawling along the bottom of the pond. I was awfully glad I hadn't jumped in to fish him out.

Monty shook his head as he emptied the excess water from his snorkel mask. Then, he began swimming back toward my side of the pool.

For a moment, I thought he must have seen me, but I kept myself tucked down in the hiding spot just in case, all the while trying to think of a plausible excuse that would explain my presence here in the Sutro Baths ruins crouched behind a pile of concrete.

It seemed to be taking Monty much longer to cross the pool this time. Carefully, I peeked back over the concrete to check on him. He was swimming much slower than before; his stroke was awkward, somehow labored.

It wasn't until he reached the nearest edge of the pool that I realized he'd been carrying something in his left hand. With a splash, he swung a goose-pimpled arm up out of the water and dropped a small, soggy package onto the concrete rim of the pool.

Monty left the soggy lump on the ledge and swam back out into the water, returning to his more effective side-stroke. He resumed his methodical sweeps of the pool, his eyes scanning the bottom through his snorkel mask. Back and forth he swam, each lap moving another yard further across. Every so often, he dove down to retrieve yet another soggy package, all of which he piled together on the

ledge. Before long, a heap of soggy lumps had accumulated on the opposite side of the concrete pile, just a few
feet away from me.

As I stared at Monty's collection, trying to imagine
what might be wrapped up inside, I realized that the pros-
pect of Sutro's lost fortune would have been far more in
line with my Uncle Oscar's interests than a tribute to the
man's populism. Now more than ever, I was certain that
there was more to the Vigilance Committee story than I'd
been told.

Monty continued to sweep the pool, presumably searching for more packages. I waited for a safe moment while
he was swimming in the opposite direction; then I sprinted
out from my hiding place and snatched one of them up.

After racing back behind the concrete pile, I slowly
unwrapped the soggy gray rag. I stared in awe at the item
I'd uncovered.

Sitting in my palm, shining in the full light of the
morning's sun, sat a green-tinged, bronze-colored frog.

Chapter 27

THE CLIFF HOUSE

I HELD THE bronze frog in my hand, studying it closely. The creature was seated with its head poked forward in a curious fashion. There was the slight edge of a smile on its wide, lipless mouth.

The frog seemed heavy for its size, as if its bronze metal had been mixed with a denser material to weigh it down. Or, I thought as I searched for a way to open it, maybe something was hidden inside. Perhaps the frog was designed like a piggy bank and hid a secret compartment somewhere within its rounded middle.

But despite a close inspection, I couldn't find any obvious seams or cracks in the molding. There were no unusual fissures or depressions in the metal. It was, inexplicably, simply a bronze statue of a frog. What about this item made it worth hiding in the bottom of the pool in the Sutro Baths ruins? Even more importantly, what made it worth retrieving from that cold, dank water?

I peeked back over the concrete barrier to the pond. Several disgruntled ducks had formed an armada and were swimming along after Monty's snorkel tube, no doubt plotting their revenge.

From Monty's position in the water, I estimated that he had nearly canvassed the entire span of the pool. He must be freezing by now and would surely be finishing up soon. It was time for me to make my exit.

I tucked the bronze frog into my coat pocket and carefully retraced my steps across the top of the crumbling seawall, leaving Monty to complete the last laps of the pond unobserved. I had no desire to see him in those tight-fitting swim trunks ever again.

I scampered back up the path circling the ruins, breathing a sigh of relief when I reached the higher ground above the wave warning signs. At the bottom of the terraced steps, I turned to look back down at the pool. I couldn't see Monty in the portion of the water that was visible from my location, but, I noticed with relief, he wasn't yet following me up the trail from below.

I began hiking up the steps, proceeding at a much slower pace due to the steepness of the climb. My leg muscles were burning from exertion by the time I finally topped the summit at the trailhead and exited into the parking lot.

I paced back and forth across the lot, considering my options for getting a ride back to Jackson Square. The rear door of Monty's van was unlocked, but it seemed unlikely that I would make it through a second cargo ride undiscovered. I still wasn't entirely sure that Monty hadn't seen me down in the ruins by the pool.

I fished around in my shoulder bag to check for my wallet. It was a splurge that I really couldn't afford, but I decided to treat myself to breakfast at the Cliff House and, I thought ruefully as I calculated the fare in my head, an expensive cab ride back to the Green Vase.

Glancing every so often down the hill at the ruins, I headed off on the sidewalk that skirted the highway from the parking lot to the bunkerlike structure of the Cliff

House. Only the edge of the roof could be seen from this upper angle; the rest of the building was stacked up against the cliffs below the highway.

I reached into my pocket and clutched the little bronze frog in my fingers, wondering again what had driven Monty to search that cold, nasty water for it—and how soon he would realize that one of his treasures was missing.

At the entrance to the Cliff House, I paused on the steps to look up at its white concrete edifice.

The contemporary design featured sharp, dramatic angles, framed by the exposed structural elements of shiny steel and aluminum. An overabundance of stone and cement cinched the building into the scraggly outcropping of the cliff, giving the impression of a solid, immovable block, invincible to the crashing waves below.

After strolling along a concrete landing that flanked the outside of the building, I arrived at a triangle-shaped observatory overlooking the ruins. From this position, I had a clear view of the pool where Monty had been swimming. Green and brown patches of algae masked the concrete bottom beneath the water. I was amazed that Monty had been able to see anything in that muck.

The family of ducks had adopted a more relaxed posture, and the pile of rag-wrapped bronze frogs was gone from the edge of the pool. Monty, I concluded, must have departed.

I left the observatory and backtracked along the landing to the building's entrance. Just inside the foyer, I was greeted by a picture of Sutro's dramatic eight-story rendition of the Cliff House. The differences between it and the current structure were striking.

Sutro's palacelike Cliff House had hung precariously off the edge of the cliff, its wide base held in place, it seemed, by no more than a wish and a whim. The edge of the enormous foundation extended out far beyond the support of the rocky cliffs. Wooden struts stretched back toward the rocks from underneath the building, straining to hold on to the earth like the exposed roots of a tree fighting erosion.

I continued further inside, walking along the main interior corridor. The entire width of the building's ocean-facing wall was made up of nothing but windows. Looking out, I felt as if I were on a boat, floating on top of the water, not anchored to the cliffs beside it.

From this interior perspective, the boxy bunker formation of the Cliff House's exterior was almost imperceptible. The precarious notion of the spot combined with the outcropping of the location to defy all architectural attempts to box it in. No matter the changes to the outer shell over the years, I suspected that the Cliff House view, and the phenomenal sense of exposure to the ocean and the air above it, remained substantially the same.

I left the expansive corridor, entered the restaurant, and asked for a table. A mosaic of cream and tan one-inch tiles spread across the floor, complementing a dining room full of wicker-backed furniture. The wall of windows continued into the restaurant, dwarfing a massive mahogany bar that lined the cliff side of the building.

A waitress led me to a table overlooking the beach on the opposite side of the building from the Sutro Baths ruins. I turned my seat to face the water, still infatuated by the stunning view.

The restaurant was filled with tourists, obvious in their bright-colored sweatshirts and constant comments about the weather. I tuned them out as I pulled the bronze frog from my pocket, wiped it off with a napkin, and set it on the corner of my table. The frog turned out to be the perfect Cliff House dining companion, quietly appreciating the scenery without offering any unnecessarily verbose commentary.

After placing an order of eggs, I flipped the menu over to read the historical information printed on its back. A short essay described the rise and fall of the Sutro Baths along with an amusement complex that had occupied the now empty beach my south-facing table overlooked. Playland-at-the-Beach had boasted carnival rides, arcades of shooting games, and a fanciful, ornately decorated merry-go-round.

Like the rest of the bygone structures that had once populated Lands End, the amusement park was long gone, but some of its rides had been preserved and were on display at various locations throughout the city. The merry-go-round, my menu noted, was now in use at the Moscone Convention Center complex downtown.

A steaming plate of food arrived, and I dug in, hungry after the morning's stress of spying. A seagull soared by my table outside the window, eying my plate of fruit and scrambled eggs, but I ignored him. Everything looked delicious, and I had no plans to share.

I was midway through the breakfast, my stomach beginning to fill, when a disturbance at the front of the restaurant caused me to turn around in my chair.

A tall, skinny man in tight blue swim trunks marched through the dining room toward my table, dripping an algae-tinted trail of water on the tiles beneath his feet. His curly brown hair was wet and slightly slimy. He held a snorkel in one hand and a net bag filled with bronze-colored frogs in the other.

Oblivious to the startled stares of the brunching tourists and the efforts of the waitstaff to detain him, Monty proceeded straight to the edge of my table.

"Aha!" he cried loudly, pointing at my frog. "I knew I was missing one!"

Chapter 28

THE FRENCH RESTAURANT

HAROLD WOMBLER GIMPED up Bush Street in downtown San Francisco, making his way toward the red and yellow storefront of a restaurant. A sign above a circular red awning flashed the name of the establishment, but the curvy script of the neon piping was difficult to read without a night's black canvas. Harold's watery, bloodshot eyes slid over the vertical red lettering painted onto a yellow wall that split the two sides of the entrance, confirming that he'd reached the designated meeting place.

Harold scrunched his lips together as if he were about to swallow something bitter. The lunch hour was approaching, and his stomach was beginning to rumble, but this was not one of his usual eating stops. He scanned the menu posted in the nearby window.

Just as he had suspected. *French.*

With a disgusted grunt, Harold slumped through one of the building's curtained glass doors and entered the restaurant.

The interior was ambiently lit, too dark for Harold's aged eyes. He liked to be able to see what he was eating, especially if it were some fancy foreign food. Plus, you never knew what kind of weird item the chefs in this town might try to slip onto your plate.

Harold peered around the entrance as his eyes slowly adjusted to the dimmer light.

Red brick walls filled with artsy framed posters flanked the length of the dining area. Harold sidled up to the nearest poster and tilted his head to look at the mounting behind it. The picture was hung on a hook that had been drilled into the brick wall.

Harold scowled disapprovingly. It was a shame to see masonry abused in such a fashion. It was early on in his lunch, but Harold was determined to dislike everything about this meal.

The restaurant was already cramped with suited businessmen and women who were preparing to enjoy a long Friday lunch in celebration of the end of another workweek. Several bottles of wine had been opened on the long wooden bar where a busy barkeeper polished a rack of long-stemmed wineglasses as he stood ready to pour.

A man wearing dark slacks, a white button-down shirt, and a black squarely positioned bowtie rushed up to the entrance, eyeing Harold warily and with haughty contempt.

After nearly two weeks of repeated wear, Harold's overalls were now suitably stained with the backsplash from several construction projects. Various spots and smears of drywall, glue, building putty, and paint covered the cloth. Rips and tears had begun to stretch out along the fabric covering his knobby knees, and he'd worked up a rank, pungent body odor.

"No," the waiter pulsed out through tightly pursed lips, his voice heavily accented. "No, no, no . . ."

Harold gave the waiter a grim look and stepped aside. He wasn't concerned. Harold didn't have a reservation; he had better. He was expected by one of the restaurant's most famous patrons.

The waiter glared at Harold, his stern expression clearly transmitting an unwelcome message.

Seconds later, an elderly man dressed in a tailored dove gray suit walked up behind the waiter and calmly put his arm around his shoulders. The gold glint of an expensive watch flashed on the man's wrist. The brown skin on his hand was silky smooth, the nail on each finger manicured to a round, even curve.

"It's all right, Francois," the man said genially. "He's with me."

The waiter issued a startled pleading look, but the Previous Mayor simply smiled patiently in return. The waiter's mouth opened and closed, wordlessly guppying his displeasure, but he eventually yanked out a menu and motioned Harold forward.

"Can I take your . . . er . . . hat?" the waiter asked, his eyes surveying Harold's dingy baseball cap with morbid apprehension.

Harold reached up and scratched his scalp; then he lifted his cap from his thinning head of greasy black hair. Silently, he handed it over. The waiter took the cap gingerly between his thumb and forefinger.

"Right this way, sir," the waiter said stiffly.

Harold hobbled through the indicated path, brushing up against the well-heeled patrons sitting at the bar. Stares and whispers followed in his wake as he made his way to the honorary window table the Previous Mayor occupied every Friday for lunch.

BACK IN THE kitchen of the French restaurant, a deliveryman pushed a dolly filled with fresh produce through the service entrance. A sous-chef smocked in a white apron pointed to an open spot on a nearby table.

"Right over there, please."

The deliveryman nodded and wheeled the dolly over to the indicated location where he began lifting up the crates and stacking them on the table. Midway through unloading the dolly, he paused to wipe his brow.

"Oh, and I've got one more container for you," the deliveryman said casually. "It's still in the truck. A special delivery."

The head chef heard his comment and rushed over. "*Ah bon! S'il vous plait*, er-um, please, bring them in right away."

He poked his head out of the kitchen and yelled at the head waiter. "Francois, update the staff. The special of the day has just arrived."

OUT IN THE dining room, Harold was still surveying the menu, his face souring as he read through the list of French dishes. Nothing on offer was the least bit appetizing to him. It was all so froufrou. Too much sauce; too little substance.

Harold put down the menu, picked up his water glass, and guzzled several inches of the ice-chilled liquid.

The Previous Mayor seemed to be enjoying all of the attention his latest guest was drawing to his table. He loved to create a stir, to be the center of attention, especially if it was for one of his many eccentricities. He and his lunch companion were the topic of conversation throughout the restaurant, of this he was certain.

But today's lunch was more than just a casual meeting. He and Harold had business to attend to.

"Is everything in place on your end?" the Previous Mayor asked, keeping his voice low enough so that he could not be overheard at the next table, whose curious diners were desperately trying to listen in.

Harold grunted his affirmation and leaned over in his seat so that he could reach the back pocket of his overalls. He pulled out a folded sheet of paper and spread it open in front of the Previous Mayor.

The sheet contained a map of San Francisco's Lands End area, focused in on the region containing the Sutro Baths ruins, the Cliff House, and the beach below.

"Good, good," the Previous Mayor said as he glanced over the map. Surreptitiously, he slid a page of diagrams depicting the interior design of a large dome structure across the table. "Here's my contribution."

As Harold and the Previous Mayor studied the second document, a waiter crept up on the table and tucked a green flier into the center of each of their menus.

Harold flicked a grimy finger at the flier. "What's this?" he grunted, showing it to the Previous Mayor who read the added menu item with surprise.

"Oh, I'm so sorry," he replied, an apologetic look on his face. "I had no idea they would be serving that dish today." He shook his head ruefully. "It's the latest food fad. Restaurants across the city are rushing to get it on their menus."

Harold motioned to the waiter who was still hovering near their table.

"This item you've got on the special?" he asked grumpily. "Is it *fresh*?"

"*Oui, bien sur,*" the waiter assured him. "Hopping around in the kitchen as we speak."

"That's what I'll have then," Harold announced. "But I'll take mine alive," he instructed. "I'll take every one you've got—make sure you keep 'em all *alive*."

Chapter 29

SUTRO'S MISSING FORTUNE

MONTY AND I rode along in stony silence as the van retraced its path back through Golden Gate Park. We had been politely asked to leave the restaurant inside the Cliff House. Apparently Monty's wet swimsuit attire had constituted a dress code violation. It had certainly shocked the out-of-town tourists sitting at the table next to me.

I let my shoulders rest against the soft, cushioning bucket of the front passenger seat. This was a much more comfortable place to ride than the metal floor of the van's rear compartment. My knees were still sore from crouching on the hard surface during the trip to the ruins earlier that morning.

I glanced over at the driver's seat. Water was seeping through Monty's blue sweatpants into the underlying seat fabric. Large drops collected on the coiled tips of his curly brown hair and occasionally plopped down onto the shoulders of his white T-shirt.

The bronze frog I'd stolen from the pile by the pond sat in my lap, its molded eyes gazing up at me serenely. I picked it up, thinking as I stared into the frog's little metal face.

"So," I said, clearing my throat. "You were recruited by the Vigilance Committee—to do what, exactly?"

Monty's green eyes stared resolutely out the windshield as he gripped the steering wheel with both of his pale, bony hands.

"That's classified information," Monty said through stiffened lips. "I really can't tell you."

I could see that Monty was struggling to keep this tidbit to himself. If I could just get him talking, I thought, surely he would break. Monty was not one to bear the burden of a secret for very long.

"It must have been awfully cold in that water," I said conversationally.

Monty nodded numbly. His shoulders shivered beneath the thin T-shirt. He'd turned the van's heater up to its highest setting.

"I'm just trying to imagine what would be worth diving down into that cold, mucky water. There are only a few things that come to mind . . ." I gestured toward the driver's seat with the hand holding the bronze frog. "This isn't one of them."

"Not *exactly* what I had expected to find," Monty muttered under his breath.

I looked over at him expectantly, eyebrows raised, frog still tauntingly outstretched, waiting for him to continue. Monty's eyes shot briefly toward me, but he shook his head firmly and returned his resolute stare to the windshield.

"It was just a man and his frogs, out for an early morning swim," Monty said tersely, sternly facing the road ahead of us. "You should give it a try sometime. I feel much healthier for having done it." He huffed up his chest, setting off a spastic coughing spell.

I took in a deep breath, trying to summon patience. "Oscar's Vigilance Committee—it was about more than trying to influence city politics, wasn't it?"

Monty coughed again, this time more to create a distraction than out of necessity. His fingers fiddled with the heater controls, adjusting the vents to optimize the airflow.

I tried to press him further with my speculations. "I mean, where did the VC get all of their money? The funds that they were funneling into the Board initiative and then the Milk campaign? As far as I know, none of the VC members were independently wealthy."

Monty flattened his lips, still refusing to budge.

I decided to cut to the chase. "I think they found someone else's money." I paused, drew in my breath, and leaned toward Monty. "Does this have something to do with the funds missing from Adolph Sutro's estate?"

Monty tilted his head, as if considering his reply. He pulled the van over to the side of the road and parked in a shaded spot near the center of Golden Gate Park. With a shrug of his shoulders, he turned the key in the ignition and stopped the engine.

"Okay, here's what I know," he said quietly. "The original members of the VC were all history buffs. San Francisco history, that's what they had in common. Wang, Dilla, Oscar, and—Napis."

Monty brushed his hand through the damp curls on the top of his head, spraying water against the back of his seat. "Of course, his name wasn't Napis at that time. He was using another alias and a different disguise."

Monty stretched his free hand out toward the windshield and peered down at his fingertips. Curving strips of green algae were stuck into several fingernails. With a sigh, he recurled his hand around the steering wheel.

"Sutro was an obvious target—historically, I mean. It's well documented that his disastrous term as Mayor left him a bitter, vindictive old man. His entire life, he'd never failed at anything. Suddenly, he had to endure the humiliation of a very public defeat."

Monty drummed his fingers on the steering wheel and ran his tongue across his front teeth.

"Sutro had always been a private person, but after he

left office, he became even more isolated. He holed himself up in the library of his mansion on the bluff above the Cliff House. He became hostile to everyone around him, especially his children. It may have been his increasing paranoia, but he suspected that some of them were secretly aligned with the business interests that had undermined him at City Hall.

"When Sutro died, his finances were in a mess. Sutro had emptied several accounts and dumped his shares in multiple businesses. A sizeable portion of the liquid assets from his estate had gone missing."

Monty tapped his nose with the tip of his algaed finger. "The Vigilance Committee started tracking down Sutro-related memorabilia, old letters, news clippings, and the like, looking for clues to where he might have stashed the money."

I leaned forward in my seat as I listened to Monty's story, my excitement growing. "So, did Oscar find it? Did he find Sutro's hidden fortune?"

Monty wiped a nervous hand across his brow. "Yes—at least, according to Dilla he did. The VC pumped some of the money into the initiative to change the seating structure for the Board elections. They set aside another chunk of it to help fund Milk's next Supervisor campaign, to try to get him elected as the President of the Board."

I collapsed back into my seat and stared up at the van's ceiling, my thoughts racing. "But that election never happened," I said. "Because of the shootings." I turned to look back at Monty. "What happened to the money?"

Monty reached over to the center console where I'd set the bronze frog. He snatched it up and thrust it into my face.

"Well, it sure didn't end up in the bottom of the Sutro Baths ruins, I can tell you that much."

UP IN THE steeple above the dome in City Hall, Sam the janitor creaked open a door and walked into the attic.

The space was filled with several glass aquariums, each one receiving a small trickle of water that pooled beneath a collection of rocks and green plants. With the combination of the heat rising up through the building and the moisture Sam was piping in for the tanks, the attic had begun to take on a moist, rain forest-like atmosphere.

Inside the aquariums, countless frogs slid amongst the greenery, splashing in the water and lazily sunning themselves beneath heat lamps. The lids on each of the tanks had been removed, leaving them open at the top, so that the frogs could hop in and out at will.

Sam opened up a large cardboard container he'd carried with him into the attic. He popped off its lid, reached inside with a grubby hand, and pulled out a handful of squirming bugs and scrambling crickets. He dropped a generous amount of both into each of the aquariums, where the insects were quickly devoured by the waiting frogs. A chorus of appreciative croaks echoed through the attic chamber.

On a ledge next to the row of tanks, the highly polished bronze statue of a frog glimmered in the light filtering in through the window.

Chapter 30

THE MERRY-GO-ROUND

A FEW BLOCKS away from City Hall, a group of children crossed the street in front of a glass-enclosed merry-go-round. Located within the several-block campus of the Yerba Buena complex, the merry-go-round was strategically positioned across the street from a multiplex theater, kitty-corner to the Moscone Convention Center, and just outside of a kid-friendly art and media museum.

The boisterous crowd of six- and seven-year-olds chatted excitedly with each other, eagerly anticipating the afternoon's birthday party. It would be the kind of wild, frenzied affair typical for their age group, complete with pizza, cake, presents, and an exuberant hour and a half's worth of merry-go-riding.

The children were escorted to their party destination under the watchful eye of an elderly caretaker. She ushered her charges through the crosswalk, hurrying the children along to ensure that the last partygoer cleared the street before the light changed.

A tangle of helium-filled balloons bounced in the air beside the woman as she walked. Each balloon had a long twine tail, which was tightly tied to a loop near the waist of the woman's furry green frog costume.

The main part of the frog outfit comprised a green jumper with frog-ish spots spaced evenly across a jiggling spring-form belly. Gloves in the shape of green webbed mitts covered the woman's hands. A frog-shaped head mounted on her shoulders featured round googly eyes that rolled in their sockets when shaken.

A car waiting at the intersection for the children to pass gave a playful honk at the woman's frog costume. The nearest child squealed in delight as the human-sized frog waved and mock-hopped in front of the car.

The children had been amused, at first, by their furry green chaperone. But with the merry-go-round in sight and the smell of hot pepperoni pizza tickling their tummies, their attention was focused elsewhere. Curiosity concerning their amphibian friend's bright green go-go boots had long since lapsed.

The merry-go-round was mounted on a circular concrete platform accessed by a short flight of steps that curved around the circumference of its base. A decorative topper of metal flashings mounted on the ride's aluminum roof spun spastically in the breeze. Undulating waves cut into the concrete paid tribute to the merry-go-round's earlier home near the Cliff House in the Playland-at-the-Beach amusement complex.

The merry-go-round was well traveled for such a stationary device. Manufactured in Rhode Island in the late 1800s, the ride was first featured at a park in Seattle, Washington, before moving down the coast to San Francisco. After nearly fifty years of service in Playland-at-the-Beach, the carousel was purchased by a private collector and stored for several years at a warehouse in New Mexico. The merry-go-round then changed owners and was put on display in Southern California, before it finally made its triumphant return to the Bay Area. Now fully restored, the ride was a favorite treat for children and parents throughout the city.

A protective glass-walled enclosure surrounded the merry-go-round, ensuring that the ride could be enjoyed in both wet and sunny weather. In addition, the enclosure prevented vandals from marring the brightly painted creatures inside.

Dilla herded her charges up the stairs to the glass door entrance where she fished a key out of a furry green pocket and fed it into the lock. The key still retained a slight fishy smell from its time spent in Lily's custody behind the oyster bar, but the odor did not affect its primary function. The key turned easily within the casing of the lock.

A jubilant rush of laughing children swarmed past Dilla as she held open the swinging glass door. A few kids stopped at the pizza table, but most continued straight into the maze of animal rides inside the merry-go-round's carousel. Each child climbed up into a carved seat, their tiny hands wrapping around the gilded poles that anchored their chosen steed to the platform.

Dilla pressed a button and the carousel began to turn. The poles pushed the painted animals up and down, and countless swinging tails, bucking heads, and prancing feet swung into action. Each animal was adorned with a checkered jacket and a generous coating of sparkling plastic jewels. Mirrors in the ceiling and base reflected back the pumping motion of the ride's glittering beasts, to dizzying, multiplying effect.

At each stopping interval, the youthful riders switched from one animal to the next. The merry-go-round offered a broad sampling of carved creatures, including horses, lions, giraffes, goats, dragons, and a single gold-trimmed frog.

Eventually, the birthday candles were lit, the celebratory song sung, and the frosted chocolate cake devoured. Dilla allowed the children one last spin on the carousel as their parents began stopping by to pick them up.

Throughout the birthday party, Dilla had struggled to keep track of her short-statured charges. The mesh screen in the frog costume's head only allowed her to see the space directly in front of her; she had no side vision. As the parents filtered in to pick up their offspring, Dilla was relieved to find that no one had gone missing. Each parent was easily matched with a child.

In her concerned monitoring of the children, Dilla failed to take notice of the non-parent entrant who slipped in through the door of the glass enclosure and shimmied around to the opposite side of the carousel.

Two hours after they'd begun, the last guest departed, and the birthday boy and his pile of presents were trundled out the door. Dilla leaned up against the glass pane, a smile on her face as she watched the boy's father scoop up his exhausted son and carry him down the stairs.

Dilla's own tired eyes rested for a moment on a cluster of purple tulips sprouting out of a round, globular planter near the merry-go-round entrance. Finally, she thought wearily as she pulled off one of the green mitted gloves, it was time to check that frog.

Dilla rotated the key in the lock of the glass enclosure, unaware of the malicious eyes pinned to the furry green back of her costume.

After loosening the straps that connected the frog head to the shoulders of the jumpsuit, Dilla pulled the contraption up and over her sweating forehead, appreciating the unobstructed freedom of her face. As she crossed the glass enclosure and climbed up onto the merry-go-round's platform, she let out a deep breath, releasing months of pent-up tension. In that brief moment of relaxation, with her senses dulled by the suffocating hours spent wrapped inside the frog costume, she didn't hear the footsteps sneaking up behind her.

Dilla bent over the front of the frog ride and ran her fingers along the animated creature's wide, smiling mouth. The lever that triggered the jaw to open was tucked into the side of the metal frog's head, disguised by the gold-painted harness that looped around its body. The lever was rusted and frozen in place from lack of use, but, with effort, she was able to force it into position. Slowly, the rim of the frog's metal lips began to part.

As the frog's bottom jaw rotated downward and Dilla peered inside, her mouth fell open in surprise. The cavity was an empty void—vacant except for a couple of dusty spiders and a small folded piece of paper.

Dilla snatched the paper from the cavity. The expression on her face registered disappointment and confusion as she unfolded the paper and quickly scanned the message written inside.

Dilla leaned back from the frog—and froze at the image of the man reflected in one of the many mirrors that covered the merry-go-round's center spoke.

Slowly, she turned to face the intruder. Her voice trembled with frustration and fear as she showed him the paper and said, "We're too late. The gold is gone. Oscar must have moved it."

Chapter 31

UNCLE OSCAR'S FRIED CHICKEN RECIPE

I RETURNED HOME from the grocery store Friday night with a package of organic free-range chicken legs and a variety of replacement spices for the containers in Oscar's spice rack. Unwilling to risk another sleepless night with a despondent, chicken-obsessed Rupert, I had decided to try to recreate Oscar's fried chicken recipe for myself. If the startup chef at the Mission frog leg restaurant could reverse engineer the coating mixture, so could I.

I carried my bundle of chicken-related ingredients up to the kitchen and spread them out across the counter. Rupert sat down on the floor nearby, closely surveying the spread as I searched through Oscar's cookbook shelf for *The Art of Chicken*. Oscar had never actually used the book when cooking his dish, but I had planned to start with a traditional recipe and then proceed with the most likely modifications. I was on my second pass through the bookshelf when I heard a banging on the front door downstairs.

With a stern, admonishing look at Rupert, I sprinted

down the steps to the showroom. Isabella leapt past me as I ducked my head to dodge the low-hanging beam above the sixth step. She was already on top of the cashier counter, sharply eying our visitor, when I reached the showroom.

I groaned at the image of the man whose face was plastered up against the front window. I'd had more than my quota of Monty for one day. It had only been a couple of hours since we'd returned from the Cliff House. Reluctantly, I turned the lock to let him in.

"Greetings and good evening," Monty said, rolling the words as he pushed open the door. He strolled jauntily inside and paced to the back of the showroom where he plopped down onto the dentist chair. In a single smooth motion, he kicked back the recliner lever and propped his leather pointed-toe shoes up on the footrest.

I brushed my hands against the front of my apron, thinking nervously about my exposed chicken upstairs. Rupert couldn't be trusted to act against instinct for very long.

"What's up, Monty?" I asked briskly.

Monty raised a knobby forefinger into the air. "The other day, I believe you mentioned that your cats had chased down a frog—here in the Green Vase?"

Isabella chirped affirmatively before I could respond. Monty swung his finger to point it in her direction.

"Yes!" he exclaimed as Isabella licked her lips. "That's what I thought."

Monty sucked in his breath and jumped up from the recliner. Slapping his hands together, he announced, "I need to borrow your cats."

"No," I replied immediately, no thought needed. "Absolutely not."

"Wait, wait," he said, waving his hands in the air. "You don't understand."

I heard a suspicious thump against the ceiling. Isabella and I looked at each other, and, in unison, both of us moved toward the stairs.

"Come on up to the kitchen," I said as I sprinted up the steps. "I've got to rescue my chicken."

"SO, ABOUT THE cats," Monty mumbled through a mouthful of fried chicken. "I just need to borrow them for one night—to sneak them into City Hall."

Monty was seated at the kitchen table, an attentive Rupert on the floor near his feet, both of them sampling my efforts to duplicate Oscar's fried chicken recipe.

"No," I repeated automatically as I dropped another leg into the black wrought iron skillet. I had been unable to find Oscar's chicken cookbook, so I was estimating the appropriate amounts for each ingredient. So far, I had tried a different coating combination on each piece of chicken.

"Wait, what?" I asked as I covered the skillet to shield against the popping grease. Monty's request had finally registered in my chicken-distracted brain. "Why would you want to take them to City Hall?"

Monty peeled off a small piece of meat from the latest sample and dropped it into a bowl on the floor near his feet. With a loud smacking sound, the chicken instantly disappeared into Rupert's stomach.

"You're still missing something," Monty said, tasting another bite. "Oscar's chicken had a lightness to it. There was something else in the crust. I think you need to add another ingredient."

"Monty, you never tasted Oscar's chicken," I protested.

"Ah, but I smelled it every Saturday night before I left the studio," he replied. He closed his eyes, remembering. "The scent floated across the street. It soaked into everything. I used to dream about that chicken." He held up a bare bone. "This isn't it."

"Hmm," I said, studying the lineup of spices. I selected a different collection of bottles and began preparing the next coating mixture.

Monty got up and scraped the pile of bones from his plate into the kitchen trashcan. Rupert's blue eyes followed him, his fixed stare never leaving Monty's greasy fingers.

I peeked under the lid of the skillet. The current batch was about ready to turn. "Next round should be up in a minute or two," I said as I grabbed a pair of tongs and flipped over the simmering chicken legs. "I hope you're still hungry."

Monty glanced down at Rupert, who smacked his lips enthusiastically. "Keep 'em coming," he replied. Monty wiped his mouth with a napkin and cleared his throat. "So I need the cats to help me find the frogs," he said casually.

"More metal frogs?" I asked as I rolled a chicken leg in the newest coating mixture. "Don't you have enough of those?"

"Oh no, real-life frogs." Monty tapped his forehead. "Like the one that beaned me on the noggin."

I checked the skillet again. This time, I pulled one of the legs out and dropped it onto his plate.

"You see," Monty continued as he chomped down on a mouthful of the most recent sample, "I received new information this afternoon about the Sutro money—it's gold actually—from my Vigilance Committee colleagues."

"Did you?" I asked, looking up from the stove to the kitchen table.

"*With* apologies for this morning's initiation exercise," he added, as if he were still soothing his wounded ego. "I passed the test, by the way," he said defensively.

"Congratulations," I replied, trying not to laugh.

"You see, the VC have discovered a new clue to the gold's location," Monty said, clearly excited at the development.

I returned my attention to the skillet as Monty wiped off his fingers, reached into his coat pocket, and pulled out a small piece of paper. "They think your Uncle Oscar moved it from its original hiding place."

I turned away from the stove to face Monty. He held a small piece of paper up in front of his face and read out in a serious tone, "*Follow the frogs.*"

"That's it? That's your new clue?" I asked. "What does this have to do with taking my cats to City Hall?"

Monty fed a last sliver of chicken meat to Rupert. "I'm sure that's the place. There have been numerous frog sightings throughout the building recently. Apparently, one even made its way into the Mayor's office—caused quite a fuss."

Monty leaned back in his chair and patted his full stomach. "I have a theory . . ."

"Oh no," I groaned. That phrase never passed through Monty's lips without being followed by some sort of preposterous supposition.

Monty proceeded, undeterred. "Oscar hid the gold in City Hall, and the frogs are guarding it—kind of like leprechauns. If we follow the frogs, they'll lead us right to it."

I stared up at the ceiling. If nothing else, Monty was consistent.

"It's perfectly logical when you think about it," Monty insisted despite my skepticism. "Adolph Sutro was totally destroyed by the big-business interests that ran *City Hall*. The first part of Sutro's gold was used to support a change in the way the Board of Supervisors were elected—the Supervisors are the driving force in *City Hall*. Another portion of the gold was used to fund the Milk campaign—to help him change the political dynamics in *City Hall*. It only makes sense that Oscar would have hidden the remaining gold somewhere within—*City Hall.*"

He flicked the piece of paper. "*Follow the frogs.*" he repeated. "Couldn't be simpler. I just need your cats to help me track down the frogs, so that I can *follow* them."

Wincing dubiously, I plucked the piece of paper from Monty's fingers. "Here, let me see it."

The paper was yellowed and curling around its edges. A smear of grease bleared the right-hand corner. In the middle of the paper, the phrase Monty had just read was written in a round, looping scrawl I instantly recognized.

The note had been written, presumably some time ago, by my Uncle Oscar.

I stared into the skillet, watching the coating on the chicken legs slowly turn from creamy white to golden brown, the unfolded piece of paper clasped tightly between my fingers.

Follow the frogs, I repeated to myself. I thought of the mysterious webbed footprints in my kitchen and the frog the cats had found in the basement. The message could just as easily have been referring to the Green Vase, but the VC apparently thought differently.

I sighed tensely. I couldn't imagine what would have inspired Oscar to write such strange instructions, but there seemed to be only one way to find out.

"All right," I said with determination. "But I'm coming with you."

"Excellent," Monty replied, surprised at my sudden agreement.

Monty carried his empty plate from the table to the stove and nudged it toward the skillet. I clamped the tongs around another fried leg and shifted it onto his plate.

Monty bit into the crust of the latest sample. "Still not quite right," he assessed. "Oscar's was lighter, fluffier, almost unexpectedly floral . . ."

I glanced sharply up at Monty. He and I both landed on the missing ingredient at exactly the same time.

"Ooh—ooh," he cried out, jumping up and down.

Wordlessly, I crossed the kitchen to the chair where I'd dropped my shoulder bag and pulled out a small vial filled with tulip petal extract. I'd been carrying the vial around with me as a security precaution ever since our Napis-engineered bus misadventure.

Monty leaned over the kitchen counter as I added a couple of the pungent drops of extract to the coating mixture. Almost instantly, I could tell that I'd finally found the right combination.

"You've done it," Monty whispered, his voice filled with awe.

I stepped back from the stove, my hands on my hips as I pondered this revelation. All of that time, I thought, shaking my head, my Uncle Oscar had been cooking up his fried chicken with the antidote to Frank Napis's poison.

Chapter 32

IN AN ABANDONED PLACE

THAT SAME NIGHT, in a nearby Jackson Square kitchen, preparation of yet another skillet full of fried chicken was under way.

An elderly Asian man watched from a wobbly three-legged stool as his daughter cooked the meal. Her long, silky ponytail of black hair swished back and forth as she combined the ingredients, carefully following a recipe taken from a cookbook spread open on the counter. The title printed on the book's cover read *The Art of Chicken*.

The kitchen was in a small loft apartment above an abandoned antique store. The loft was sparsely furnished but pleasant enough for its most recent resident. The large open space of the loft's living area overlooked the store's empty showroom. Sheets of brown kraft paper covered the building's floor-to-ceiling windows, sealing off the showroom and the loft's occupants from street-level view.

Despite the use of numerous air-freshening devices, stale, stuffy whiffs of sandalwood and hibiscus still floated through the air in the loft, remnants of the endless incense sticks burned by the previous tenant. The whole place had been cleared out a couple of months earlier following the tenant's sudden and unexpected departure. A highly polished fat-bellied Buddha sat on the loft's kitchen table, the only item that remained from the showroom's previous inventory.

The building was not as tall as its neighbors up and down the street, comprising only two stories instead of three, and its construction was of a much more recent vintage. The previous Gold Rush-era structure on the lot had been leveled in the late 1970s, during a period of much looser regulation of the city's historical properties.

While there had been quite a furor at the time of the original demolition, the new building was constructed with the same type of red bricks as the older structures up and down the street. Nowadays, almost no one remembered that the establishment next door to the Green Vase didn't share its lengthy history.

The owner of the plot had been surprised during the older building's teardown to find a secret passageway leading between his property and a low-hanging stairwell above the first floor of the Green Vase. With the assistance of his construction manager, a perpetually disgruntled man named Harold Wombler, the new owner had ensured that a covering of tarps concealed the opening to the passageway until the new construction was complete.

A hidden door in the loft's back bathroom now provided access to this passageway. Behind the door, dusty steps led into a narrow tunnel, the exterior of which, to untrained eyes, appeared to be an oversized ventilation duct. On the other side of the tunnel, a trapdoor opened up over a low-hanging beam just above the sixth step on the stairs leading from the Green Vase showroom to the second floor kitchen.

The old man chuckled, remembering Oscar's excitement about the secret passageway. Who knew what kind of mischief it had been used for during the Gold Rush days? It had certainly come in handy of late.

Luckily, the old man was short enough to make the

trip without too much discomfort. He had even managed to navigate the passage carrying a plate of freshly fried chicken.

The old man leaned back in his stool and reached for the plastic tubing connected to his oxygen tank. He had recently turned in his pipe for a nicotine patch, but his teeth were permanently etched with tobacco stains from his years of smoking. His frail fingers poked at the patch, prodding its surface to ensure that the medicine was still oozing out; then he reached for a plastic chopstick and slid it between his thin lips as if it were a cigarette. He had cheated death for now, but he knew it wouldn't last.

His hand travelled to his face and the long, wispy growth that spun out from his chin. He had let his facial hair grow during the past months of self-imposed incarceration, and he was rather enjoying the effect.

Of course, he'd had plenty of company during these months of seclusion. His wife and daughter had visited him frequently, nursing him through the tulip extract resuscitation from his self-applied spider toxin coma.

The man's fingers twirled the chopstick as he thought back thirty years ago to his Vigilance Committee days. Such a long time had passed since he'd posed in the black-and-white photo in front of Harvey Milk's Castro Street campaign headquarters. His reflections on that period always brought a solemn moment of sadness. The bright excitement of that heady time had been forever darkened by the City Hall murders.

Oscar had been so excited when he'd guessed the location of Adolph Sutro's hidden fortune. It had been Oscar's first major discovery, the beginning of a long line of successes. It was so like Oscar, the man thought, to see into someone's soul through the artifacts they'd left behind.

Sutro wouldn't have hidden the funds on his estate, Oscar had reasoned. It would have been too likely that one of his heirs would find it. No, he had reverted true to form.

As Oscar had imagined it, Sutro had walked down the

hill from his estate to the amusement park spread out across the beach. The area would have been packed every weekend with working-class families—along with the city's beautiful children, full of hope and laughter, a life-time's worth of opportunity ahead of them. Sutro had se-creted the money within the most popular ride in the park, a brightly painted merry-go-round whose pole-mounted seats were fashioned into all manner of animals: horses, giraffes, lions, goats, dragons, and a Sutro-era substitution provided by an anonymous donor—a single gold-trimmed frog.

The key had been in Sutro's library. His extensive liter-ary collection had at one time been the largest in the city. Most of the books were sold when the estate was liqui-dated, but Sutro's daughter had managed to hold on to one volume, her father's favorite green-covered text that con-tained several Mark Twain essays. One of the selections was particularly dog-eared: the famous *Celebrated Jump-ing Frog of Calaveras County.*

It had not been easy to track down the Playland-at-the-Beach merry-go-round. Oscar had had to negotiate long and hard with a collector in New Mexico before he con-vinced the man to part with the antique ride. Their agree-ment had required that the merry-go-round be made available for a short display period in Southern California before coming north to San Francisco.

But the effort had been worth it. Sutro's hidden fortune had been right where Oscar had suspected, in the secret mouth cavity of the gold-trimmed frog. In place of the buckshot that had filled the mouth of Twain's frog, Sutro had taken a mountain of gold coins and melted them down into a collection of gold ingots, specifically shaped so that they fit like puzzle pieces into the curved contours of the frog's oral cavity.

Once Oscar tracked down Sutro's hidden gold, every-thing else fell into place. The initiative to change the Board of Supervisors seating structure had passed, and Harvey Milk had begun to lead a progressive coalition of newly elected representatives. The VC were excitedly preparing for the next election, energized by the impact they were having on their city. The morning of the shootings, however, changed them all forever.

John Wang rubbed his pallid face, the paper-thin skin wrinkling beneath his fingers. Thirty years later, he and Dilla had decided to bring back the VC. It was a much smaller initiative that they were now pursuing, more limited in scope, more personal in motive. But, he had to admit, he was enjoying the entertainment.

Mr. Wang stood up and tottered toward a card table in the middle of the room, dragging his oxygen tank behind him. His body was rail thin; the dark trousers cinched around his bony waist swallowed up his entire lower half. A dinner of fried chicken and mashed potatoes, supplemented with Oscar's life-boosting tulip juice, should help bulk him up a bit. His daughter was concerned about his plummeting weight.

As Lily began to pull the chicken from the pot, Mr. Wang offered a fried cricket to each of his dining companions, a friendly pair of frogs he had recently rescued from a traveling circus. Their antics, he found, amused him.

The frogs, in turn, seemed quite enamored with their new props—a frog-sized pair of feathery orange mustaches.

Chapter 33

THE BREAK-IN

DARKNESS HAD FALLEN when Monty's white van pulled out of Jackson Square Saturday evening and headed toward City Hall.

Rupert, Isabella, and I had each been thoroughly briefed by Monty on his plan to sneak the cats into City Hall so that they could track down the source of its growing frog population. Monty had drawn up endless schematics of the two entrances we planned to use, supplemented by hand-sketched floor plans and stick-figure diagrams. He had painstakingly walked us through the sequence of events that would allegedly allow us to breach security. I could recite every detail by heart. I was certain we would all end up in jail.

But that is how I found myself dressed up in a spare pair of Sam the janitor's rumpled overalls, crouched on the metal floor in the back of Monty's van, holding on to a rolling cart with an orange-shaped air freshener tied to its handle. The cart was almost identical in size and shape to the one Sam typically pushed around, but instead of hauling refuse, mine carried two cats sitting on top of a mound of old blankets and towels.

I glanced down at the faded nametag on the overalls. Monty had assured me that Sam was off work today and probably wouldn't miss this extra pair, which normally hung on a peg in his cleaning closet. I hoped Sam wouldn't notice that I had run them through the wash before putting them on.

The cuffs at the bottom of each leg were rolled up several times to make way for my feet, which were clad in an old pair of Harold Wombler's similarly loose-fitting construction boots. Additional rolls of cloth were wound up around my wrists. I felt as if I'd been mummified.

The driver of the van was an extraordinarily grumpy Harold Wombler. "You look too clean to be a janitor," he had crankily opined when he helped me load the cart into the back of the van.

Monty had assured me that Harold was a perfect accomplice for this mission. The Vigilance Committee's roots, he had told me with a brash confidence, spread far and wide. I was not convinced, but as I reached into my pocket and folded my fingers around the piece of paper containing my late Uncle Oscar's handwriting, I was determined to find out more.

Harold slowed the van as he drove down Van Ness. A block away from City Hall, he pulled up next to a red-painted curb. Engine idling, Harold removed a walkie-talkie from his tool belt and grumbled into the receiver.

"You in position, Carmichael?"

The van was filled with a moment of static, followed by Monty's crackling voice.

"No fear, we're here, Wombler."

At that moment, around the opposite side of City Hall, a shiny black Town Car pulled up in front of the entrance facing the Civic Center Plaza, just beneath the winding gold railing of the balcony outside of the Mayor's office suite.

The car's chauffeur had tied her wavy auburn hair into a tight bun at the nape of her neck. A prim flat-topped cap with a hard rim that hid her heavily mascaraed eyes had been secured to her head with bobby pins. She clicked the tips of her long, curved fingernails against the steering wheel as she waited for Monty to finish preparing himself.

At exactly ten past nine, he called up to the driver's seat. "I'm ready."

Cursing under her breath, the chauffeur opened the driver's side door and stepped out.

The rounded curves of her figure were flattened out by the bulky fabric of the chauffeur's uniform. A neatly pressed coat overlaid a matching pair of slacks with black piping running down their seams. Miranda Richards had never looked so androgynous.

The rubber soles of Miranda's black industrial-issue shoes squeaked against the pavement as she walked around the side of the vehicle and opened the passenger side door.

Monty carefully unfolded his long legs from the back of the Town Car, trying to mimic the man he'd watched depart from a similar ride outside of the Cliff House a few days earlier. Miranda scowled at him as he planted his shiny dress shoes on the sidewalk and smoothly stood up.

"This will never work," she said tartly as she slammed the car door shut behind him.

Monty flashed her a toothy smile, one that had been artificially brightened hours before. The square shoulders of a velvet-fronted tuxedo almost doubled the width of his narrow frame. In his left hand, he carried a velvet-trimmed top hat—which, of course, he would never bring close to his carefully styled mountain of hair.

He had pulled out all of the stops with tonight's Mayor-shellacking pompadour. The crest of the molded wave topped out at nearly two and a half inches above the rim of his forehead. Several of the pigeons snoozing in the eaves above the entrance to City Hall poked their heads up out of their roosts to take notice.

It had been heavily publicized that the Mayor would be

attending a charity event at the Museum of Modern Art this Saturday night. Several celebrities had flown up from Los Angeles to lend their support, ensuring that there would be significant coverage by the local news media. Everyone, including the night shift security guards manning the Civic Center entrance of City Hall, expected that the Mayor would be outfitted in his finest garb this evening.

The weekend night shift, who generally didn't see much of either the Mayor or Monty, was also the least likely of City Hall's security crews to see through Monty's Mayor impersonation. If he kept his head down and moved fast enough through the scanners, it was our hope that the guards would assume he was simply running up to his office suite to pick up a forgotten last-minute item. Monty had practiced his mayoral voice for several hours that afternoon, but, having heard a sample, we all recommended against him using it.

Monty thoughtfully rubbed the pointed tip of his chin with his right hand as he paced deliberately up the steps in a carefully constructed rush. The Mayor's hurry was always a controlled motion, even when he was pressed for time. Any sudden jerking motion might disrupt the care-· ful balance of his hair.

At the top of the steps, Monty waved his top hat at the security station, pulled open one of the heavy glass iron-framed doors, and walked inside.

Miranda hissed into her walkie-talkie as Harold pulled the white van into the service entrance parking lot on the opposite side of City Hall. "I can't believe it. He's in."

The small parking lot was brightly lit but, at this late hour, completely deserted. Harold backed the van up so that the janitorial services sign Monty had affixed to its side was clearly visible to the video cameras feeding live pictures to the security guards at the front entrance. At this precise moment, in any event, we expected that the guards would be preoccupied by Monty's mayoral entrance.

Holding my breath, I lifted the handle on the back door

of the van and pushed it open. It took longer than I had anticipated to wrestle the cat-filled cart out onto the concrete sidewalk leading up to the service entrance. I could see Harold, still sitting in the driver's seat, watching me skeptically through the rearview mirror.

With a grimace at Harold, I finally began rolling my cart down the ramp to the entrance. I gripped the security badge Monty had borrowed from Sam's closet and hopefully waived it in front of an electronic scanner mounted onto the framing of the door. An internal latch clicked, releasing the lock. I swung the cart in front of me and through the open door as quickly as possible.

Once inside, I stood still for several seconds in the dimly lit basement level of City Hall, waiting for the sound of sirens or the halting voice of a security guard.

There was nothing but a still, eerie quiet.

Chapter 34

FOLLOW THAT FROG!

THE BASEMENT HALLWAYS of City Hall were far more desolate and foreboding at night than they had been in the afternoon of my last visit. The flat white non-coloring of the walls and floor soaked up the darkness, merging into a shapeless shadow that seemed to close in on me from every angle.

The wheels on my cat-filled cart squealed against the tile floor as I pushed my cargo forward, my feet shuffling loosely in Harold's oversized boots.

Isabella propped her front feet up on the interior edge of the cart so that she could look ahead down the hallway. Her own sharp vocal sounds added to the squawk of the wheels as she tried to give input to our speed and direction.

Rupert cautiously eased the top of his face over the opposite side of the cart, nervously surveying our dark surroundings. After a brief assessment, he popped back down inside and tunneled under the blankets.

We came to the end of the first hallway, and I struggled to steer the cart into a left-hand turn. One of the wheels skidded on the tile flooring, refusing to make the appropriate swivel. Isabella leaned over the top edge of the cart to try to determine what was causing the impediment.

"Whoop! Watch out Izzy," I called out as the stubborn wheel suddenly gave in and the cart lurched forward.

Isabella's claws dug into the heavy plastic of the rim as she worked to regain her balance. Further cart instructions in a much harsher tone were subsequently issued.

The light that had fed into the previous hallway from the service entrance was snuffed out when I made our left-hand turn. The cramped darkness of the second hallway immediately began to squeeze tighter and tighter around the edges of the cart.

I reached for my flashlight. Tension crept across my back as I fumbled with the switch, desperately anticipating the broad beam that would appear from the lens at the end of the flashlight's long canister.

No sooner had the light flicked on than a sliding swoop rushed up on me from behind. In the two seconds it took my eyes to convince my brain that the black-clad form popping his top hat was Monty, my knees nearly collapsed beneath me.

"Everything go according to plan?" he asked jovially, spinning around the cart, clicking his heels in the air. "It turns out there was no one at the guard station. We could have just walked in."

I glanced anxiously around the dark hallway. The absence of security guards in the building was not exactly reassuring.

Isabella sniffed skeptically at Monty's top hat as he bent over the cart to check on the cats. A two-inch stripe of Rupert's face peeked out from beneath the pile of blankets.

"There's my ace team of frog hunters," Monty boasted proudly.

Isabella suddenly shifted her stance as she picked up a movement on the floor further down the hall.

"Wrao," she said as she angled around Monty and leapt out of the cart.

Rupert wiggled halfway out of his nest of blankets and poked his head over the rim. He watched briefly as Isabella stalked across the tile floor in a hunting crawl; then he turned back toward me with a pleading look.

"All right," I sighed and pushed the cart forward, now with Rupert at the helm.

The group of us inched down the hallway, following Isabella as she slunk after a small, springy body hopping along the tile floor. Her shoulders rocked slowly back and forth as she homed in on her prey. The frog paused and looked back, a fearful expression on his flat green face.

Isabella licked her lips. Her tail swirled back and forth behind her, the orange-tipped end snapping with anticipation.

"Uh, Monty?" I asked as Isabella prepared to pounce. "You know, she's about to gulp down that frog."

Monty shot me a startled look; then he bounded forward.

"Whoa! Whoa! Whoa!" Monty called out, swooping up Isabella by her midsection as the frog fled down the hallway. "Hold the phone, there, girl! We've got to *follow* the frog, not eat it," he admonished as he dropped her back inside the cart.

Isabella issued a long, disgusted hiss.

"Let's get going," I said, giving the cart a shove.

Monty cocked his head sideways. "Flashlight?" he asked, holding out his free hand as he stared down the dark corridor.

I handed the light to Monty, and he aimed it into the darkness. Isabella's frog was now gone, but as Monty waved the beam in an arc around us toward the opposite end of the hallway, his arm suddenly froze.

"Check it out," he said, intrigued.

Ten feet past the intersection where I had turned into the second hallway, the flashlight illuminated a pilgrimage of at least half a dozen frogs, all of them heading straight toward us.

"Where are they coming from?" Monty murmured as he walked toward the parade of frogs.

Isabella chirped impatiently from her perch on the rim of the cart. With effort, I swung the cart around and reversed course.

As we progressed down the hallway, Monty trained the flashlight on the line of locked doors. The beam brushed over door after door until he focused it on one at the far end that was slightly ajar. A small green face poked out of the opening and hopped into the hallway.

"Monty," I whispered cautiously as I suddenly realized where we were. "Isn't that your office?"

"Mine's the one next to it," he replied, shaking his head in puzzlement. "That's Sam's cleaning closet. It shouldn't be open. I locked it up myself this afternoon." He flicked the sleeve of my overalls. "When I picked up this for you. Sam is supposed to have the day off."

Monty raised a cautioning hand as we crept up on the cleaning closet. He eased over to the door and placed one ear against its surface. Then, he nudged the door open a few more inches and stepped inside.

"Well, I'll be," he said, sounding surprised.

Isabella leapt out of the cart and followed him through the doorway. With a sigh, I scooped up Rupert and stepped around the cart to take a look for myself.

Several tiles had been removed from the center of the cleaning closet, creating a square hole in the floor, each side of which was about two feet long.

Monty knelt at the edge of the opening, set his top hat on the floor beside it, and trained the beam of the flashlight into the darkness below.

"Whoa," he called out in amazement as he leaned down into the hole. Isabella filled in the remaining space, sticking her head next to his. Between Monty's bent-over frame, Isabella's swishing tail, and the bulky top hat, my view was blocked.

"What do you see?" I asked curiously. Rupert squirmed in my arms trying to get his own view of the action.

"Wrao," Isabella called out informatively as Monty's feet suddenly kicked back in repulsion.

An indistinguishable squelch issued from beneath the floor. "Whap . . . right in the face," Monty muttered. "Oh no. Here he comes again . . ."

I stepped aside as Monty jerked his head up, trying to extract himself from the opening in the floor. He misjudged the size of the hole and caught the back of his head on the front edge of its rim.

Bonk.

"Ow!" Monty cried.

The rebound from the impact threw him off balance, and his hands lost their grip on the slick tile floor. Isabella dodged Monty's flailing legs as the flashlight and top hat toppled down into the hatch after him. The subsequent racket that ensued seemed to indicate that he was rolling down a short hill in the substructure beneath us.

Isabella stuck her head back into the hole to watch Monty's tumble. When the commotion beneath us quelled to silence, she looked up at me to report her findings.

From the tone of her voice, I gathered she didn't think much of his chances of returning.

"Wrao."

Chapter 35

THE MOAT

I NUDGED ISABELLA aside and leaned over the edge to look down into the hole. Nearly twenty feet away from the opening, the flashlight's beam cascaded out across the foundation's substructure, illuminating an intricate network of scaffolding and pilings. Monty's prostrate shadow lay on the edge of the lighted area.

Rupert and Isabella stuck their heads next to mine as the three of us peered into the darkness.

I hesitated and then called out, "Monty? Are you all right?"

He sat up and brushed off the front of his tuxedo jacket. "I've still got my hat," he said, holding it up to the light.

As I waited for Monty to right himself, my senses began to adjust to the darkness beneath me. A dank, earthy smell oozed up out of the hole, accompanied by a quiet humming sound. A mingling chorus of higher and lower pitched murmurs seemed to be rising out of the substructure. The longer I listened to the sound, the more its individual components began to stand out—the croaking vocal cords of hundreds, if not thousands, of frogs.

Isabella had apparently come to the same conclusion.

"Wrao," she said, her voice awed.

There was a shuffling sound on the mounded dirt just below the opening in the floor. I rubbed my eyes, trying to focus in on the shaded spot.

A small green frog looked timidly up through the hole, as if it had been waiting for me to detect its presence.

"Ribbit."

Isabella stiffened on the ledge beside me. Instinctively, I grabbed for the loose fur on the back of her neck as the intrepid frog leapt up from the darkness and onto the floor of the janitor's closet.

Isabella's blue eyes shone. Despite my efforts to hold her back, she lunged forward, her front feet swiping at the tile floor as the little creature sprang up into the air and vaulted away from the hole in the floor.

I managed to slow Isabella just enough for the frog to escape her reach, but I had, unfortunately, forgotten about Rupert, who faced no impediment to his frog pursuit. His fuzzy white mass launched toward the springing frog, his front legs floundering wildly through the air.

There was never really any contest; the frog was far too nimble. It was halfway to the door leading out of the janitor's closet when a surprised Rupert realized, too late, that he had ill-timed his leap. He dropped down through the opening in the floor, following the same trajectory as Monty into the substructure of City Hall.

Isabella and I leaned back over the hole, listening to Rupert's scrambling feet as he slid down the dirt embankment.

"Wao-ooo," Rupert's frightened voice called up.

Down at the bottom of the short hill, a white glow hopped up into Monty's arms.

"Oh, hello there, Rupert," Monty welcomed him, now apparently recovered from his own tumble. "Nice of you to join me. Let's see what we've got down here."

I pushed up off of the hatch and swung my feet over its ledge, trying to find a more comfortable seated position.

Isabella lay down beside me and stretched her mouth open into a yawn. She was quickly becoming bored with frogs she wasn't allowed to chase.

From this position, if I tilted my head to the right angle, I could follow the beam of the flashlight as Monty and Rupert explored the substructure.

"Hey! Here's some of those base isolators," he called up. "They look just like the one in the display. Look here, Rupert. See the rubber lump in the middle of the column? It separates the building above us from the ground we're standing on."

I sighed, anticipating the demonstration Rupert was about to receive.

Monty's voice echoed through the substructure. "When there's an earthquake, the ground moves like this . . ."

Whump. The flashlight's beam bounced wildly across the substructure.

"What happened?" I called down through the hatch.

"It turns out it's rather slippery down here."

I glanced over at Isabella and shook my head. Stretching my back, I leaned away from the hatch again, this time surveying the surroundings of the janitor's closet.

Sam's cleaning cart, far grungier than the one I had been wheeling around, was pushed to one side. A collection of mops, brooms, and a dingy-looking mop bucket filled in the rest of the space. On the back wall, running just beneath the ceiling, a rectangular window similar to the one in Monty's office let in a streak of light from a streetlamp outside.

"Why don't you come on back up?" I asked, shivering from the eerie emptiness of the basement. "And make sure you bring Rupert."

Monty's voice seemed far away. "Yep, yep, yep. Don't worry. We're headed back your way . . . hey, what's this?"

I leaned back over the hole. Monty panned the flashlight toward the edge of the underground area. The lip of the concrete moat that surrounded the foundation was barely visible in the beam of light. The earth around the moat seemed to be undulating with mounded movements.

I watched as Monty bent over the side of the moat and trained the flashlight into its curved depth.

"It's full of water," he said, his voice transmitting bewilderment.

I glanced up at the ceiling in the janitor's closet. "It's a moat, isn't it?"

Monty cleared his throat authoritatively. "That's just a term of art . . . in, ah, earthquake retrofitting technology. This isn't a castle. It's not supposed to have water in it."

"Who knew?" I whispered, raising an eyebrow at Isabella. She looked unimpressed.

Monty's voice continued to report up through the hatch. "The moat is completely full. There must be hundreds of gallons of water in it. All flowing around in a circle. Round and round and round . . ."

I jerked my shoulders to the side as a second frog popped up from the substructure and into the janitor's closet. Isabella watched as it hopped out the door and into the hallway. With a petulant sideways glance at me, she rested her head on her front paws.

Monty was still inspecting the moat. "There are millions of tiny black things swimming around in the water. Comma-shaped dots with tails."

I stared down into the darkness, trying to interpret his observations. "Tadpoles?"

Monty's response came echoing back. "Yes, yes, the moat is teaming with tadpoles."

"That explains where all of the frogs are coming from," I replied.

"Ooh! Hey, there goes one with legs. Half-frog, half-pole. Look at that, Rupert. Fascinating."

Rupert made a murmur that sounded like concurrence.

"The note said to *follow* the frogs," I called down into the hole as I dodged yet another exiting frog. "There appears to be a number of them leaving your area."

There was a splash, followed by a sliding scramble.

"Ha, ha, get back here buddy," Monty said, laughing loudly. "Hey," he called up. "Rupert and I nearly landed in the moat."

"Are you two coming back already?" I was starting to get impatient.

Another sliding slurp emanated from the substructure.

"Whoa, watch out there Rupert, the ground is really—slick."

A deep silence filled the hatch.

"Is it muddy from the water?" I asked.

"No," Monty replied, sounding somewhat perturbed. "All of the water is in the moat." He grumbled a further comment beneath his breath.

"What's that?" I yelled down to him. "I couldn't hear you."

"There's an awful lot of frogs down here. Thousands of them, I'd guess. I can't hardly move without stepping on one. All of these frogs have . . . ahem . . . left their mark. The ground is covered with, well . . . it's quite unpleasant really."

Monty's voice took on an anguished tone. "I'm afraid it's frog"—he sighed in disgust—"fecal material."

Chapter 36
THE WINDOW

THE CAT MONTY hoisted up through the hatch was far less white and decidedly less fluffy than the one who had dropped down it. Rupert's furry, round body was covered with sticky patches of brown smudge; his mottled coat was now redolent with the musty, earthy smell of the substructure.

Rupert looked at me gratefully as I wrapped my hands around his belly and gingerly pulled him up into the janitor's closet. I carried him out to the hallway and carefully deposited him on top of the old towels inside the cart. Suspicious brown smears were now streaked up and down my front. There was no longer any need to worry that Sam might realize that I had washed his spare overalls, I thought ruefully.

Monty's head and shoulders emerged from the hatch as I returned to the janitor's closet. He was besmirched from head to toe with the same brown smudges.

"Here I come," he announced, dropping his battered top hat on the floor beside the opening. With a heave, he hauled his body midway up the ledge so that he could squeeze a knee over onto the floor. After a moment of groaning exertion, he managed to stand up next to the hole.

"Well, now we know where the frogs are coming *from*," I said, staring at Monty's rumpled tuxedo. I pulled the piece of paper with Oscar's scrawled handwriting out of one of my pockets. "Now we just have to figure out where they're *going*."

Monty raised a soiled finger and then pointed it down into the hole as yet another green frog zoomed up onto the floor of the janitor's closet. Monty's finger traced the frog's path as it hopped out the door.

The tiny frog glanced back at us nervously as we stepped into the hallway. Then, it took a long leap forward. "There it goes," Monty said enthusiastically. "The same direction as the frogs we saw earlier."

A second frog peeked out the door of the janitor's closet. It blinked up at us as its hind legs squirmed back and forth with indecision, and then it, too, scooted down the hallway.

Isabella sniffed the air with renewed interest and made as if she were about to go after them. I scooped her up and siphoned her into a spot in the cart next to Rupert.

"Let's go," I said as I grabbed the cart's handle.

"Hold on for just one minute," Monty said briskly. "I've got a roll of paper towels in my office." He pulled a key out of his pocket and unlocked the door next to the janitor's closet.

As I waited for Monty to rummage through his office for the paper towels, I glanced up at the window running along the top of the back wall.

"Monty," I called after him, remembering Sam's troubled expression at the end of our last meeting. "What's the story with your window?"

"Ah yes," he reflected. "The window." He ran his hand over his head, trying to smooth out the mangled crest of his pompadoured hair. "You don't want to get Sam started on the window story. We'd still be here listening to it if I hadn't dragged you off down the hallway."

Monty strode behind his desk to peer out the rectangular opening, absentmindedly tapping the wall next to the Mayor's photo as he walked past it.

"You see, this is the window the Supervisor came through the morning he shot Milk and Moscone."

Monty turned back to face me. "The basement windows didn't have bars over them in those days. The man simply slid in here with his guns and ammo, took the back stairs up to the second floor, and bullied his way into the Mayor's office. He shot Mayor Moscone; then he walked down the second floor corridor, pretty as you please, and shot Harvey Milk. It all happened so quickly, the guy was gone before anybody realized what had happened."

Monty leaned over his desk toward me. "The janitor saw the shooter sneak in through the window. He asked the Supervisor what he was doing, but the man just gave him the brush-off. The janitor was outranked, you see."

Monty shrugged. "It wasn't the first time a Supervisor had squeezed in one of the basement windows. Apparently several of them had the habit of going through the basement to get around the security scanners on the main floor."

Monty bent down to the desk and opened a side drawer. He pulled out a roll of paper towels, ripped one off, and began wiping the larger smudges from his tuxedo. "At least this is a rental," he muttered glibly.

Another frog hopped past my cart in the hallway. "There's another one," Monty called out. "Keep an eye on it, will you? I'll be ready in just a second."

I stood in the doorway, staring at the little green frog, watching its determined progress down the hallway. Monty dropped the used paper towel into a trashcan, strolled around the desk, and ushered me the rest of the way out the door.

"Look! It's turning the corner," Monty cried as he sped

off down the hallway. The slick soles of his dress shoes left a trail of brown smudges on the floor tiles behind him.

"Wait," I said, still pondering Sam and the window story. "The janitor who saw the Supervisor come in through the window, was that . . . ?"

Monty was already ten feet down the hallway when he spun around to face me. "Sam's father," he said, nodding. "It wasn't his fault. He couldn't have done anything to stop it. But the man was never quite the same afterward. They say the guilt tormented him for the rest of his life."

I rolled the cart toward Monty as he spoke. He grabbed the opposite side of it and leaned toward me for a loud whisper.

"The man finally killed himself about fifteen years after the murders, I think. That's when Sam took over as head janitor."

Monty leaned back and tapped the side of his head knowingly. "Trust me, you don't want to get Sam going on about his father. It's a bit creepy. He talks about him as if he's still alive."

Monty swirled his finger in the air suggestively. "Don't get me wrong, I like Sam, but he's a bit cuckoo, in case you haven't noticed."

Chapter 37

THE MYSTERY OF THE MIGRATING FROGS

WE FOLLOWED A very self-conscious frog all the way down the dimly lit hallway. Every so often, the frog paused to look back at the motley caravan trailing behind him.

Monty pranced back and forth across the tile floor, swishing his top hat and tails as he circled dance steps around the cart. I shoved the cart forward, ignoring his antics and trying not to trip over the rolled-up pant legs of my overalls.

The frog neared the end of the hallway and turned toward us, his green face twitching with consternation. Monty bent his lanky body toward the floor, dropping to one knee to bring his face closer to eye level with our amphibian ambassador.

"Hello there, little friend," Monty said cordially. "Don't mind us. You continue on about your business. We're just here to observe."

Monty whispered a loud aside in my direction. *"And follow you to the pot of gold."*

Eying Monty warily, the frog thumped its right leg against the tile floor.

"Ah!" Monty cried out. The soles of his shoes slapped against the floor as he lifted off of his knee and jumped up onto both feet. Monty bent at his knees, so that he assumed a crouched position somewhat similar to that of the frog. With a dramatic flick of his top hat, Monty tapped his right leg against the floor, miming the frog's thump.

The frog took a moment to consider this overture. His red tongue slid out and slapped the side of his mouth. I watched, shaking my head, as Monty attempted the same.

Isabella hopped up on her haunches to look over the edge of the cart. Exhausted by the lateness of the hour and his adventure in the substructure, Rupert snuggled down into the pile of blankets and settled in for a nap.

On the floor in front of us, Monty continued to ape and impersonate the frog. "Come on, little guy," Monty wheedled, still in his crouched frog-imitating stance. "Where are you going? I'm a frog, just like you. Lead the way."

I don't think that the frog was the least bit convinced by Monty's ruse, but he did finally turn and hop the rest of the way down the hallway. With a last disconcerted glance back at us, he turned the corner and disappeared.

Monty's face gleamed with excitement. "I really think I got through to him," he said proudly. "I think we connected—you know, on a man-to-frog level."

I sighed, ruefully reflecting that I had willingly involved myself in this ridiculous caper.

With exaggerated hand gestures, Monty motioned for me to follow him as he tracked after the hapless frog. Reluctantly, I wheeled the cart forward, flicking on the flashlight I'd commandeered from Monty when he emerged from the hatch in the janitor's closet. As Monty and I rounded the corner, I swung the beam down the length of the corridor.

I had to set aside my doubts regarding the logic of

Monty's frog theory as he and I both stopped and stared at the scene in front of us.

A pile of frogs had congregated on the tile floor at the bottom of the basement stairs that led up to the first floor. There were hundreds of frogs, waddling this way and that as if they were mingling at a cocktail party—a moist green ribbiting mass. We watched, amazed, as one by one, they each took their turn leaping up the stairs.

Isabella was plastered to the edge of the cart, her eyes fixated on the surreal landscape in front of the stairs.

I glanced down into the middle of the cart to check on Rupert. He had rolled over onto his back so that his stomach pouched upward. All four feet were folded and hanging limply in the air.

The frogs didn't seem to notice us at first, but as we edged toward them, the flashlight's focused beam grew stronger, and the throngs began to stir. Their croaking sounds took on a more concerned tenor.

The wheels on the cart ran over a divot in the tile floor, causing a loud squeak. Like a flock of wild birds, the frogs took off, en masse, up the stairs.

It was an amazing sight—a dark, flying tangle of muscular back legs and webbed, streaming feet, the bodies of individual frogs almost indistinguishable in the hurtling pack. The frogs reached a flat mezzanine midway up the stairs and rounded its turn in perfect unison, disappearing almost instantly up the rest of the staircase.

Monty and I stood at the foot of the stairs, struck dumb by what we'd just witnessed.

"Wa . . . wow!" Monty's stuttered exclamation broke the awed silence. He rotated his head toward me and shrugged his shoulders questioningly.

I had no response for him; I'd never seen anything like it.

"Wrao," Isabella ordered sternly, her eyes plastered on the stairs. Her tail whipped wildly back and forth, fanning the air above Rupert's snoozing head.

"Here, Monty," I said, turning off the flashlight and tucking it into one of the overall's many pockets. "Help me carry this thing up the stairs."

Monty grabbed one side of the cart while I latched on to the other. Together we hefted it up the stairwell, our progress closely monitored by Isabella, who switched from side to side to look down at the steps. Rupert rolled back and forth with the shifting equilibrium of the cart, never once opening his tightly shut eyelids.

We rounded the mezzanine and began the second half of the ascent. A croaking murmur, similar to the sound from the substructure, echoed off of the stone walls around us, drowning out the clumsy clunking of my footsteps.

Isabella draped her body over the edge of the cart. Her front legs slid down the outside as she surveyed the floor around us, checking for any straggling frogs that might have been left behind by the larger group.

The frog sounds continued to increase in volume as we reached the first floor, the crescendo resulting in a near deafening chant.

"Wrao," Isabella called out insistently, urging us on.

I complied with her instructions and pushed the cart forward into a short tunnel-like foyer. A narrow slice of the rotunda could be seen through the opening on the opposite side, shining with a ghostly spectral glow.

Monty walked beside me, his earlier bravado diminished, his top hat trembling in his hands. The slapping of the flat soles of his dress shoes was barely audible over the energetic humming of the frogs.

We stepped out onto the pink marble of the rotunda. The colonnades and balconies above us were showered in moonlight streaming in through the ring of arched windows circling the dome's false ceiling. The moon's meager lighting amplified as it reflected off of the polished marble, throwing shadows that enhanced the shapes carved into the stone and plaster, giving darker, more menacing expressions to the frozen faces.

On the floor around us, a myriad of green forms dotted

the radial designs spiraling out from the foot of the central staircase. The group of frogs we'd followed up from the basement was but a small fraction of the numbers populating the rotunda, milling on the pink marble, and slowly making their way up the staircase.

Chapter 38

UP, UP, UP

MONTY AND I left the unwieldy cart in the center of the rotunda so that we could continue to follow the trail of frogs up the central staircase.

Isabella leapt out onto the pink marble floor, causing a scattering of frogs in the two feet of space surrounding her front feet. I carefully rolled the sleeping Rupert over and scooped him up into my arms. His mouth stretched open in a sleepy yawn that he cut short when he caught sight of the surrounding sea of frogs.

Familiar brown smudges were beginning to appear on the floor beneath the dome. City Hall, I thought, was going to need an extra cleaning crew in the morning.

Isabella started immediately up the stairs, continuing along the path of the frogs. I took a step forward to follow her, but suddenly stopped, perplexed.

"Monty?" I asked nervously. "Where are the security guards? Even if they weren't at the front desk when you came in, shouldn't there be at least one person on patrol in here *somewhere*?"

Monty shrugged, unconcerned. "They probably went out

for a doughnut. I imagine it's a pretty boring post most nights." He waved his arms across the frog-filled expanse of the rotunda. "But wait until they get a look at this."

It seemed awfully strange to me that this enormous frog invasion had so far gone unnoticed by anyone responsible for the upkeep or security of City Hall. Apprehensively, I began the climb up the central staircase.

Monty used his top hat to clear a path along the steps, fanning it at the frogs to usher them away from our feet. One slanted-eye look from Isabella was all it took to convince even the largest, most stubborn frog to step aside.

The frog numbers began to thin as we reached the Ceremonial Rotunda at the top of the staircase. Several frogs had gathered around the bronze bust of Harvey Milk as if it were a designated resting spot along their pilgrimage.

Monty paused to investigate the grouping around the bust, but Isabella cut him off with a herding blow to his calf.

"Wrao," Isabella meowed sharply at him before setting off down the second floor hallway. Her tail waved in the air like a flag as she followed the dwindling numbers of frogs—the few who still had the fortitude to plod onward to their unknown destination.

"She's even more eager than I am to find this stash of gold," Monty said, glancing back at me.

I nodded grimly and wrapped my arms tighter around Rupert. I hadn't yet voiced my concerns to Monty, but I had the sneaking suspicion that something else entirely might be waiting for us at the end of this odyssey.

I looked out over the railing to the open space of the rotunda as we continued around the second floor hallway. More and more frogs were coming up from the basement. The first floor seemed to be alive, thousands of individual movements coalescing into the single pulse of a massive green beast.

All along the hallway, we continued to pass frog after weary but determined frog. Some irresistible inner force seemed to be driving them forward.

At the opposite end of the second floor, just past the turnoff for the Mayor's office suite, we trailed an exhausted but resolute frog to a side staircase leading to the third floor. Isabella crept up a few feet behind the frog as it hopped along the marble.

Once the frog entered the stairway, Isabella leapt past it and began trotting up to the third floor. Monty's dress shoes skipped along behind her as I brought up the rear, still carrying Rupert in my arms. The group of us continued on, traveling ever higher within the upper reaches of the rotunda.

By the time Rupert and I stepped out onto the third floor corridor, Isabella and Monty had already keyed in on yet another pilgriming frog. This one was resting in front of a door marked "No Entry."

The lock on the barred passage had been released. The door was cracked open a couple of inches, ample space for a frog's width.

The frog scooted through the narrow opening as we approached. Isabella nosed at the crack, trying to wedge her head into the frog-sized space. Monty stepped up behind her, grabbed onto the handle, and swung the door wide.

Inside, a narrow stairway scaled skyward, lit only by an occasional bare lightbulb mounted onto the sides of rough stone walls.

"Up again," Monty called out as Isabella hiked the stairs ahead, leaving the panting frog bested in a corner of the steps.

The already slim width of the staircase shrank further as the steps began to spiral in the ascent. The cramped walls of this off-limits section of City Hall were far less polished than the creamy stone balusters below. Dusty wooden panels and beams began to replace the marble siding.

There was only one possible direction for the path to take from here. Isabella hurdled up the steps, her pace now unhindered by frog escort. Monty huffed after her, struggling to keep her in sight.

Rupert and I trailed behind, the cumbersome bulk of Harold's oversized construction boots and Sam's rolled-up overalls slowing my navigation of the steps. But I couldn't blame all of my slow pace on the burdensome clothes. A gnawing nervousness was growing in the pit of my stomach as we grew nearer to the end of the frog trail.

Several turns up from the third floor entrance, I passed the first firmly shut door I'd seen since the hallways in the basement. A sign mounted on the wall identified this locked passage as the entrance to the Whispering Gallery, the highest balcony visible from the floor of the rotunda.

I thought back to the wooden model of the dome in the ground floor display area and the spindly steps that stretched up into the dome-topping spire. We would soon be passing above the dome's faux drop ceiling; the spire's attic seemed our inevitable destination.

The spiral of the stairs tightened again as I continued to climb, the passageway constricting down into a throttling two-foot width. The lightbulbs were interspersed now at greater distances, so that the already dim lighting disappeared on the farthest corners of each turn. The stale, musty air trapped within the tubular staircase did nothing to diminish the sweat beading across my forehead.

I hadn't seen Monty and Isabella for several minutes now. Even the dull thud of Monty's footsteps had vanished into the stuffy atmosphere of this elevated hideaway. It was deadly quiet in the isolated upper heights of the dome.

Rupert dug his claws into the front fabric of the overalls as a *slap, slap, slap* accelerated toward us, signaling Monty's return. His lanky body popped suddenly out from around the spiraled corner of the staircase, his hands awkwardly wrapped around Isabella's middle as he held her at arm's length to avoid her scratching claws. All four of Isabella's feet stabbed out in protest as Monty descended the steps toward me.

"Come on," he urged breathlessly. "You're almost there."

"What did you find?" I asked, observing the irritated expression on Isabella's face.

"The attic," Monty replied in a hoarse whisper. "Filled with, well, you'll see." He made an up-and-down motion with Isabella, as if he were trying to make a silencing signal. "But keep it quiet."

Sucking in my breath, I hurried up the remaining steps. Rupert squirmed nervously in my arms as we cleared the last turn of the stairs. The climb terminated in a flat, open room at the base of a steepled spire—the building's uppermost feature, situated above the crest of the dome.

A cool evening breeze filtered in through the many decorative arches and windows that ringed the gilded structure. Protective screens prevented a mass of pigeons on the surrounding circular balcony from entering the room. But the coolant of the fresh air and the stunning vastness of the city view could not draw my attention away from the oddity of the interior.

The room was cluttered with twenty or thirty glass aquariums. Each one had been plumbed so that it received a light trickle of water to feed the aquatic plants living inside. Resting under and alongside the plants was a nirvana of hundreds, if not thousands, of frogs.

The roof of each of the aquariums had been removed, facilitating easy access for the inhabitants. Every so often, a frog hopped up into the air, transferring itself from one tank to another.

Several burlap bags lined the floor beneath the tanks, each one filled with an assortment of frog-keeping paraphernalia. On the far side of the room, near one of the larger screened windows to the outside balcony, a narrow cot had been unfolded. An unrolled sleeping bag stretched out along the cot's length.

A couple of books lay on a bench positioned next to the entrance. Three of the texts related to frog caretaking and maintenance. The fourth had a familiar shiny green cover; it was a collection of Mark Twain essays.

But the room's most intriguing feature was seated right in front of us at a card table.

A redheaded man wearing dingy gray-striped overalls sat on one side of the table, carefully studying an array of cards fanned out in his hand. He appeared to be carrying on an animated conversation with the unoccupied seat across from him. The seat was empty except for a collection of cards, turned facedown, and a feathery orange mustache.

Chapter 39

ABOVE THE DOME

SAM SEEMED OBLIVIOUS to our arrival; his eyes were fixed on his cards. His grubby fingers strummed the surface of the card table as he considered his options. At long last, he ran his tongue across his top lip and laid down a card faceup on the deck stacked in the middle of the table.

"Ha!" he cried out to the empty seat and the orange mustache. "I've got you now." He leaned back in his chair and grinned broadly to his invisible opponent. "Let's see you wiggle out of this one."

Monty raised an eyebrow at me as he bent down to set Isabella on the floor. She quickly stepped away from him, snapping her tail into the air to communicate her offense at the undignified manner in which she'd been carried.

Monty cleared his throat and rapped his knuckles on the threshold of the entry, trying to draw Sam's attention.

Sam glanced over at us, his expression welcoming and disturbingly unsurprised. "Hey there, Mr. Montgomery and, uh . . ." His face clouded, as if he were struggling to remember my name. He shrugged good-naturedly. ". . . and Monty's friend. Nice to see you both."

Sam laid his cards down on the table and pointed at Isabella, who was sniffing the aquariums, and Rupert, who I had shifted in my arms to try to block the "Sam" nametag on my overalls. "You know, cats aren't allowed inside of City Hall."

But frogs, apparently, were perfectly acceptable, I thought to myself.

Monty appeared to have had the same idea. He struggled to straighten a smirk from his face. "Please don't tell on us, Sam," he pleaded. "We brought them in for an after-hours tour, when no one else would see them." The honest tenor of his voice was almost convincing. "They're very well behaved, for cats."

Isabella hopped up on one of the counters holding the aquariums and stuck her head inside the nearest tank. Monty looked at me beseechingly to intervene, but I motioned at Rupert, who I was afraid to put down lest I reveal the "Sam" nametag on my overalls. Monty replied with a sour look, threw his hands up in the air, and rushed over to grab Isabella. He received an annoyed "wrao" in return.

Between the artificial frog habitat, the disembodied mustache, and the delusional card-playing janitor, I was unsure how to proceed.

"So, uh, Sam, how long have you been living up here?" I asked gently as Monty grappled with an irate Isabella. One of her sharp, stabbing claws nicked his right cheek.

"Just a short while," Sam replied with a sheepish shrug. "I'm not supposed to be sleeping up here, but this is such a nice spot for a nap." His ruddy face broke into a broad smile. "Beautiful views, even at night. Check out the city lights."

I carried Rupert over to the east-facing window for an appreciative look out at the sky-high panorama of the surrounding city. Not far in the distance, a cluster of towering concrete buildings marked the edge of the financial district. Just beyond, the lighted lines of the Bay Bridge spidered across the water toward the Oakland Hills.

Behind me, Monty cursed under his breath as he continued to struggle with Isabella. I took a wide circle around them and returned to Sam.

Another pair of tired frogs emerged from the stairwell as I approached the card table. Once inside the attic, they waddled, without hesitation, across the room to the frog tanks. An electronic box, I noticed, was mounted on the wall behind the row of aquariums.

"What's this?" I asked, pointing at the box. Two round speakers on the front side of the device faced up against the tanks. A dial on the top of the box had been turned to a marker indicating three-fourth's power.

"Yeah, that's a radio," Sam said blithely. "My mom gave it to me for the frogs. It plays music on a spectrum that only they can hear." Sam nodded his head toward the tanks. "That's why they keep coming—for the music."

"That's what's bringing the frogs all the way up from the basement?" I asked, amazed. "This box? Is it sending out sonar or something?"

"Oh no," Sam said confidently, "just music. That's what my mom told me. The frogs don't dance or anything silly like that. They just like to listen to the music."

"Sam," I said, still puzzled. "There are an awful lot of frogs headed up here. The moat in the substructure of the foundation is filled with water—"

"And about a million tadpoles," Monty interjected, despite his ongoing duel with Isabella. "Who put those in the moat, Sam?"

Sam thumped his chest proudly. "My mom showed me where to put the hose. She took me down there about a week ago—through the trapdoor in the janitor's closet. She knew about it from when my dad worked here. You know, all this time, I never thought to look down underneath the building into the foundation layer. It's really a different world down there."

He strummed the grubby stubs of his fingers on the table, remembering. "We dumped a couple of packages of tadpoles into the water. I was afraid, at first, that they wouldn't make it all the way up here to the top of the dome, but Mom told me the music would get them going, give them inspiration. She knows how much I like frogs. It's been great to have them up here with me. They keep me and my dad company—it turns out he's a frog-man, too."

Monty was losing his battle with Isabella. His hands and arms were bloodied from numerous scratches. I turned my back to Sam, set Rupert on the floor, and held out my arms for her. She leapt easily over to me and put her front paws on my shoulder to cover the nametag, all the while glaring haughtily at Monty. Rupert yawned sleepily and trotted over to Sam's cot.

"Your father?" I asked, turning back toward Sam as Monty shook his head emphatically back and forth, trying to ward off my inquiry. I bit my lip, but decided to press on. "I'm sorry—I thought he had passed away."

"Yes, you're right. He did." Sam acknowledged cheerfully. "But, he came back a couple of months ago."

Sam leaned forward in his chair. "I was a bit surprised, right at first. You know, you sometimes hear of this sort of thing occurring to other people, but you never think it will happen to you." Sam arched an eyebrow at me. "You've got to keep an open mind, that's what my dad always says."

Monty rolled his eyes toward the ceiling, but Sam was already off and running with his story.

"That's why I've been spending so much time up here, you see," Sam explained. "So I can hang out with him and the frogs. You never know how long something like this will last."

Sam leaned back in his chair and stroked the red stubbled hair on his chin. "One day, not too long ago, I was running a sweeper on the third floor hallway. I looked up and saw a man standing next to the door for the stairwell that leads up into the dome."

Sam rubbed his eyes. "I thought, for sure, I must be seeing things, because this guy looked just like my old dad. Next thing I knew, he was waving at me."

Monty put his head in his hands, but Sam seemed not to notice.

"I couldn't believe it at first. My dad's been dead now for nearly fifteen years. But, sure enough, the closer I got, the more it looked just like him. He motioned for me to follow, so I did—all the way up to this room in the steeple."

The chair creaked as Sam shifted his weight to cross one leg over the other. "I got to tell you, it's so quiet when you reach the higher parts of the dome. I was starting to get kind of scared as I climbed up all of those steps, especially since I was following a ghost. Kind of creepy if you let your mind go there. But when I walked into this room, there was my dad, nice as you please. Sitting right here at this table."

There was a gleam in Sam's eyes as he spoke, and I realized that this reunion, however much imagined, meant a lot to him.

"It's amazing how fast we reconnected. Just like the old times. I've been coming up here as often as I can ever since. See, look, my dad and I, we started this game of cards. Of course, you have to be patient when you're interacting with a ghost. Sometimes, it takes him a while to make his next move."

Monty stared down at the empty seat and the downward facing, immobile playing cards. He clearly wasn't buying Sam's ghost story.

I leaned toward Sam and asked cautiously. "And do you, er . . . uh, see him sitting at the table, right now?"

Sam gave me an incredulous look. "Of course not." His eyes narrowed as if he, Sam, were questioning *my* sanity.

"But, you're . . . playing cards with him?" I asked tentatively.

"With his ghost," Sam replied, in a matter-of-fact tone. "He can't always be visible, you know. It takes a lot of work to make himself seen." Sam pointed to his chest. "But he's always with me in spirit, even if I can't see him with my eyes."

Monty had given up on this conversation. He began snooping around the room, peeking into the bags underneath the frog tanks. He was still searching, I suspected, for the hidden Sutro fortune.

I was more concerned about the role of the fake mustache. I was beginning to suspect that *it* was the reason we'd been led to this location. *Follow the frogs* I thought with growing apprehension—and find Frank Napis.

"Uh, Sam," I said, my voice trembling as I pointed to the object occupying the seat on the opposite side of the card table. "What is that doing in your father's chair?"

My fingers gripped into Isabella's thick fur as Sam chuckled. "Oh, that's just a placeholder. I found it lying around City Hall somewhere. I figured one of the tourists probably lost it."

Sam got up from his chair, walked around the card table, and picked up the mustache. "It gives me something to focus on when I can't see him in person. You see, Dad always has a bit of facial hair, a stubble, you know, like me. He doesn't shave much."

Every nerve in my body tensed as I forced myself to ask the next question. "Does your father sometimes have a mustache like that one?"

"Well, not exactly," Sam said affably. He dropped the mustache on the card table and strolled over to the bench near the entrance of the attic. He picked up the Mark Twain book, flipped open its green cover, and pulled out a black-and-white photo.

"Here's a picture of him," Sam offered, pointing at a group of four people standing in front of a Castro Street storefront. It was an exact copy of the photograph I'd found in the wardrobe in my basement. "He's the guy here on the end."

"The end?" I stammered. "No, you mean there in the middle." My shaking finger lined up with Frank Napis.

"I think I know my own father," Sam replied with a wary look. "He's the one with the big white beard. This one."

Sam shifted the photo to the right, so that my paralyzed finger now pointed to the image of my Uncle Oscar.

Chapter 40

DILLA CHECKS IN

I CLIMBED OUT of the white van in front of the Green Vase and stumbled wearily up the steps to the front door, struggling to carry both cats in my arms.

After the adventures and revelations of the last two days, I thought, I might never leave home again. My head was pounding, unable to process the implications of my conversation with Sam. I felt exhausted; the stress and emotion of recent events had completely drained me.

But as I set the cats on the top step of the entrance and reached out my hand to insert the tulip-shaped key into the lock, I noticed that the front door was slightly ajar. Someone had stopped by while I'd been out. I had a pretty good idea of who it was—but, at this point, it wouldn't have surprised me if Oscar himself had greeted me at the entrance to the Green Vase.

Sighing tiredly, I pulled the door open to allow Isabella to slide through. Then, after scooping up a sleepy Rupert, I stepped inside.

With an alert chirp, Isabella trotted through to the back of the showroom where an elderly Asian woman was stretched out on the dentist recliner. Her bright green go-go boots were propped up on the footrest, and she appeared to be dozing quietly. The fingers of the woman's left hand were wrapped around a key with a tulip-shaped handle, similar in size, shape, and function to the one I had just slipped back into my pocket.

"Ah, there you are, dear," Dilla said drowsily. "I hope you don't mind, but I let myself in."

"Not at all," I replied as I turned back toward the cashier counter. "Here, let me get your package."

"You've been out late," she said, bending her head to check her watch.

I smiled to myself. Dilla, I suspected, knew exactly where I'd been.

I leaned behind the counter and carefully slid Dilla's book back into its wrapping. With the flat of my hand, I pressed the tape down along the seams of the refolded paper. "I've got your package," I said, glancing cautiously toward the recliner.

"Excellent," Dilla replied. She flipped the lever to collapse the footrest and bounded up, her energy apparently restored.

I met her halfway across the room and handed her the package. She studied it for a second, examined the wrapping, and then looked up at me.

"Did you open it?" she asked. Her eyes had an eager gleam to them.

I thought about trying to cover up my unauthorized examination of her book, but I didn't have the energy to even make the attempt. I shrugged my shoulders apologetically and grinned sheepishly.

Dilla clapped her hands together in delight. "Good!" she said. "That's exactly what your uncle would have done."

My uncle, I thought—that phrase had never elicited a more muddled image.

At this point, I honestly couldn't guess what Oscar would have done while couriering such a package. My memory of him seemed to be slipping away from me, the sharpness of his features eroding even as my mind tried harder and harder to hold on to them.

Dilla's eyes sparkled. "Did you compare it to the older book?" she asked. "The one Harold left for you? Did you see the extra essay about the Cliff House?"

"Yes," I replied with a short laugh. "It's one of my favorite Twain pieces of those I've read so far."

Dilla held up the brown-wrapped package. "It's located right after the story about the jumping frogs." She leaned forward and looked at me intensely, gesturing with the book. "Don't you see? It *follows the frogs!*"

I rubbed my eyes, feeling another wave of exhaustion. After the discovery about Oscar I'd made in the steeple room above City Hall, I was done looking for hidden treasure. I didn't want to know any more of his secrets.

I reached into the pocket of the overalls and pulled out the folded-up piece of paper with Oscar's handwriting on it.

"We followed many, *many* frogs tonight Dilla," I said tiredly as I handed her the paper. "But all we found was a janitor named Sam who seemed to believe that he's being visited by the ghost of my Uncle Oscar."

Dilla made a confused stirring noise beneath the mask as she reached for the paper. She held it up to her face so that she could read the writing.

"Oscar?" she asked, her voice as hidden as her face.

It was too much to recap, too much that my mind just couldn't grapple with. "Dilla," I sighed. "Sometimes, I think maybe I never really knew him at all."

I pulled my version of the black-and-white photo out of a pocket in the overalls. "Sam had a copy of this."

The smile visible through Dilla's mask was oddly frozen. She brushed her hands against the front of her ratty wool sweater and tugged self-consciously at the scarf around her neck.

"Ah yes, the old Vigilance Committee days." Dilla sighed, the air fluttering out of her like the restless tweet of a small bird as she studied the photo. "That was a dif-

ferent era, dear. That photo was taken before . . . before
the Milk and Moscone assassinations." Her voice darkened slightly. "When that man snuck into City Hall through
the basement window."

"The window in the basement . . . next to the janitor's
closet." I struggled to find my voice. "Oscar's window?"

Dilla put a comforting hand on my shoulder. "Yes,
dear. Your Uncle Oscar was working as a janitor at City
Hall when the murders occurred. He felt so responsible
for what happened." She tutted her disagreement. "But,
of course, he wasn't. Not in any way. He couldn't have
known what would transpire that day. Even if he had, I
doubt he could have stopped it." She sighed sadly. "That
event changed him. He holed himself up afterward, here
in the Green Vase. He spent all of his time hunting through
the past . . . searching for a way to change it."

Dilla tucked the paper into a pocket of her sweater.
"I've got to go, dear," she said abruptly. "Think about that
extra essay. It follows the frogs!"

And with that, she stepped out the door and took off at
full speed down Jackson Street. I stood on the steps outside, watching until she and her green go-go boots disappeared around the corner.

Chapter 41

ISABELLA TAKES CHARGE

THE OTHER OCCUPANTS of the apartment above the Green Vase were still fast asleep Sunday morning when Isabella poked her head above the blankets and looked out across the bedroom. Her pupils stretched wide to catch the thin threads of light dropping through the slats in the blinds on the window facing the street.

In a single graceful movement, Isabella leapt off of the bed onto the floor and paced silently through the room. Noiselessly, she slid her head beneath the blinds and looked down onto Jackson Street.

The rusted-out pickup truck was parked in its usual spot, about a hundred yards up the street, barely visible in the leafy shadow of a short tree. The white blur of a man's wrinkled face could be seen through the truck's cracked windshield; the rest of his body hunched behind the steering wheel. His weary, bloodshot eyes looked up at Isabella's window, and, with the slightest nod of his dingy baseball cap, acknowledged her presence.

Isabella turned away from the window as her person staggered groggily out of bed. Her person hadn't slept

well, even after being out so late. She'd tossed back and
forth all night, occasionally murmuring something about a
feathery orange mustache. Isabella had kept watch, concerned. That kind of restless sleep, in her opinion, did
nothing but numb the senses.

Isabella quickly crossed the room to herd her person
toward the bathroom, taking care to avoid the person's
stumbling zombielike steps. Once she was satisfied that
her person had found the shower and managed to turn on
the water faucet, she returned to the bedroom to roust her
brother.

Isabella sidled up next to a Rupert-sized lump in the
covers. Flexing her claws, she snagged the edge of the
blanket and flipped it up, revealing Rupert's peacefully
snoozing face.

He was still slightly damp from the quick bath he'd received when they returned home from City Hall the previous evening. At least, Isabella thought, he no longer smelled
like a frog.

She bent over Rupert's head, gently licked his ear, and
emitted a smooth wake-up growl. There was a faint flicker
of recognition in Rupert's whiskers, but nothing more.
Isabella stood up and paced around to the opposite side of
his still-buried lump. She crouched down, wiggled her tail
back and forth as a warning, and pounced.

A startled white blur shot out from beneath the covers
and skidded across the bed. Rupert gripped his front claws
into the edge of the blanket as his back end rolled over the
side of the bed. He clung on for a short fabric-ripping
moment, and then thunked onto the floor.

Mission accomplished, Isabella strolled toward the bathroom to confirm that her person's shower water was heat-
ing up. Her tail stuck bossily up into the air, hooking
sideways at its orange-tipped end.

Rupert pounded past Isabella as she made her way
across the room. Now fully awake, he was predictably en
route to the red igloo-shaped litter box. It was already

rocking when she leapt up onto the edge of the bathroom sink.

A moment later, Isabella and her person watched as Rupert burst out of the box and thundered down the stairs to the kitchen. The person sighed sleepily and entered the shower.

Isabella set up her surveillance, enjoying the steam that rapidly built up in the room. It was such a warm, pleasant humidity. She began to clean one of her front paws, dipping it every so often into the drip from the faucet. Once the top fur was thoroughly licked and inspected, she flipped her paw over and started to work on the underside, stretching her toes out so that the rough edge of her tongue could reach the spaces in between.

The sensitive hairs that lined Isabella's pointed ears pulsed with intensity as they soaked in the early morning sounds. Her sharp mind filtered through the collected data, identifying and categorizing each entry.

A police siren wailed as it chased an errant motorist through the financial district several blocks away. A taxi bottomed out on a pothole on the next street over. A stray dog dug through a Dumpster in the alley behind the Green Vase. A rusty spring creaked in protest as the hidden door above the sixth step on the bottom flight of stairs swung open, and a thudding, froglike plunk squashed against the floorboards in the showroom below.

Isabella stopped midway through a long grooming lick. Nimbly, she leapt off of the bathroom sink, trotted out of the bathroom, and hopped down the stairs to the second floor. Her dainty feet padded across the kitchen's tile floor, bringing her to the top of the stairs leading to the showroom.

At this early hour, the windowless passageway was void of all but the dimmest reflection of light. Isabella felt her way down the stairs, pausing at the sixth step to look up at the low ceiling. The intuition of her heightened feline senses told her that the secret door had just been reshut.

A tiny scuttling sound issued from the showroom below. Isabella trod lightly down the rest of the steps, expertly avoiding putting pressure on the areas that would creak under her weight.

As she reached the ground floor, she looked out across the showroom. Hulking bookcases partially blocked the beams of light that had begun to stream in through the front windows, but, to Isabella's skilled eyes, the room was well lit. Every nook and cranny opened up under her gaze.

From the darkness at the back of the showroom, she saw that the front door was slightly ajar. Two men stood on the sidewalk outside where they appeared to be having a serious discussion.

One of the men wore a pair of baggy ripped overalls. Isabella easily recognized his hunched shoulders and droopy, wrinkled skin.

Harold Wombler reached over to pat the second man on the shoulder. Isabella tilted her head, studying his body language. He seemed to be giving assurances about a small box with airholes that he held in his left hand. Harold finally turned and, carefully carrying the box, gimped off toward his pickup truck.

The second man hobbled through the front door of the Green Vase, walking as if each step took an extreme amount of effort. Leaving the front door slightly ajar, he slowly shuffled around the corner of a bookcase and disappeared behind the cashier counter. The stool behind the counter scraped against the wood flooring as the man hefted his frail body up onto it.

Isabella's nostrils flared, keying in to his scent. It was imbued with the sweet, succulent fragrance of fried chicken, the signature smell of her secret friend, Mr. Wang. What a wonderful surprise. She hadn't had breakfast yet.

A floorboard creaked behind her, and Isabella tensed. Rupert suddenly rushed up, his claws scrambling on the slick wood floor. Her eyes narrowed as she prepared for his inevitable retribution pounce. Just as his heavy body leapt into the air, she sidestepped nimbly out of the way.

She watched as Rupert landed with a sliding whomp on the floor beside her and then scooted off underneath the dentist recliner to regroup for his next attack.

Unconcerned, Isabella sauntered hopefully up to the front of the store. As she rounded the bookcase next to the counter, her eyes searched for the plate of fried chicken that Mr. Wang usually carried with him on his visits. She didn't see any sign of the plate, but she rubbed her head affectionately against the leg of his baggy trousers, just in case.

"Miss Isabella," the man said genially, his voice soft and raspy. "Good morning to you, too."

As Mr. Wang patted Isabella on the head, she heard the sound of her person entering the back of the showroom from the stairs. Isabella slipped through the legs of the stool and peeked around the corner of the bookcase. Her person was approaching them, but, for some reason, she looked apprehensive.

"It's okay. Come over here," Isabella tried to communicate with the tilt of her head. It was sometimes hard for her person to understand these things, but she seemed to have picked up her pace. Isabella turned back to the man on the stool.

"My person's coming," she expressed with her sharp blue eyes as she rubbed against him once more. "She'll be so happy to see you."

The man smiled down at her and scratched the top of her head.

Mr. Wang was quite accomplished for a human, Isabella thought as her person's tentative feet slid around the corner of the bookcase. He always seemed to know everything that was going on.

PART IV

The Final Frogs

Chapter 42

NOT SO DEAD AFTER ALL

"YOU SEEM SURPRISED to see me."

The phrase rocked back and forth in my head as I stared at the man sitting on the stool behind the cashier counter, a living, breathing Mr. Wang.

"I . . . I thought you were dead." The stunned phrase was all I could spit out.

Mr. Wang grinned, his thin, anemic face straining under the spreading stretch of his lips.

He was alive; it was true. But he looked far worse than he had the last time I'd seen him. I leaned up against the front side of the counter as Mr. Wang scratched the silky top of Isabella's head.

"I *was* dead," he said ruefully, "for a while." The scratching rasp of Mr. Wang's laugh confirmed his poor health. He looked as if the slightest puff of breeze might disperse him into a shattering of dust. A long, wispy beard trailed down from his chin, further enhancing his ghostly, corpselike appearance.

Following Frank Napis's attempt to poison me, Mr. Wang explained, he had convinced his wife and daughter to help him fake his death, using the same spider venom toxin and tulip extract recovery potion.

"Not a very pleasant process," he said wryly with a knowing wink at my concerned expression.

"You look pretty good . . . considering." I managed to speak the words, but the lie was obvious. Mr. Wang's arms and legs were skeletal sticks, and his deoxygenated skin was the gray, lifeless color of decay.

"Why?" I asked. "Why did you go through all of that?"

Mr. Wang leaned back on the stool, thoughtfully stroking the wispy tail of his beard. "It seemed like the best way to outmaneuver our friend Frank." He coughed wheezily. "Frank Napis had too much invested into the history of this place, into your Uncle Oscar's research, to give it all up. We knew he'd still be around, trying to recoup some of the treasure Oscar unearthed."

The "we" he referred to, I assumed, included both the Vigilance Committee and the local police department, where Mr. Wang had worked prior to his retirement job running the flower stall.

Mr. Wang tugged on the tip of his beard. "Once Frank was ousted from his antique shop and his latest cover blown, he became much more difficult to keep track of—and, as a consequence, much more dangerous."

While his law enforcement colleagues were keeping an eye out for Napis, Mr. Wang had set up camp in the loft above the now abandoned antique shop next door to the Green Vase.

"It is, after all," he said, shrugging his narrow shoulders, "my own building. I rented it out to Frank a couple of years ago—through a real estate agent who kept my ownership interest in it a secret."

He picked up the black-and-white photo from the counter where I'd left it after my discussion with Dilla the previous evening.

"We thought we'd draw him out of hiding with the VC money," Wang said, tapping the edge of the photo. "If we hung the right bait, we figured, he'd consider it easy pickings."

"So that's why Dilla restarted the Vigilance Committee?" I asked.

Mr. Wang nodded with a polite smirk. "That, and she was really excited about the VC's latest political project." He noted my puzzled expression. "Those frogs have a friend in Dilla, that's for sure."

He reached down to scratch Isabella's head. "But, getting back to Frank Napis. You see, only the members of the Vigilance Committee knew where the Sutro fortune was hidden. So, I faked my death, and Dilla began running around in a disguise." He chuckled. "One that was meant to draw more attention to her, not less—it wasn't long before Frank found a way to contact her."

I crinkled my forehead, confused. "I thought Napis was one of the members of the VC. Didn't he already know where the gold was?"

"Ah, dear, you've misunderstood," he said slowly, the tone of his voice flat and even. "There were only three members of the Committee. We never let Napis join."

LESS THAN AN hour later, I walked out the door of the Green Vase, watched closely by Isabella from the top of the bookcase and Rupert from behind the first row of books on the bottom shelf.

"I'll be back," I assured them, trying to sound confident as I locked the door and crossed the street toward Monty's van.

It was parked in the same spot where he had left it when we'd returned from City Hall the previous evening. I wasn't sure how Mr. Wang had obtained the key, but I suspected Monty would be concerned when he woke up and saw it missing.

I didn't see anyone else around as I slid the key into the ignition, started the motor, and headed off down Jackson Street, but Mr. Wang had been certain my movements were being carefully monitored by a number of interested parties. He hoped that Frank Napis would be among those that followed me out to the Cliff House and the Sutro Baths ruins. I wasn't so sure that I shared that aspiration, but Wang had assured me I would be safe.

I turned the van at the bottom of Jackson Street and, before long, found myself rumbling along through the Broadway tunnel. The wide boulevard of Van Ness was vacant except for the light traffic of churchgoers, the Sunday schedule of MUNI buses, and the morning's blanket of fog. Most of the citizens of San Francisco were enjoying a languid start to their morning.

Long before I emerged from the Pacific edge of Golden Gate Park, I could see the ocean in my mind's eye, fiercely lapping up against the remains of Sutro's seawall.

I kept thinking of what lay ahead, Mr. Wang's parting advice playing over and over in my head.

"Just be sure to watch your footing. There's a high surf warning in the forecast."

Chapter 43

RETURN TO THE RUINS

I PARKED THE van at the far end of the Lands End parking lot in an open slot close to the trailhead. A scattering of cars, presumably carrying Sunday morning hikers, had arrived before me. Just over the cliff beyond the parking lot, the ocean spread out into the horizon, a sparkling crystal blue. From this distance, I noted with relief, its surface appeared smooth and placid.

As I closed the driver's side door, I tried not to look back toward the rear compartment of the van. I didn't want to give any hint of my awareness of the extra passenger crouched down in the back.

"Don't fall in," she'd called out before I exited the van.

With a grimace, I slung a small duffle bag carrying Monty's snorkel apparatus across my shoulders and strode purposefully toward the trailhead.

A slight whisper of a breeze lifted up off of the ocean, dancing with my hair as I began the descent. The surrounding carpet of succulents shimmered a brilliant emerald green as the plants' delicate green fingers curled up from the hillside.

I kept my focus forward while navigating down the steep hill, but, as I reached the bottom of the manicured steps, out of the corner of my eye, I was pretty sure I saw a pair of bright green go-go boots sneaking along behind me.

My own worn tennis shoes proceeded further down the path, skipping recklessly as I passed the first wave warning sign.

I tried to look confident and excited about my destination, no matter how much the sight of it, looming off in the distance, struck me with terror.

The closer I got to the foaming brim of the ocean, the more aggressive and agitated the churning water became. By the time I reached the bottom of the ruins and steeled myself for the balance beam walk across the top of the crumbling seawall, an endless procession of belligerent waves had lined up to make violent chops against the boulders beneath my feet.

On the hill above me, a hundred yards behind Dilla's green go-go boots, yet another figure emerged from the parking lot. The second follower was a tall, stringy man in a hurriedly constructed outfit of blue jeans, T-shirt, and a brown-smudged tuxedo jacket. Montgomery Carmichael ran a comb through his unwashed, gel-stiffened hair as he stepped off from the trailhead.

I smiled to myself. So far, Mr. Wang's predictions were turning out to be correct.

Temporarily dismissing all thoughts of my audience, I trained my attention on the slippery rock wall and the onslaught of waves thundering against its base. There was a full twelve inches' worth of wall width beneath my feet, but that ample support seemed to narrow each time my gaze strayed to the waves crashing just below.

It was with a grateful sigh that I stepped off of the far end of the wall and onto a flat patio of razed foundation that bordered the long algae-filled swimming pool. I brushed my hair back from my eyes and took a quick glance up at the hillside.

Behind both Monty and Dilla, a furious-looking woman in a red suit and heels had begun a precarious stomp down the trail. Miranda Richards was clearly not dressed for the occasion, but that didn't appear to be slowing her down. Her scowling red lipstick was so ferocious, it threatened to scare the succulents from the side of the hill.

Down in the bottom of the ruins, I nervously slid past the concrete piling where I'd watched Monty diving for the bronze frogs. I proceeded along the embankment that formed the ocean edge of the pool, heading toward a rocky beach that skirted a pile of boulders about fifty yards beneath the Cliff House.

A concrete piling on the opposite side of the pool provided another opportunity for me to sneak a peek up at the trail.

At the top of the hillside, I watched as a thin, aged Asian man tacked on to the end of my parade. He hobbled down the steps just beneath the trailhead entrance, his stilted legs moving far more nimbly than I would have thought possible.

I sucked in my lower lip with determination and scrambled across the rocks at the periphery of the ruins to where a narrow ledge of boulders formed a fragile landing that jutted out into the ocean. The water rushed through the rocks at my feet; a wet hissing spray dampened my shins.

The view from the bunkered building melded to the cliff above me had been spectacular, but the glass enclosure of the Cliff House had shielded me from the ocean's wild roaring objection to the intrusion on its privacy. Now, standing on the bouldered beach below, I received the full, hydrous brunt of that complaint.

One slip and I would fall right off of the edge of the continent, into the same rocky depths where a countless number of sailing vessels had met their splintering end. Foaming fingers skimmed across the turbid water's surface, shamefully covering the evidence of the wrecks that lay beneath.

I set the duffle on the rocks and bent down to unzip it. Hoping that Dilla wasn't too far behind me, I pulled out the snorkel and began fiddling with its mask to adjust it to the size of my face. Thankfully, I didn't have to proceed very far with my pretended snorkel dive.

Dilla's voice called out to me as her boots slid over the rocks. "Wait!"

Sucking in my breath, I looked up from the snorkel to face her.

As I did so, I caught sight of a familiar figure looking down from the observation deck of the Cliff House. It was a man with a flat, featureless face that had previously sported a fake, feathery orange mustache.

Chapter 44

A FAKE-OUT FOR FRANK

"WAIT," DILLA CALLED out again as she teetered toward me on the slippery wet rocks. She had removed her rubber mask, revealing what appeared to be a panic-stricken and tearstained face.

Lips firmly pursed, I stood up and tried to put on a stern look as wave after wave pounded near our feet. The onslaught of the ocean's bellowing swagger rendered us both nearly mute. Certainly, it would be impossible for the man observing from the Cliff House landing above us to make out much of the conversation.

"How do I look?" she asked leaning toward me, her voice pleasant while her expression remained convincingly angry.

I cleared my throat. This charade was going to be much harder than I had anticipated.

"He's watching us," I said tensely, trying not to move my lips. "From the Cliff House observation deck."

"Excellent!" she replied, "We just need to keep him there a little bit longer. Now, as loud as you can. Make sure that he can hear you."

"This is where Oscar hid the Sutro fortune," I yelled at the top of my lungs. "The gold left over from the Vigilance Committee!"

"You figured that out from the Mark Twain book?" Dilla replied, her voice echoing against the rocks above us.

"The extra Cliff House essay," I hollered back. "It followed the one about the frogs!"

"Why didn't you tell me?!" she demanded before hissing in a whisper. "Throw your hands up in the air! You've got to sell it!"

I drew in my breath, trying to strengthen my hoarse voice. "I'm nearly broke," I screamed. This part, unfortunately, was true. "I could use the money for myself!"

Dilla rolled her hands into the loose hem of her wool sweater as she looked down into the foaming confluence of rock and water just beneath the rocky ledge.

"It's impossible!" I screamed, gesturing with the snorkel. "There's no way to reach it!"

"I have to find that money. Frank . . ." Her lower lip trembled as if she were about to cry. She was a far better actor than me. She looked pathetic as she stood there, the wind flapping the loose legs of her putty brown pants. "If I don't figure out where Oscar hid it, Frank's going to . . ."

As Dilla broke into a sob, I caught a glimpse of the man looking down on us. He had the faint twist of a grimace on his thin lips. He didn't look convinced of the scene unfolding on the rocks below.

"Frank got to you, didn't he?" I said, trying my best to sound angry and betrayed. "He pressured you into helping him find the gold."

I risked another quick look at the landing. "I don't think he's buying it," I whispered tensely.

"Stop looking at him," she replied. "The police should be there any minute now." Her voice rose in volume. "Tell me what happened to the money!"

Swallowing hard, I put on my stoniest scowl and screamed out the lie I'd rehearsed earlier that morning with Mr.

Wang. "Oscar dumped it here after the murders. He was so disgusted at what the money had led to. He threw it away. It's impossible to retrieve it!"

Dilla gave me the quickest of winks before she turned and craned her neck up at the rocks above us.

"Did you hear that Frank?!" she yelled angrily. "The money's gone! Gone for good this time!"

But the overlook was now empty—empty except for a puzzled-looking pair of uniformed policemen frantically staring down at us from the overlook. Frank Napis had vanished once again.

DILLA PULLED ME back in toward the cliff wall, hugging me tightly. "Well, thank goodness that's over," she said, collapsing with relief.

I wasn't sure a celebration was in order. The routine hadn't gone according to plan. Frank Napis hadn't been persuaded by our performance, and he hadn't been apprehended. He was still on the loose, as dangerous as ever.

But before I could voice this concern, Monty stepped up from around the bank of boulders and poked his finger toward my chest.

"*You*!" he said accusingly. "I look out the window this morning and see *you* driving off in my van!"

I smiled apologetically. "Just borrowed it really . . ."

"*You*! You knew all along where the money was!" Monty cut in, flapping his arms in my face. "I can't believe you didn't tell me!"

I'd never seen Monty so irritated. He looked at me with disgust as he shrugged out of the battered tuxedo jacket and slipped off his shoes. "Here, Dilla, let me do this." He stepped toward me and snatched the face mask from my limp hands. "After all, it is *my* snorkel."

Apparently, someone had forgotten to tell Monty that this had all been a hoax to lure Frank Napis out into the open. To my knowledge, there was nothing of value hidden in the treacherous sinkhole of rocks below us—nothing but the remains of the countless ships that had wrecked on this rocky point over the last two hundred years.

Monty stepped up to the edge of the precipice and fitted the snorkel mask over his head.

Dilla and I rushed after him. "Are you crazy?" I yelled over the sound of the crashing waves.

Monty turned to me, the skin on his reddened face distorted by the snorkel mask. "I'm thuh Lowne Wranger," he replied, pointing proudly at his chest.

Mercifully, the voice of Miranda Richards shouted from behind the boulders. "Don't any of you fools jump into that water! You'll be sure to drown!"

Miranda stepped confidently out onto the rock ledge, her red suit unmarred by the hike through the ruins. I turned and stared, amazed at her ability to handle the rough terrain in her high-heeled shoes.

"You should have let me take care of this, Mother." Miranda's commanding voice seemed to quiet even the ocean.

Dilla wrung her hands. "I'm sorry, dear, but I knew you wouldn't approve." She put on the saddest of hound dog expressions. "We thought if we could just tease him out into the open, the police would be able to pick him up. Frank was right up there on the landing. I don't know how they could have missed him."

Miranda crossed her arms in front of her chest, clearly not moved by her mother's display of emotion. "Is that all you did? Really, Mother? Right now, there are several thousand frogs swarming City Hall. The whole place is a mess."

"Yes, well, you know how much Sam likes frogs," Dilla said, her voice switching instantaneously to an excited gush. "And if I was going to bring back the VC, there had to be frogs. That was the only way Frank would think we were serious."

Dilla turned to give me an aside. "When Oscar ran the Vigilance Committee, we always had frogs."

Miranda looked as if she were about to reach out and strangle her mother.

"You know," Dilla continued, ignoring Miranda's icy glare, "the VC part has been the most fun of this whole gig. I had a private meeting with the Mayor—he's such a charming man. I think I finally got through to him on the amphibian refuge. The Board of Supervisors will be voting on the proposal in the next couple of days. It's sure to pass now. My son will really enjoy that."

"Son?" Monty and I repeated in unison.

"Yes, yes, my son Sam," Dilla replied offhandedly, as if this fact were common knowledge.

"Sam is your son?" I asked, my head spinning. "But then, his father is . . ."

Dilla self-consciously rubbed her hands against her cheeks. "Yes, well, you understand, I had to protect him from his father. When Frank disappeared from his janitorial job fifteen years ago, no one knew what had happened to him. I didn't want Sam to go out looking for him, so I told Sam his father was dead. It seemed like the best way."

"You told everyone at City Hall that Sam's father committed suicide!" Monty interjected.

"That was better than the truth," Dilla replied defensively. "Honestly, Frank never took any interest in the boy." She tutted with disapproval. "He just tried to use Sam as a way to get back at me. Even now, these last couple of weeks, he's been threatening to contact Sam as a way to coerce me into telling him the location of the Sutro gold."

I sucked in on my bottom lip, trying to process all of this information. Mr. Wang had failed to mention this familial relationship during our conversation earlier that morning.

"But what about Oscar?" Another wave crashed on the rocks, nearly drowning out my words.

"Oscar?" Dilla asked, her face truly puzzled.

Monty pointed the snorkel at her. "Last night, Sam told us *Oscar* was his father."

I gulped, blinking as the scene from the attic flashed before me.

"What are you talking about?" Dilla demanded. "Frank Napis, or whatever name he's using today, that man is Sam's father. He was my, let's see"—she began ticking off on her fingers—"third husband, I think. Not a good choice, I'll grant you that."

Miranda's painted lips curled tightly. She raised four fingers on her left hand and, scowling, mouthed, "Fourth husband."

I pushed back a strand of flying hair and tried to tuck it behind my ear. "But, Sam said . . ."

Dilla clapped her hands together. "Oh look, there's hubby number eight, hobbling down the trail through the ruins." She hopped up and down, trying to draw his attention. "Wang, you old coot! We lost him." She winced, watching his progress over the rocks. "Oh dear, if he falls, he's going to break a hip."

"Mr. Wang? He's your current husband?" I demanded.

"Number eight," Miranda confirmed flatly.

"Yes, yes, dear, I've been with Wang for several years now. Why else would I have come up with that costume? I wanted us to match for once."

Mr. Wang, I thought, was going to have some explaining to do the next time I cornered him for a conversation.

Miranda rolled her eyes and began to walk back toward the ruins. She waved toward Mr. Wang, who had almost made his way down the hill; then, she pulled out her mobile phone and began to dial.

Dilla leaned toward me. "I knew Frank was hiding behind that ridiculous mustache the whole time he was running that antique store next to the Green Vase. We all knew it, even Oscar." She shook her head sadly. "Wang and Oscar thought it was better for us to keep an eye on him, so that we knew what he was up to."

Dilla waved her hands dismissively. "I was fine to let Frank parade around in all of his silly costumes, so long as he stayed away from Sam. I didn't want Frank showing up out of the blue, upsetting him."

She shook her head. "Sam's my son, but even I have to admit he's a little, well, just a wee bit off sometimes. Lately, he's been trying to tell me that he's communicating with Frank's ghost." She scrunched her face in frustration. "That's why I wanted to get Frank out of the picture for good this time—to protect Sam. Frank threatened he'd pay Sam a visit if I didn't find the missing VC gold and hand it over to him. I don't know how the police managed to miss him up there at the Cliff House."

I was still struggling to keep up with Dilla's disclosures. "But, Sam pointed at *Oscar* in the picture . . ."

"Trust me, dear," Dilla said bluntly. "I'm rather an authority on this subject. Sam's father is Frank. Frank Napis."

I suddenly saw an image of Frank Napis, dressed up as Mark Twain, playing cards in the attic with Sam.

"Frank Napis has been hiding out in City Hall for the last several weeks," I said with a rush of concern. "He's been with Sam the whole time."

Chapter 45

SAM TAKES A SWIM

SAM WOKE UP Sunday morning on the cot in the attic above the dome of City Hall. He yawned and stretched his arms as he looked out across the sparkling view of the city. Behind him, a gentle chorus of waking frogs murmured in the glass tanks. In his opinion, there could be no better place to greet the day.

He glanced over at the card table and smiled. His father had been there sometime during the night. Sam rubbed his stubbled chin thoughtfully as he examined the card his father had played.

"Cunning, old man," Sam mused. "I didn't see that coming."

Sam plopped down into the folding chair next to his hand of cards. A square plastic container had been placed in the center of the table. Moist droplets had condensed on the interior of the lid from the hot food inside.

Fried chicken, Sam thought. It was one of his favorite meals. It was so nice of his dad to have left the food for him. The security guards that worked the night shift were fond of it, too. They were always appreciative when a box of fried chicken unexpectedly appeared at the security station.

He thought back to the previous evening. It was just like his dad to warn him ahead of time that he would have visitors. The conversation had played out just as they'd planned. The woman had been shell-shocked when he'd brought out that old black-and-white photo and re-directed her pointing finger to the man in the white suit and false beard. Sam smiled, remembering the woman's stunned reaction. Yes, he was certain, she had believed his little fib about his father.

Still reflecting on the scene from the previous evening, Sam cracked open the lid of the plastic container and took a whiff of the chicken.

It was slightly different from the concoction his dad usually left him. A handwritten note taped onto the lid read "Extra Spicy Recipe." Perhaps, Sam thought, that explained the burnt red color of the crust.

Sam pulled out a leg and tentatively bit into it, testing the heat of the spices. The crust was still crispy, the meat underneath tender and juicy. He smacked his lips together, savoring the treat. He was a little disappointed, he had to admit. Despite the warning, the flavors weren't that spicy after all.

Sam walked over to the bench near the entrance of the room and picked up the book with the bright green cover. His dad had dropped it off for him a couple of days ago.

The frog story in the book was a bit distressing, Sam thought, as he continued to munch on the chicken, but he had assured all of his frog companions that they needn't worry. He wouldn't let anything like that happen to them.

As Sam flipped through the pages with his greasy fingers, he thought he heard a slight gurgling sound somewhere in the room. One of the hoses he'd hooked up to the frog tanks must have come loose, he thought. Sam lay the book on the card table and began searching through the tanks, exchanging pleasantries with the frog inhabitants as he checked the tubing.

He paused at the card table to pick out a second leg of chicken. This piece wasn't nearly as good as the first. There was some sort of strange aftertaste in the crust.

"Probably the spices," Sam reported to the frogs as he made a sour face.

A small pool of water began to form on the floor of the attic as Sam returned his attention to the tanks. All of the tubing appeared to be functioning properly, but the dripping sound had now increased to a trickling stream. A pool of water seeped out around his feet, soaking the soles of his boots. At this flow rate, the source of the water should be easy to spot. He continued to look through the tanks. Where was the leak?

As Sam passed from tank to tank, he began to notice a flush, feverish feeling on his forehead. He wiped a cold, clammy hand across his face. The plump of his cheeks pulsed with a steamy heat.

The water was rising faster now, threatening to soak his cot and the few personal belongings he had stored in the room. Sam dashed around trying to lift items up off of the floor.

His head started to pound with the drum of an excruciating headache. He'd never known any sickness to come on so fast. He'd take an aspirin, he told himself, as soon as he dealt with the water leak.

The water continued to creep up his legs; the level was now just below his knees. He sloshed through the room, still fruitlessly searching the water lines feeding into the aquarium tanks.

Several of the frogs hopped out of their tanks into the water flooding the attic, splashing joyfully as they swam about the room, their aquatic realm suddenly expanded.

In no time at all, the water rose another foot. Sam glanced down, disbelievingly, at the liquid circling around his waist. He could no longer see his feet—the water had turned green from the amphibian bodies zooming through it, their muscular back legs kicking with the force of a foaming frog frenzy.

The water soaked through his overalls so that the fabric stuck to his skin, increasing its weight. It was becoming difficult to wade through the heavy, pressing liquid.

The card table began to float, the playing cards sliding on its surface. His father's chair toppled over. Sam watched, panicked, as the feathery orange mustache slid off of the metal seat. He thrust his hands down into the water, trying to catch the floating hairpiece.

The water was cold and frigid against the feverish heat of his skin. His arms and legs flailed about, bumping up against a myriad of swimming frog bodies. The mustache was nowhere to be found.

Struggling, Sam lifted himself up from the water. As his head rose above the surface, he saw a movement in the spired ceiling of the attic. Balanced on top of one of the rafters, the two sides of its long, feathery hairpiece fluttering like wings, sat the missing mustache.

Sam watched, awestruck, as the mustache flew gracefully from one beam to the next. He had never known it to behave in such an odd fashion.

Sam held his hand up above the water, stretching it out as if offering a human perch. The mustache's hairy wings beat back and forth with contemplation. Sam cooed at the tiny beast, trying to entice it toward him.

He soon regretted the action. As the mustache approached, it sharpened into a hostile arrowlike shape, targeting Sam's head. Sam ducked down into the water, trying to fend off the attacking creature's sharp pecks.

As Sam's head sank beneath the water, the dark liquid grabbed hold of him, pulling him down with forceful icy fingers. Multitudes of green bodies swarmed over his face, blocking his view of the ceiling above. His arms and legs flailed about as he struggled to gain leverage on the slippery floor. Fluid began filling his lungs, constricting his breathing. His body was burning, screaming for oxygen. He had to get back to the surface.

A grim, wrinkled man appeared as if from out of nowhere. The edges of his grisly black hair floated in the water as he stared down at Sam. He wore a ripped-up pair of overalls that were far more frayed, Sam thought, than his own.

The man came at him, arms outstretched, reaching for his face. Sam resisted, but the wiry old man was much stronger than he looked. The man's fingers clawed at Sam's mouth, trying to pry it open. Sam knew he couldn't let that happen; he was holding his breath beneath the water. It was all the air he had left.

But the man could not be stopped. He was relentless in his assault. The skin on his hands was so loose and wrinkly that it slipped beneath Sam's grasp.

The water pressed down on him, stealing his last seconds. It was over; he was done, slipping from consciousness.

A cool flowery liquid filled Sam's mouth and sank down his throat. His tense muscles relaxed. His jaw slackened as he savored the rush of air that accompanied the sweet floral taste that, for some strange reason, reminded him of fried chicken.

The next minute, Sam felt a compote of crushed tulip petals being crammed into his mouth. He began to chew, releasing the petal's fresh, flowery juice.

The strength slowly seeped back into his body, and he sat up on the quickly draining floor. Mystified, he watched as the water rushed through the windows, gushed out over the balcony, and flowed down the gold detailing of the dome.

Looking around the room, he found himself alone. The strange intruder who had nearly strangled him beneath the water was gone.

Chapter 46

THE CAMERA SHOP

ABOUT A WEEK later, Monty and I climbed aboard an orange and white MUNI bus at the corner of Jackson and Battery. After carefully scrutinizing the number and destination listed on the front of the bus and comparing it with a detailed map of the city's bus routes, I had convinced myself that we were headed for the Castro.

Nervously, I gripped the curved corner of my seat cushion as I watched other patrons enter and exit the bus with a relaxed normalcy I was still unable to muster. I turned my gaze to the window and tried to tamp down the sickening brew of anxiety that was stirring in my stomach.

Monty leaned back in the seat next to me, not the least bit concerned about our rumbling speed or the identity of our driver—I had asked to see his MUNI identification card before boarding.

The bus slowed to an idle at the triangled corner of Market and 17th, waiting for the light to change and release us for the broad, sweeping left-hand turn onto Castro. Monty nudged my shoulder.

"You'll need to pull the rope to get the next stop," he

said, grinning at my white-knuckled fingers, which were still clamped down on the seat cushion.

Gulping with apprehension, I released my right hand and swung it up to catch the rope that hung beneath my window. A slight buzz registered my signal, and I saw the driver nod toward me in the rearview mirror, acknowledging my request.

Monty used the back of the nearest bench seat to pull himself up as the bus made the wide turn onto Castro. The afternoon sun shone down on the street, the gentle downward slope shielding it from the day's otherwise brisk breeze.

The bus came to a creaking halt outside of the Castro Movie Theater. The vehicle's accordion doors unfolded, and Monty bounded out onto the sidewalk. With my nervous, shaking feet, I followed him as quickly as I could, but Monty had already strutted halfway down the block by the time I was clear of the bus.

I caught up to him at the corner and together we waited for the bus to drive past before crossing the street and entering a small card shop at address number 575.

A Warhol-style mural took up much of one wall. The bright, stylized painting depicted Harvey Milk's wide, grinning face, positioned so that he was looking out through the card shop's glass fronting to the street.

A small bell rang as Monty pushed open the door, and we walked inside. A counter at the back of the store was manned by a red-haired, clean-shaven gentleman in a crisp white T-shirt and jeans. He looked up from a newspaper that was spread open across the counter and beamed at us in recognition.

"Hello!" Sam greeted us joyfully, almost unrecognizable in his clean clothes and recently showered state. He stepped around the counter and swung his arms around Monty's shoulders, pulling him into a tight bear hug.

"Hi, there, Sam," Monty managed to squeeze out from inside the smothering embrace.

"What do you think of the store?" Sam asked, clearly

excited by his new job. "I get to use the cash register and everything."

"It looks great, Sam," I said, trying to stay out of bear hug range without seeming standoffish.

Sam thumped his chest and grinned bashfully. "My mom put in a good word for me," he said sheepishly. "She said this would be a much safer job than City Hall—what with all of its recent flooding."

Monty and I nodded along. I knew from personal experience that the powerful spider toxin hallucinations were difficult to shake. It seemed easier to let them drift slowly from Sam's memory than to try to convince him that it had all been a dream.

"Course, I'm just here part-time," Sam said as he leaned up against the counter. "The rest of the day I spend out with the frogs."

He picked up the newspaper from the counter and pointed to the lead story. "They wrote all about it in today's paper. There's even a quote in here from me!"

I had read the article myself earlier that morning. In the aftermath of the frog invasion of City Hall, the Mayor had been more than eager to support the initiative turning the Sutro Baths ruins into a frog preserve—not the least because this provided a convenient location to relocate the hundreds of thousands of frogs that had taken up residence in the rotunda. Crews were working around the clock to implement the desalination renovations to the seawall. Accommodations for City Hall's non-native frog species had been hastily prepared in an empty pavilion at Golden Gate Park, which was now destined to become a permanent frog exhibit.

It had taken the better part of the previous week to round up all of City Hall's amphibian inhabitants. Occasional brown smudges on the rotunda's pink marble were still being found by the early morning cleaning crew.

The story had been extensively covered by both local and statewide news media—and endlessly mocked by the nation's late-night comedians. The image of the Mayor's horrified face as he fled down the steps of City Hall was now deeply embedded in the minds of the state's potential voters. Seizing the opportunity, several additional contenders had entered the gubernatorial race, including the President of the Board of Supervisors. Most political observers expected the Mayor to announce his withdrawal shortly.

My gaze travelled to the feathery orange mustache that lay on the counter next to the newspaper. Sam picked it up when he saw me staring at it.

"It's so my dad's ghost can find me again," Sam explained. "Since I'm no longer working at City Hall." He seemed puzzled at my worried expression. "You know, the next time he comes back to visit."

Chapter 47

NINE LIVES LAST FOREVER

MR. WANG AND I slowly walked along a shaded sidewalk in Redwood Park, passing trunk after soaring trunk until we arrived at a bench near the frog fountain.

I pulled Mr. Wang's wheeled oxygen tank behind me, carefully maneuvering it so as not to disturb the plastic tubing wrapped around his head. As we sat down on the bench, Mr. Wang closed his eyes and took a deep, fortifying draw from the tank.

From my coat pocket, I pulled out the worn piece of paper with Oscar's handwriting on it. "So," I said, hopefully holding out the paper. "*Follow the frogs*?"

Wang reached out with his bony hand and patted me on the knee. "Amazing little creatures," he replied with a chuckle. "Frank knew something was up the minute those frogs started showing up at City Hall." He struggled to clear his throat. "Unfortunately, I had no idea he was hiding in its dome." His expression turned serious. "We got to Sam and the security guards just in time with the tulip antidote."

I sighed ruefully. "Monty was convinced we would find Sutro's missing gold up there."

The narrow corners of Mr. Wang's mouth dipped downward. "Well, you did, didn't you?"

He grinned at my puzzled expression. "For a while after the shootings, Oscar left the remaining gold ingots in their original hiding place inside the merry-go-round's frog. Then an opportunity came along to put them to a good use—one that the entire city could enjoy. I think old Adolph Sutro would have approved."

"What was it?" I asked, shaking my head in bewilderment.

"The frogs did their best to show it to you. They took you to the closest possible viewing location." Mr. Wang's thin lips smirked. "You were standing right beneath it."

"The dome!" I said, finally catching on. "It went into the replating of City Hall's dome?"

Mr. Wang nodded and took another concentrated pull from the oxygen tank. "Anonymous donation, of course."

Mr. Wang's bony fingers fiddled absentmindedly with the plastic tubing that fed into his nostrils. "You know, Oscar never got over the Milk and Moscone murders. He always suspected the shootings were part of a greater conspiracy, one that involved Frank Napis."

Mr. Wang heaved out a rasping sigh. "Frank and Oscar were fellow janitors there at the time. Frank switched shifts with Oscar for the morning of the shooting. Otherwise, it would have been Oscar who caught the Supervisor sneaking in through that window."

Mr. Wang shrugged. "Oscar never found any concrete proof to back up his suspicions, but when Napis popped up in Jackson Square, Oscar vowed he would keep a closer eye on him this time." He shook his head sadly. "His surveillance of Frank had seemed like a fairly innocuous obsession—at least until a couple of months ago."

The water from the fountain surged, and the bronze frogs sparkled in the splash. I couldn't help but wonder about my uncle, all of his secrets, and the questions that still lingered about his death.

"It's strange to be with you again," I said slowly. "After I thought you were dead."

Mr. Wang's gray eyes gazed blankly into the pumping water of the fountain.

"I sometimes wonder . . . about Oscar . . . about his death?" I gave him a pleading, questioning look.

Mr. Wang leaned back on the bench and looked skyward, his expression unreadable. "You know, Rebecca, your Uncle had a great fondness for cats. He thought a person could glean a great deal of wisdom and insight from the feline species."

I laughed. "What does that have to do with . . . '?"

Mr. Wang smiled wryly and tugged on his wispy trail of beard. "Your uncle used to say, if you used them wisely, you could make nine lives last forever."

Enjoy the rich
historical mysteries from
Berkley Prime Crime

Margaret Frazer:
Dame Frevisse Medieval Mysteries
Joliffe Mysteries

Bruce Alexander:
Sir John Fielding Mysteries

Kate Kingsbury:
The Manor House Mysteries

Robin Paige:
Victorian and Edwardian Mysteries

Lou Jane Temple:
The Spice Box Mysteries

Victoria Thompson:
The Gaslight Mysteries

Solving crimes through time.

penguin.com

Penguin Group (USA) Online

What will you be reading tomorrow?

Patricia Cornwell, Nora Roberts, Catherine Coulter,
Ken Follett, John Sandford, Clive Cussler,
Tom Clancy, Laurell K. Hamilton, Charlaine Harris,
J. R. Ward, W.E.B. Griffin, William Gibson,
Robin Cook, Brian Jacques, Stephen King,
Dean Koontz, Eric Jerome Dickey, Terry McMillan,
Sue Monk Kidd, Amy Tan, Jayne Ann Krentz,
Daniel Silva, Kate Jacobs...

You'll find them all at
penguin.com

*Read excerpts and newsletters,
find tour schedules and reading group guides,
and enter contests.*

Subscribe to Penguin Group (USA) newsletters
and get an exclusive inside look
at exciting new titles and the authors you love
long before everyone else does.

PENGUIN GROUP (USA)
penguin.com